TO MARRY A DUKE

ANNA AYSGARTH

ISBN: 979-8-88653-159-6

Published by Satin Romance
An Imprint of Melange Books, LLC
White Bear Lake, MN 55110
www.satinromance.com

Published in the United States of America.

Cover Design by Ashley Redbird Designs

To my lovely children, Jamie and Emily and my equally lovely daughter-in-law, Helen. What a wonderful legacy you all are.

CHAPTER 1

*V*erity watched as her sister slowly put down her pen, blotted her work, and looked up from the ledger. "Well?" she prompted. Ella did nothing without due consideration, and this morning was no exception.

"I have checked the ledger a thousand times, Verity. Father sold much of the land as well as, well, anything of value, really, while he was alive and there have been many debts since his death, though the fact that he sold Swallowfield out from under us just before he died was something none of us could have foreseen. I had thought that the estate was entailed and that Father could not sell any of it, but it appears that it was not, or Father found some loophole." Ella looked at her sister and took a deep breath. "There is only one solution, which is that one of us must marry, definitely a man with money, and preferably Elliott Thorne."

Verity's eyebrows shot up, she hardly knew which part of the sentence to respond to, that Swallowfield, their home, was no longer their own; that the estate was, quite unusually, not entailed; and that one of the two sisters must marry—and for money!—or the fact that Ella had suggested the notorious Elliott Thorne, the man she had almost been betrothed to seven years before. The man who had nearly ruined her. The man who had broken her heart. "Elliott Thorne?" was all she could manage.

"Who is now Duke of Rydale," Ella continued smoothly.

"I know exactly who he is and what he is," Verity replied.

"And you must be the one to marry him."

"I beg your pardon?" Once again, Verity could scarcely believe her ears.

"You must marry Elliott Thorne. He is the only wealthy man we are actually acquainted with. There is no time to go through introductions, courtship, betrothal and so on." Ella's tone was business-like.

"Absolutely not. Never. No."

"Verity Grainger," Ella began, her voice a little sharper. "You now know how precarious our finances are, there being three sisters and no male heir. However, even if some distant relative is found to inherit Father's title, who is to say that he will want whatever is left of the estate, and he certainly won't want us. You remember Charity Longthorn from school? When her father died and her cousin inherited, she and her mother were tossed out of their home almost before her poor father was cold in his grave, they now live in a little cottage in Portsmouth, Charity teaches at a little school and her mother is reduced to taking in sewing. Charity, you may remember, was to have married Lord Worsely; they had been betrothed since childhood, but when he heard that the cousin had cut them off with barely enough to live on, he cried off. As to our situation, it may be that what is left, if anything of the estate must be sold anyway, if we are lucky there might be a cottage we might just be able to rent, though how we shall manage that I cannot yet imagine, so I repeat, one of us must marry well and quickly. I, of course, have no history of suitors of whom to turn, and of course Caroline is too young, so the duty must fall to you."

Verity looked around her, the once-opulent silk wallpaper was faded and peeling and there were patches of damp around the windows where the rain had penetrated the stone walls. There were paler spaces where paintings had once hung, and the oak sideboard had long been denuded of silverware. Not for the first time she noticed that the Persian rug had threadbare patches and there was a space where her mother's beloved pianoforte had once stood. They clearly had to do something in order to survive, but what Ella was asking was surely too much. She had not forgotten what happened between her and Elliott Thorne, and she doubted that he had. She would never forget standing at the window of her chamber, tears running down her face, seeing him ride down the drive without a backward glance after his meeting with her father when he told her father that he would not marry her without a sizeable dowry. That had obviously been all she was to him, a chance to gain her fortune. He had professed love and it had just been a sham. Now there was not even a fortune to attract a suitable husband, or any husband, let alone Elliott. She shook her head. What was done was done and there was no point in dwelling on things she could not change.

"What about you? You are the eldest. Should not you be the first to marry?"

Ella smiled at her sister, walked round the desk and wordlessly held out her hand, together they walked to the looking glass above the marble fireplace. As they looked at their reflections, Ella pulled back her dark hair which had been carefully dressed to hide most of the scar down the side of her face and neck, where she had been burned as an infant when the candle next to her bed had set the curtains alight. The careless nursery-maid had been dismissed, but the scar would remain forever. "I think you are wrong to hide yourself away Ella," Verity said softly. "Any man who loved you would see beyond the scar to the real person."

"The trouble is," Ella replied without emotion, "that few people see anything other than the scar. It is just human nature," she added. "Why would a man marry a woman with a disfigurement when he could marry one without?" She looked at Verity whose skin was clear and creamy, her green eyes fringed with thick, dark lashes and her heart-shaped face framed by unruly auburn curls some of which had already escaped their chignon. "Don't you see, Verity? You are our only hope if we three are to have any chance of staying together."

"But why Elliott? Why not some other man? You know what Elliott did to me." Even now, seven years on, Verity still felt the pain when she remembered how Elliott Thorne had used her and left her. She had been prepared to lose everything for him, and almost had.

"Elliott is now one of the richest men in the country and, as far as I know, all down to his own efforts. It seems that he has a talent for investments, discovered after he left the army. His business interests expanded beyond all expectations. I imagine Father would have been kicking himself had he known how rich Elliott would become," Ella commented, "and from poor Charity's experience you know life is not kind to single women without a husband, father or brother to protect them.

We have no discernible skills, though you and I could perhaps earn modest livings as governesses, Father, or more to the point my mother, at least made sure that we were educated, but that would mean us being separated and then what would become of Caroline? With no money for school fees, I doubt she would even be able to gain work as a governess, or even a lady's maid. She would probably end up as a nurse-maid or a companion to a cantankerous elderly lady whose family cannot be bothered to take care of her. Either way, she would be at the beck and call of people to whom she was once equal and you know how the ton enjoys nothing more than to gloat over the fall of one of its own." As ever, when faced with a problem, Ella chewed her lip. "The fact is, like it or not, and I appreciate that you do not, we need someone who will take care of us. Rydale has to marry and produce an heir, why not to you? At least you know Elliott."

Verity could not fault her sister's logic.

"I have racked my brains for another solution, any solution, but there is nothing else. We must face the fact that we have no money, no prospects and few discernible skills. If you do not marry well, we shall end up in the poor house," Ella went on. "You are our only hope."

"But Elliott of all people? We have nothing to recommend us, apart from the fact that we are the daughters of an earl, a disgraced earl at that. We have no dowries, and there is nothing to attract any man, especially Elliott to marry me."

"Elliott fell in love with you once, you can make him do it again."

Verity smiled sadly. "You're forgetting one very important thing Ella."

"What?"

"Elliott Thorne, Duke of Rydale, hates me."

CHAPTER 2

*E*lliott Anthony Thorne, Duke of Rydale, sat opposite the elderly lawyer, barely hiding his impatience as the old man read the documents for what seemed at least the fifth time. "I can assure you that the documents are entirely in order, notarised and witnessed," he growled. Mr. Govan looked up, his once-piercing eyes now faded to a pale blue beneath snowy white brows drawn into a slight frown. "I am sure they are, Your Grace, but as lawyer to the late earl, it would be remiss of me if I did not make certain, as this will certainly change the lives of the young ladies beyond their reckoning," he mused with a fierce tone.

"As you can imagine, I am keen to settle the matter as soon as possible." In truth, he had only seen the lawyer out of a politeness he did not feel. The deeds were his, and Swallowfield Park and its estate were legally his property, bought at a fair price. Although, he admitted inwardly, that had the late earl known to whom he was selling, he would no doubt have sold everything at half the price to the devil himself if he had known that the buyer was the man he had thrown out of his house for having the tenacity to offer for his daughter seven years ago.

In truth, he acknowledged, it was the actions of the earl and his treacherous, faithless daughter that had spurred him into taking control of his life. As the third son, he knew he would inherit nothing. He either had to marry a rich woman or go into the army, the church had never been an option. Verity's father had suspected that he was a fortune hunter and now, he could accept that there was perhaps more to the earl's accusations than he would have cared to admit at the time.

He had indeed spent two years in the army and made a successful soldier, his tactical brain and streak of ruthlessness meant that he had quickly been promoted. He could have continued and had a successful military career, and although he enjoyed the comradeship, camaraderie and discipline, the waste of war sickened him.

Many times, on the battlefield, he saw generals prepared to risk the deaths of too many men for the sake of half an acre of land. Men who had no choice but to follow orders, to charge directly into the cannon fire because their commanding officers thought that by ordering charge after charge, they would somehow overcome the enemy from the sheer weight of numbers of brave men sacrificing their lives. He deplored the lack of ability of officers who had bought their commissions, as indeed had he, but the level of incompetence astounded him. Officers who led from the rear, some who delighted in handing out harsh discipline to their men who were so often ill equipped, it was a wonder that any battles were won. Some were dedicated and he thought with affection of his own commanding officer, but many saw battle as a means to make a name for themselves, their victories and medals were won at the cost of their men.

So after two years, he resigned his commission and used the same tactical brain to build a business empire. His former commanding officer had advanced him a loan which he had used to buy his first ship, the world was opening up and Elliott had quickly realised that trade would determine the prosperity of nations. He began importing silks and spices, wine, tea and coffee as well as exporting coal and iron but soon bought shares in canals; there was no point in getting goods into the ports if they could not reach markets in other parts of the country.

The original loan had been repaid many times over. He now had interests in land, shipping, trade and banking all over the world and was taking a keen interest in the developments of railways, they were not quite ready for commercial use yet, but he had no doubt that they would be and he had already formed one company which was experimenting with using steam engines to move coal from the mine to the docks. As his commanding officer had said, part of Elliott's talent was in seeing not only what was but also what might be.

Five years later, the son who would not inherit anything was not only one of the richest men in the country but also a man of immense power, who had the ear of royalty as well as politicians. He had even inherited the all-important title when his mother's cousin who had been impressed by his achievements, had died without children and adopted Elliott as his heir. He was now wealthier than his own family, Verity's father, and the man the earl had selected as a suitable match for his daughter put together. It was even rumoured that he was richer than Prince George, the Regent—though as the Prince was perennially in debt, this, Elliott knew, meant little. As the Duke of Rydale, those in the ton who were inclined to dismiss men who made their money in trade were prepared to overlook his business interests, especially now that he had that respectable title. In fact, many of them quietly sought his advice on investments. He had everything he could ever want, except one thing.

Vengeance.

Verity Grainger had brutally refused him seven years ago, not even having the courage or courtesy to see him that day in her father's library, merely sent a message, a brief note on a torn scrap of paper to say that she did not want anything to do with him. He had been merely an amusement, a flirtation, a diversion until she found a husband who could afford the lifestyle befitting the daughter of an earl and that she never expected or wanted to see him again. Even now, seven years later, his jaw clenched when he thought of her. She had led him on, flirted and teased until he was dizzy with wanting her. He had offered her his heart and she had ripped it apart and stamped her pretty little feet on it.

He had never been in love before Verity, nor since. He would not make that mistake again. He certainly enjoyed women, he enjoyed their company and definitely their bodies, but since Verity, there had been no-one to whom he gave more than a moment's thought. Once they became too needy, he ended it. Pleasantly, usually with jewels and money, but ruthlessly and without emotion. No woman had touched him like Verity, no woman had hurt him like Verity, and he would make sure no woman ever did. Now that her odious father had sold the house from under her, he could, should he so desire, toss her out on her ear. The late earl had squandered his fortune several times over and the selling of his estate must have cost his pride dear, though Elliott would never summon up a scrap of sympathy for the old bastard who was everything Elliott despised, a man who expected everything to come to him because he had been born in the right bed, as apparently did his daughter. By his death, he had squandered everything his ancestors had built up, their reputation as well as their wealth. He was a man who knew neither the price nor the value of anything.

Presently, the plump lawyer looked up. "The papers do seem to be in order, Your Grace. It is just that the situation does seem to be most irregular, most irregular indeed."

Elliott smiled sardonically. Most people were intimidated by him, by his physical presence or his razor-sharp brain, both of which he had used to his advantage both in the army and in business, but this little lawyer appeared not to notice it at all. "I do not see why. The estate was bought legally and above board by my bank, I purchased the estate from the bank at a fair price. The earl had nothing to complain about." Even if the old fool did work out who had actually bought his property. "You will find nothing amiss; I assure you."

"I have been searching for an heir of the late earl, rest his soul, as he was not blessed with a son. The earl would not have wanted the title to die with him of course, no nobleman wants that, do they? You yourself, I imagine, will be thinking of an heir to continue the ducal line. There is," he continued, conversationally, "a young man in

Canada I believe, a distant relation, the son of the earl's cousin, though getting in touch with him has proved to be something of a trial. He is either involved in logging or trapping, there is some doubt as to which, and they have snow, a lot of snow," he mopped his brow, "and bears."

"Be that as it may, but you know the earl sold his estate, there is nothing to inherit besides the title, which I'm sure the earl would have sold as well if he could have thought of a way to do it. If this young cousin does turn up to claim that, good luck to him." This had gone on long enough. "Now, if you have nothing further to add, I intend to ride out and inspect my property." He stood up and drew on his leather gloves.

"There is just one more thing, Your Grace. The late earl had no sons but there are three daughters."

Elliott shrugged. "I am aware and assume that the late earl made some provision for them."

The lawyer scratched his head. "Well, that is the perplexing thing. Until I read it just now, I would have said the same, one would obviously expect a father, as is his duty, to provide for his children, but it seems that without the money from the estate which you now own, they have nothing."

"That is hardly my concern."

Mr. Govan smiled shyly. "Well, it appears it might be, Your Grace. In the ninth codicil, see here, in Latin, '*In omnia parati.*' It means be prepared for everything."

"I know what it means," Elliott snarled.

"And here, '*duo uno fiant,*' two become one, and '*matrimonium.*'"

"What the hell are you talking about?" His eyebrows all but disappeared into his hair.

The lawyer cleared his throat. "It would appear, Your Grace, that in selling his estate to you as it happens, the late earl has also included a marriage contract for one of his daughters."

"What?" bellowed Elliott.

"It's all here in black and white and Latin," wheezed the lawyer, "or *coracinus* and *albus* if you will." He giggled at his own joke, quickly turning it into a cough when he saw the thunderous look on the duke's face.

"Let me see." Elliott took the sheaf of papers from the lawyer's plump hand and quickly scanned the documents, coming to the final page, which was almost entirely in Latin, but which, he could not deny, bore his signature, he looked up. "How the devil? There is no way on God's earth that I would have ever agreed to this, and the bloody earl knew it."

He racked his brain as he remembered signing the papers in his library in his London townhouse. It was the day he was to sail to Venice to launch his new bank. He was running uncharacteristically late due to one of his mistress' tantrums and was in danger of missing the tide. The runner had arrived with the papers as he had been about to leave.

He groaned as he remembered his lawyer in the library, waving a sheaf of papers needing his signature, most were standard business documents. Just as he was shrugging into his greatcoat, the lawyer had said, "This is somewhat irregular, Your Grace. It's an addition to the deeds of the Swallowfield estate."

"What the hell has the old fool added now? I thought the transaction had been completed, in fact I know it had, it is probably another of his tactics to get more money out of me. Refuse it."

"It's one sheet, all in Latin."

"What does it say?"

"Forgive me, Your Grace, my Latin is, I am afraid, a little rusty, but I'll have it translated and ready for you to sign when you return from your travels. Unless, of course, you are able to find a few minutes to look it over yourself."

Now, Elliott remembered what he had responded with unfortunate, absolute clarity, "I have no time for more of the old bastard's delaying tactics, I will sign it now, get it translated and if it is unacceptable keep it and we will deal with it when I return. If it is not important, send it with the rest of the papers to be notarised." The review had been overlooked in the waves of his journey.

"I think there must have been a mistake," he ground out.

"Mistake or no," wheezed the elderly lawyer. "It would seem that if you want to take ownership of the Swallowfield estate, it seems that you must also take one of the daughters, and there are three. The eldest is Lady Ell..."

The end of the sentence was lost in the sound of the door of his office crashing closed. The old lawyer stared at it, then couldn't resist a wry smile.

CHAPTER 3

Three days later, Elliott sat in his library with his own lawyer, his temper barely under control. Usually, business was conducted with good nature and politeness, even ruthless decisions were imparted with charm and elegance.

"I apologise, Your Grace," Burton stammered. "I can only think that my young clerk sent off the documents. I had kept the one in question separate, but he must have assumed that as it was signed, it should go with the rest. Once again, I apologise and offer my resignation with immediate effect."

"Do not be ridiculous Burton, a mistake has been made that is all."

"I shall at least dismiss my clerk."

"Again, a mistake has been made, and none of us would succeed without making a mistake now and again. One error, however horrid it may be, in five years is not a warrant to remove yourself. Reprimand him by all means, but I imagine that he will certainly take more care in future."

"You are more than generous, Your Grace."

"We are all entitled to a second chance, Burton." Elliott was not interested in apologies. "Is there nothing that can be done?"

"I fear not, Your Grace. If you do not marry one of the daughters, you stand in breach of contract. I need not remind Your Grace that this will do neither your, nor the young lady's reputation any good."

"I don't give a damn for my reputation," Elliott ground out.

"Indeed not, Your Grace, but what about the young lady?"

Elliott paused. He knew that a man's reputation would soon be restored, especially a man with wealth and title, but the girl would suffer. He knew the full extent of their situation—knew the money from the sale of Swallowfield had been used to pay at least some of the late earl's debts. The sisters had no money, no prospect now of marriage except to him. Once a woman's reputation was lost, she would never recover, society would shun her. At best, she would end up working as a governess, living at the beck and call of those who had once been her equals, and in fear that the slightest slip on her part would lead to her dismissal without reference. How the mighty are fallen. It was the least she deserved. The thought should have given him some satisfaction, but strangely it did not.

Of the earl's three daughters, only one was truly eligible. Young Caroline was out of the question, and Ella, though the eldest, had always been aloof and distant. Verity had the passion that had ignited him. Verity who had broken his heart. Verity, he considered, he could wed if only to ensure that his vengeance was fully carried out and would be felt for the rest of her life.

Their conversation was halted by a commotion in the hall. "Don't worry Fry, I'll see myself in." Elliott grimaced as he heard his brother's tones. There was something of a scuffle at the doorway as Fry, his butler could not countenance a visitor arriving without being properly announced, even though the visitor was the Duke of Hart, Elliott's older brother.

"His Grace, the Duke of Hart, Your Grace," he intoned, before hastily withdrawing, adjusting his wig.

"Well little brother, you have certainly set the hens cackling this morning." Stephen Thorne laughed.

"What the devil are you talking about?" Elliott replied testily. The brothers usually got on well, but his patience was as thin as a whore's garter.

Stephen looked at him with amused surprise, "You have not seen it have you?" He tossed *The Times* onto Elliott's desk. "A most joyous announcement! Rather vague, though, I must say."

Elliott almost groaned as his eye caught the boldly declared piece, "Weep, O Maidens, at the Joyous Betrothal of the Eligible Duke Rydale to Lady Verity Grainger."

"So tell me, Rydale, what is going on? Why am I the last to know about my brother's betrothal?" the older man said, helping himself to a cup of Elliott's specially imported coffee.

"Believe me, Hart, this comes as big a surprise to me as it does to you."

Hart paused, the silver coffee pot in mid-air. "What, you seem to have become accidentally engaged? That seems a little careless to me, Brother, for most men, however drunk they are, remember something of the courtship and the proposal."

Elliott almost ground his teeth in frustration. "There was no courtship and certainly no bloody proposal. It would appear that I signed some kind of marriage contract by mistake when I bought Swallowfield, and if you ever mention this to a living soul, I swear I will kill you."

Stephen looked as though he did not know whether to laugh, but a swift look at Elliott's face settled the matter. "I do not wish to seem obtuse, but knowing your head for business, how could you have signed something by mistake? You usually go through documents with the care of a monk copying a manuscript, and if you do not, this fellow does." He waved at Burton.

"It was in Latin."

"Latin?"

"Latin!" Elliott stormed.

"Well, now you know why they beat it into us in school." Hart grinned.

For the first time that morning, Elliott managed a smile. "Clearly, they did not beat me enough."

There was a pause before Stephen continued. "Isn't Grainger the name of the chit you were keen on? The one the father said would never be allowed to marry you?"

"She is." Elliott frowned.

"Well then," Stephen sipped his coffee, "there is no problem. You have to marry soon and produce an heir, so you might as well marry this Lady Grainger and be done with it."

"There is only one problem with that."

"Which is?"

"I would not marry either Lady Grainger if she were the last woman on earth. I was not good enough for her seven years ago and I'll be damned if I am going to be forced into marrying her now."

"What do you propose, if you will pardon the expression, to do?" Stephen put down his cup.

He heard himself saying, "Burton, send a letter to Lady Ella and Lady Verity to say I shall be visiting Swallowfield and wish to call on them. Send our fastest rider, as I want this settled as soon as possible."

"Certainly, Your Grace. To what purpose?"

"I want to know if they put the old man up to this. And get that damned solicitor there. That old lawyer is as wily as a fox, and I would not put it past him to have had a hand in this."

"You think the girl knew about this?" Burton's eyebrow shot up.

"Of course she did. I was not good enough for her when I was without wealth or title. Now that I have both, the greedy little schemer no doubt wants her share. It is my belief that somehow, the earl found out who was buying his property before he so conveniently died, and she saw her chance to marry a duke." There was no doubt in his mind as to which Lady Grainger he was referring.

CHAPTER 4

*V*erity put down her teacup with a quiet clink, her face white as the damask cloth on the oak table. Spread in front of her was yesterday's copy of *The Times*, kindly sent to them by the vicar when he had finished with it, the luxury of a daily newspaper now being beyond their means. "I do not understand," she stammered. "How could there be a betrothal announced for all the world to see when we have not even seen Elliott since I was seventeen? How could it be announced without us knowing a thing about it?"

Ella looked up from the letter she was reading, her face almost as white as Verity's. "It is worse than I thought, much worse. It would appear that Father left us with nothing, not even a cottage. He sold everything before he died. I thought I knew about the state of his finances, but I knew nothing."

"What do you mean, Ella? What is that letter?" Verity asked, her face grave as she registered the look on her sister's face.

"It is from Mr. Govan. He confirms that Father sold everything just before he died to pay his gambling and a myriad of other debts. However, he made provision for us. Oh, Verity, that is what this marriage announcement is all about. Father must have made an arrangement with Elliott before he died," she said, relief flooding her face. "It seems that one of shall indeed marry Duke Rydale without the necessity of undue effort! What fortune!" She left the room looking less distressed than she had since their father's death.

Verity said nothing, her mind in turmoil. Nothing made sense. Why would her father arrange for a marriage to a man he despised, a man he had virtually thrown out of the house? Money, of course. She began to realise that the parent she had always loved and respected, thought only of himself and money. Joining himself to the now-acceptably-rich duke was a way of saving his own reputation, even in death. He did not care about her or her sisters; they were a burden, three girls for whom dowries had to be found, though he had clearly never even considered funding dowries for them as he considered all his daughters a drain on his income as none of them would carry on the family line. She suddenly saw with perfect clarity the numerous small ways his disappointment had been shown, how he had been absent for birthdays and Christmases, how he had spent only a half-hour at her coming-out ball before disappearing to a gambling hall.

A half-forgotten conversation suddenly surfaced in her memory. She had been standing outside the library one day when she overheard him saying, "Of course, Ella will never marry, for no man will want her. I can barely stand to look at her myself. She will stay here and look after me in my old age. Two wives have failed to give me a son, fortunately wives are easy enough to acquire, perhaps the next one will succeed." Ella had disappointed as an infant through no fault of her own, Verity had disappointed by falling in love with a man with no money, and Caro had disappointed merely by being born another girl.

She looked round the morning room where the girls had taken to breakfasting rather than the formal dining room. It was the cosiest room, the pale lemon silk hangings reflected the weak winter sunshine streaming in through the long windows, the ormolu clock on the mantelpiece ticking comfortingly as she sat on the green sofa. It was the room that her mother had loved, and she had a faint memory of sitting curled up on the window seat while her mother dealt with her correspondence. Though she sometimes wondered whether she actually remembered it or whether it was because Ella told her the story so often.

She knew not how long she lay on the sofa, but it could not have been long before Ella approached her. "Dearest, a letter has arrived. Duke Rydale is to call upon us within the hour. Please consider carefully what you shall do and say upon his arrival. Remember that we are all in your care." Verity hardly looked up as Ella departed.

Her mind spun, crashing wildly between truth and deception, acceptance and anger. How would she approach this awful circumstance?

Her thoughts were interrupted by Caro bursting into the room. "Ella says you must come to the library now. Mr. Govan is here with two other gentlemen. I think one of them is the Duke of Hart and the other is," she shrugged, "horrid." Verity's heart sank. She had come to dread visits from the family lawyer, as he unfailingly brought bad news and the presence of the Duke of Hart was clearly linked with the announcement in *The Times*. No doubt he had come to protect his family's interests. What noble family would want the daughter of a disgraced earl associated with their name?

As she approached the library, she heard the sound of angry voices, one voice in particular. "Let me assure you, I would not marry Lady Verity if she was the last woman on earth." Clearly Elliott was the other man, the horrid one. "And as to the manner of the announcement, if you think I care one jot for public gossip, then you must think again. If Lady Verity thinks she has succeeded in blackmailing me into this marriage by placing the announcement in the newspapers, she is sadly mistaken."

Verity felt the blood rush to her cheeks. How dare he accuse her? She had rarely felt so angry, and how dare he accuse her of announcing their marriage? He was the last man on earth she would trust with her heart. She had done that once before and he had nearly destroyed her, so she was not about to let it happen again. Verity strode into the room, ready to do battle.

Elliott stood by the window, resting his arm against the glass as he fought to control his temper. He had promised himself that he would remain calm, but being in this room, the very room where Verity's father had relayed the message that Verity wanted nothing to do with him and then threatened to shoot him should he ever try to see her again, had brought back every bitter memory. It had also brought back memories of his times with Verity. He could still see the swing from the window, where he had pushed her higher and higher, heard her giggling, catching flashes of her lovely legs. He envisioned the lake where she had challenged him to a fishing competition, and won, at the cost of getting attractively damp. Beyond the formal garden was the maze where he had stolen many kisses. Looking at them now, he saw the level of neglect, evident in the once-beautiful property: One of the ropes of the swing was rotten and it hung drunkenly, swaying in the breeze, the gardens had gone to seed, and the maze was almost hopelessly overgrown. The evidence of neglect was everywhere, showing in faded wallpaper, brighter, where pictures had once hung and the absence of silverware on the sideboards and mantels.

As he turned, Verity entered the room, and his breath left his body. She was no longer the young girl of his memory as she had grown into a beautiful young woman. The once-slender girl now had lush curves and the promise of beauty had been completely fulfilled, with smooth skin and a face dominated by huge emerald eyes lined with thick, sooty lashes. Her generous mouth looked as though it had been made to be kissed, and he instantly thought of how her mouth may feel again. Much to his disgust, his whole body responded to her.

Verity came to a halt, good manners, drilled into her by various governesses asserting themselves, taking in the Duke of Hart and Mr. Govan, and curtseyed appropriately. As she stood, her eyes found Elliott. He bowed, she curtseyed, and her eyes flashed. "Your Grace, let me assure you that the thought of this marriage is as repugnant to me as it is to you. As to the notice in *The Times*, I have as little idea as to how it got there as you, and believe me, should I find the person responsible for placing it, had he not undoubtedly sold them, I should shoot him with my father's duelling pistols."

Elliott could not help smiling to himself in spite of the situation, for Verity was nothing if not direct. "Well, that is settled then," she went on, "you do not wish to marry me, and I certainly have no intention of marrying you, so presumably we print a retraction in the newspapers and that is the end of that."

A discreet cough interrupted them. Mr. Govan adjusted his wig. "I'm afraid the matter is not quite so simple, my lady."

Every eye in the room swivelled towards the elderly lawyer. "What do you mean?" Ella spoke.

"Well, your father left very clear instructions that in the event of His Grace refusing to marry his daughter, that he was to be pursued through the courts for breach of promise. I have the paperwork here." He bent and fumbled in the leather bag.

"He did what?" Elliott's voice bounced around the room.

"The late earl, God rest his soul, instructed that should the duke refuse, he should be sued." Mr. Govan repeated. "I believe he was trying to ensure that his daughters would be suitably provided for," he added helpfully.

"I sincerely hope this is some kind of joke, Govan," Elliott ground out, the thought of being dictated to by Verity's father making him beyond furious. "Why in the name of God would he do such a thing? He thought I was a scoundrel and a wastrel! He threw me out!"

"It would appear that he had a change of heart, Your Grace," Mr. Govan countered softly.

"Which no doubt coincided with my wealth and elevation to the peerage." Elliott snarled.

Verity was grasping the back of the chair so hard that her knuckles were as white as her face. "My father, no doubt, had his reasons, none of which I imagine were concerned with anything to do with my happiness," she said, her voice tightening, as though holding back tears. "However, Mr. Govan, there is no need for His Grace to be sued. He does not wish to marry and neither do I, therefore, there is no reason why there should be a court case."

Govan bowed. "Under normal circumstances I would happily agree with you, my lady, however, I am in fact still employed by his late lordship rather than you and, most irregular as it might seem, I must carry out his wishes. It is," he added, mopping his face, "most trying, having a dead man for a client."

Verity took a steadying breath. "This is the most absurd thing I have ever heard."

Elliott nodded sharply in whole-hearted agreement. Though if there was no way out of this damnable situation, he might as well get on with it and accept it. Move forward, make plans.

Mr. Govan risked a small smile. "The law is the law, my lady, ridiculous as it is at times I must confess. However, I do believe there may be a way through this maze." He took a pinch of snuff.

CHAPTER 5

The hairs on the nape of Verity's neck rose as she became aware that Elliott had moved from the window and was standing just behind her, close enough for her to feel his coat brush her gown. Close enough to feel the heat from his body. God help her, all she wanted to do was to lean against him and take comfort from his strength. She stiffened her spine. What was she thinking? Elliott had rejected her seven years ago and again today. She gave her concentration to what the lawyer was saying.

"I suggest that as the betrothal has now been made public, in order to save unnecessary scandal, you both proceed with the betrothal as though it were real, then in six months or so, you may set it aside quietly. I'm sure I shall be able to sort out the legal aspects by then." Mr. Govan beamed at the cleverness of his plan.

"Are you suggesting that we maintain a public charade for six months?" Verity asked slowly.

"Indeed, I am. The more convincing you are, the more convinced the court will be, and when the engagement is broken off, I am thinking by you, Lady Verity, there will be no more to be said. You will have followed your father's wishes, and both be free to go your separate ways.

Scandal will be avoided and neither of your reputations will suffer." Mr. Govan mopped his brow again.

Elliott gave the lawyer a steely look. "If you think I give a damn about my reputation, you are sadly mistaken."

Govan returned his gaze steadily. "Then think of the lady."

Elliott placed his hand on Verity's arm. She was so pale he thought she was about to faint. "I think you and I need to speak about this without an audience."

***

Pausing only to pick up her shawl, Verity walked quickly through the marble hall and out towards the maze. Elliott could not help but notice the swing of her hips as he followed. He gave himself a mental shake. He would not allow the strong attraction that he conceded he still felt cloud his judgement. He had offered for her, she and her father had refused, and that was that. What he felt was pure lust. He smiled wryly. There was nothing pure about his thoughts on Verity's matured body at all.

When Verity stopped, they were in the middle of the maze where a stone cupid, eternally shot his arrow into the air. This had been a mistake, he suddenly realized. The last time they had been here, he had taken her into his arms and sworn his love and kissed her until she was incapable of anything other than clinging to him, and she had returned his kisses with equal passion. His loins tremored as he remembered it in exquisitely painful detail. Within days he was gone, turned away without a word.

Verity turned. "Well, here we are, Your Grace. What is it you wished to say to me that could not be heard by the others?"

Suddenly, Elliott felt irritated by the use of his title. "For God's sake stop 'your gracing' me, you know my given name. Use it."

"I'm afraid I cannot. It would not be proper," she shot back. "Especially now that our roles are reversed, I may still be Lady Verity, but beyond that as you very well know, my sisters and I are poor, if not paupers. It is a fitting punishment, is it not?"

Elliott's eyebrows shot up. "What do you mean? Punishment?"

"For our family. Father put so much store by these things and now they are gone. It was for want of a title that..." Verity stopped herself abruptly.

Elliott's lips thinned. "Ah yes, the all important title, which it seemed that I would never possess, and now that I do, your father is still scheming from beyond the grave to ensure that you marry one."

"I don't need to marry a title sir, I have my own," she shot back, her eyes flashing.

"Indeed, you do, but were you to be a duchess, that might have satisfied your father's ambitions." He regretted his words as he noticed Verity blanch. Something had hit an unintended target.

Elliott ran his hands through his hair. He should have known that Verity would be difficult and, he didn't even know why he was prepared to go along with Govan's scheme, as the woman meant nothing to him. If he wanted to bed a woman, there were any number of women he could call on who would satisfy his needs. If he wanted a wife, there were plenty of young virgins whose mothers would lay them in front of him like a carpet if it meant snaring a duke and if he wanted witty conversations, there were plenty of women, both high born and low who would go out of their way to entertain and amuse him. Yet he heard himself saying, "I think we should give Govan's plan a try."

Verity was almost struck dumb. "That is the most ridiculous thing I have heard. I don't know who is the more insane, Mr. Govan, for suggesting it in the first place, or you for thinking seriously about it. Perhaps you should see a physician, sir, for your brains must have addled since I saw you last."

"I assure you, my lady, though much has changed since you saw me last, that my brains are completely intact," he shot back.

"Then forget this foolishness and leave, there is nothing further to say." Verity turned to leave. She had not taken more than three steps when Elliott's large hand closed around her arm. "I suggest that you at least listen to my suggestion before you flounce off in one of your unreasonable huffs," he drawled. For some reason he could not fathom, it was imperative that she should agree to Govan's plan.

Verity's green eyes flashed. "Let go of my arm, and I neither flounce nor huff."

Elliott could not help but notice that anger had put colour in her cheeks and the sparkle back in her eyes. He almost groaned aloud, as he could never resist green eyes, or more correctly, he could never resist *her* eyes and now that his thoughts and, it seemed, immediate future, had been turned to the woman in front of him, he could not seem to tear them away. He did not want to tear them away. What he wanted was to remove every item of clothing and look at her before pleasuring her until she shouted his name and begged him to take her, just as he had wished to years before. Furthermore, he promised himself, before this false betrothal was over, he would do just that.

"Think about it, Verity," he drawled. "I admit this debacle is not ideal, but this plan of Govan's could have benefit for us both. I must marry at some point in order to provide an heir, and you must marry to provide security for yourself, Ella, and Caro. To the ton, who are easily contented, this would look either like a love match, or an advantageous match arranged by your father before his death." His conscience screamed at him for exploiting Verity's love for her sisters, but he had learned in the army that one used all intelligence to one's advantage before one lost it. "If we go to London for the little season, I can look for a suitable bride without the pressure of the ton breathing down my neck and you can look for a suitable husband. I could even," he added magnanimously, "introduce you to a few potential suitors that are appropriate for one such as yourself."

Verity stared at him, evidently trying to work out whether his offer was genuine or whether there was some hidden motive. God, when she looked at him like that, he felt his whole body harden. In fact, he noted, he had been in a state of semi-arousal since he had laid eyes on her. Noticing the pulse beating wildly at the base of her throat, he smiled, knowing that whatever he was feeling, she was feeling too. "Come now, Verity, I tell you, this plan could work out well for both of us." He stepped forwards until their bodies almost touched. He took in a deep breath of the rose perfume adorning her hair, wanting that scent on his bedsheets. Both his hands were on her arms. It would take the smallest movement on his part, and she would be in his arms.

Verity lowered her head. "I cannot," she whispered.

"Why on earth not?"

She raised her head; the brief moment had given her enough time for reality to reassert itself. "In case you have forgotten, Your Grace, we have no money. Did you not notice the spaces on the walls where pictures were once hung, or the threadbare carpets or the bare shelves in the library? We cannot afford for me to go to London and take part in the season."

Her father's words echoed through her mind, causing her pain even seven years later. "Elliott Thorne is a nobody, and he has nothing and will be nothing. You will marry my friend, the Earl of Darfield, the matter has been agreed. His period of mourning for his late wife is over. Another weak woman who could not give him a living son. You will do your duty. There will be no discussion on this matter, and if you are in the slightest bit difficult, you will remain in your room until your wedding."

As it happened, there had been no need for Verity to be locked away; the Earl of Darfield had contracted a sudden fever and died before the betrothal had been formally announced. Yet her father had now reached from beyond to force her together with another loathsome man purely for the sake of a title.

"Now have your revenge." She turned to go but he would not release her.

"What do you mean revenge?"

"It is what you wanted, is it not, when you bought all this?" she gestured. "Only my father rather inconveniently died before you could turn him out on his ear, so I imagine that's what you intended to do to us and would have by now were it not for Father's ridiculous plot." He met her gaze evenly, but she could see that she was right; he had bought out the earl as revenge. Shaking free of his grasp, she turned on her heel. "As for the threat of being sued, ignore it. Regardless of what Mr.

Govan says, there will be no day in court." She held her head high as she walked away.

For the second time, she was surprised and caught, and this time she was held firmly in his arms. "Now listen to me, you little vixen, you are damn well going to go along with this plan, or I shall be suing you for breach of promise. I will pay for you and your sisters to go to London for the season. You have some aged aunt or godmother or some such I recall, so you can stay with her to ensure that all is proper. But go you shall."

"We shall never convince anyone that we are in love, for you are the most high-handed, pig-headed, arrogant..." Her words were cut off as his mouth closed on hers. Taking advantage of her open lips, he slid his tongue inside, deepening the kiss. For a moment, she was so shocked she could not move, then a warmth spread right through her body, long-repressed desire flooding through her, her arms slid around his neck, and he gathered her closer, pressing her softness into his hard length.

Breaking the kiss, he whispered, "Oh, I don't think we shall have any trouble convincing anyone that we are well suited." He stooped to pick up her shawl, handed it to her, bowed and strolled off, leaving her to wonder what madness had overtaken him.

CHAPTER 6

Three weeks later, Verity and Ella sat in the duke's coach as they approached their aunt's house. Once his mind was set on something, it seemed Elliott wasted no time in making it happen. Caro had been ecstatic when she had learned that she was able to return to school in Yorkshire and would be joining her sisters for the Christmas celebrations. Swallowfield Park had been closed down, but Elliott had assured the sisters that he would restore it and it was his intention that it be done before Christmas. The estate workers were retained to work on the land and the servants had been found other work until they could return when the house was reopened. He had even gone so far as to have included the dilapidated estate cottages in the restoration, being appalled at the condition which the old earl had allowed them to fall into.

"I do believe Elliott will restore both Swallowfield and our fortunes again," Ella remarked with a smile. "He certainly seems to be taking this betrothal business seriously." She paused, waiting for a response from her sister.

"Elliott does nothing unless there is a benefit in it for him," Verity replied testily. "Refurbishing Swallowfield is no doubt done for his benefit, not ours. It is his, he owns it, lock, stock and barrel." She turned to face her sister. "I want you to have no illusions, Ella. Once this betrothal is over, we shall be on our own, and we must plan so that we have some means of providing for ourselves."

Ella laughed. "We'll think of that in due course, but for the moment, let us enjoy our visit and make the most of our time in society."

Verity looked at her sister in surprise. Ella was usually the practical one, the one who had taken control of their finances. It was not like her to leave things to chance, nor was she usually keen, due to her scar to be seen in society. However, she did not have time to question her sister further as the coach drew to a halt and the door was opened.

"Girls, girls, it is such a pleasure to have you!" Lady Bettina Newsham, known to them as Aunt Bette, drew them both to her ample bosom. "You should have come the minute your father died. I can't bear to think of you, hidden away at Swallowfield. Now, first things first, tea, then you shall tell me everything. I must confess I am dying of curiosity regarding the duke. By the way, my dears, he has arranged for a modiste, well when I say a modiste, I mean Madame Dupont, the talk of the ton, to come here tomorrow to ensure that you have a complete wardrobe for the season. I had heard that usually one has to wait for months to see her and that she only takes on the very finest clients, so goodness knows how the duke managed that."

"I imagine he is a very good customer," Verity muttered, irritated that Elliott had made a decision about her without consulting her, let alone considering the fact that they were still officially in mourning for their father, regardless of their lack of feeling for the man who had made their lives a misery while alive and continued to do so now that he was dead. Not to mention the inappropriateness of a man having thoughts or making decisions about the very garments that would clothe her body! She blushed at the impertinence, but also felt rather touched by his very personal consideration.

Aunt Bette's words gushed over them like a river in torrent. "Now, let me look at you both. Yes, you are both exactly like your mothers, no wonder Corban couldn't cope with you. But there again, Corban was the most selfish, arrogant man to walk the earth." She held up a hand to stem the outburst that neither of them had begun to voice. "I'm sorry my dears, I know he was your father, but even as a child there was something cold about him. He was my half-brother, but I cannot mourn his passing. And," she added, handing Verity a cup of tea, "truly, neither should you. Now, do tell me about your betrothal to the duke, for I am fairly bursting with curiosity, as is the rest of the ton."

Verity gave the story that had been decided. That Elliott had gone away to make his fortune and returned to claim his bride. This was the version that the ton would be told and, judging by Aunt Bette's hearty sigh of "how romantic!" it should be enough to convince them, or rather the women, at any rate.

As she lay in bed that night, Verity's thoughts swirled round. It seemed that every time she spoke with someone about her father, the more she found that she had not known him at all. Aunt Bette had made her thoughts perfectly clear; that he was a scoundrel who had married three heiresses and squandered their fortunes after they died birthing his daughters while ever in the search for another wife and a son. As she blew out the candle, Verity decided that she would put all further thoughts of him out of her mind and concentrate on getting through the next few weeks of the little season.

———

Verity had barely coaxed her eyes open when Ella breezed into the room. "Come on you slug a bed, get up. Madame Dupont will be here in a half-hour!"

Exactly thirty minutes later, both girls were washed, dressed, and just leaving the breakfast room when Madame Dupont arrived with three assistants staggering under the weight of silks, satins, brocades and velvets. "Now mademoiselles, we shall 'ave fun making the clothes for all the occasions, no?" she said breezily.

"I think there must be some mistake," Verity interjected, "we really don't need a whole wardrobe, perhaps one ball gown and one day dress."

"Non, no, no, no, that is not right. My orders from 'is Grace were most specific. You are to 'ave ze basics immediatement and the full wardrobe by the end of ze week," she continued, as she began laying out the fabrics and pattern books. "It will be quite ze undertaking, but we will concentrate only on 'is Grace's order until it is finished. Now, come into ze light so that I may make ze measurements."

For the rest of the morning, Verity and Ella were prodded and poked, draped and pinned as Madame nodded or shook her head, her every reaction noted down by one of her assistants as though she were dictating a message from on high. Eventually, she announced that she had enough to begin the collection, the fabrics were promptly collected up, and she swept out.

The minute she left, both sisters collapsed in a heap of giggles on the sofa. "Not ze silver gauze, we are dressing a lady, not making ze candlestick," Ella mimicked.

"What are you thinking, putting ze green with ze brown, we are not planting ze tree," Verity added.

Both of them stopped laughing and sat up straight when Aunt Bette entered the room. "Don't stop my dears. Something tells me that there has been precious little laughter in your lives," the older woman said with a smile. "Madame is rather a force of nature herself, isn't she?" Coming from Aunt Bette, who was more than a match for the prince himself, it set the girls off again.

CHAPTER 7

 ays later, Verity was beginning to lose patience with herself, as Aunt Bette had insisted that she spend an hour each day practising the pianoforte.

"I know it is a chore, but young ladies are supposed to have some accomplishments, and frankly my dear, your efforts at watercolours look as though they have been done by a drunken spider, so do not even think of complaining about it. Ella, you will accompany me to see the dowager Countess of Hinton. She is as deaf as a post but has a most promising grandson."

Ella blushed. "Oh really, Aunt, there's no need. I do not expect, nor do I want to marry. Besides there is…"

"If you're talking about the scar my dear," her aunt interrupted, "dismiss it from your mind. Besides, to be honest, the grandson is no oil painting himself, but he has a kind nature and a huge fortune, more than enough to recommend him as a match."

Ella grimaced, but dutifully followed her aunt out.

Verity struggled once again through the allegro section. "If I get this wrong again, I shall hurl the pianoforte and the music through the blasted window," she muttered.

"Dear, dear, talking to yourself and cursing. I am shocked," said a deep voice from the doorway.

His sudden approach shocked her. "Oh," she squeaked in an alarmingly appealing manner, "I had no idea you were there."

"Evidently." Elliott grinned as he sauntered into the room to stand by her side. He saw her eyes trace his body and grinned to himself. He was well aware that the cut of his charcoal jacket emphasised his broad shoulders and the light grey trousers hugged his muscular legs before disappearing into highly polished hessians. His snowy white neckcloth was held in place by a ruby pin the size of a small egg. He smiled as she noticed his awareness.

"What are you doing here?" She scowled.

"Is that any way to greet your betrothed?" he teased. "At the very least, I think I should merit a kiss."

"Don't be ridiculous," she snorted. "That would hardly be appropriate even if this engagement was real."

Elliott sighed theatrically. "When you are my wife, I shall expect a much more gracious, not to mention obedient, manner upon my arrival in our home. However, if you persist in denying me a kiss, I can see I shall have to steal one."

Within a heartbeat, he had covered the space between them, swooped down, and quickly kissed her gently, then stepped back, noticing—with no small amount of satisfaction—the delicate blush he left behind. Verity swallowed nervously, making him want nothing more than to take her in his arms and kiss her like he had in the garden at Swallowfield. He could almost forget that this entire plan was a ruse to make her regret breaking his heart with her rejection. But he enjoyed her as much as he ever had.

"Why are you doing this, Your Grace?" she stammered.

"I always enjoy kissing beautiful women." He grinned.

"Oh, do be serious, Elliott! Why are you going along with this ridiculous charade? You have enough money and influence to make sure that you are not sued for breach of promise. You don't care a fig for your reputation among the ton, and in any case, that fact that you are a duke and rich beyond measure means that whatever social sins you commit, you will still be received."

He knew he would be, but she would be ruined. As much as he had wanted to pain her, he could not bring himself to destroy her life after feeling alive again simply by being near her delectable body. "I already told you, Verity," he replied airily, "so long as there is no scandal, by playing the part of a betrothed couple we can both look around for more suitable partners."

"I can just imagine the queues of men thronging the door for the penniless daughter of a disgraced earl," she shot back. "In any case, why should you care? I shall be a nobody, no-one will receive me, and the likelihood is that Ella and I shall have to become governesses."

"No-one will know about your finances, nor anything about your father, not from me," he replied quickly.

"But that is what I do not understand. After all these years of hating me, why did you not take the opportunity to take your revenge against my father and me?"

He frowned. That was what he had intended, but somehow now it seemed less important. In any case, he told himself, he wasn't committed to marriage and, in a few months, they would walk away from each other, and he would finally have her out of his system. "This situation is one neither of us could have foreseen or welcomed, but we made an agreement which I intend to honour. Now stop pouting and get whatever you need. I have my new phaeton outside and I have the inclination to show it and my new fiancée off in the park."

"I do not pout," Verity shot back at him, her eyes flashing like emeralds in fire-light.

He flashed her a grin. "Oh, but you do, and it's delightful."

Moments later, Verity was seated in Elliott's shining carriage heading towards Hyde Park. Her mind was in a whirl. Three weeks ago, Elliott had at first scarcely been able to stand being in the same room as her, then he had kissed her senseless, and now he was acting like a suitor, gently handing her into the carriage and tucking a blanket around her. She did not know what to make of him, but one thing she did know was that she had to try to keep her head; she must not allow herself to fall in love with him all over again.

It seemed that half the ton was out in the crisp, cold air. The early mist had cleared and though the sun was shining and the sky blue, frost still clung to the branches of the trees that lined the paths and horse trails. As they trotted along, Elliott seemed to be continually raising his hat and greeting fellow riders and walkers, each of whom cast curious glances at Verity. All wanted to know the woman who had snared the eligible Duke of Rydale.

After encountering the third ancient countess in her equally ancient carriage, Elliott grinned. "I think that is enough public exposure for today. No doubt, many tongues will be wagging in a multitude of drawing rooms this afternoon. At least two dowagers will probably choke over their tea. I think your ears will be burning."

Verity scowled. "I do not know why you insist on being so public about this. Surely it will make breaking our engagement easier if it is not the talk of the town."

Elliott's grin became broader. "And you insist you don't pout. Come, it's a beautiful day, I think a little walk might restore your temper." He drew the carriage to a halt, and they stepped down.

Verity shivered. Once out of the warmth of the carriage, she felt the chill of the east wind, her day dress and pelisse more suited to summer, but she had no other. Elliott looked up at the sky. "My butler is convinced that we shall have snow by the end of tomorrow. Perhaps we shall have to travel by sleigh to Sir Kenneth and Lady Howel's ball."

"It is a moot point, since I have not been invited," Verity replied, trying to stop her teeth from chattering.

"Of course you have. I guarantee that by the time we arrive back at your aunt's you will have been invited to more balls, routs, and musicales than any sane man could ever possibly want to endure."

She could not help but laugh at his disgusted expression. "You are talking about social gatherings, Your Grace, not having your teeth pulled."

"At least having one's teeth pulled is over quickly," he shot back with a grin, which made him look boyish again. "In any case," he added, "it will give me the opportunity to show off my fiancée, dressed as she should be."

Verity skidded to a halt. "Is that what I am to you? Something to be shown off, like a racehorse or a prize cow?"

Elliott frowned. "That is not what I meant. You are deliberately misinterpreting what I say."

Verity raised a delicately arched brow. "Really?"

"I merely meant that once Madame Dupont has worked her magic, your gown will do justice to your beauty." For God's sake, he was a man who could negotiate successfully in four languages, yet everything that came out of his mouth at the moment made him sound like a complete fool.

Verity's eyes narrowed. "Are you saying, in effect, that without Madame Dupont's expensive services, that I would not be fit to be presented as the future Duchess of Rydale? Because while we are on the subject of Madame Dupont, I have one or two things to say."

Elliott felt his patience slipping. He had intended a pleasant outing with a beautiful woman for whom he yearned, or at least lusted, but Verity seemed determined to argue with him over every small point. Although, he conceded, he had not enjoyed the company of a woman so much for years. For the first time in a long time, he felt alive. But by God, she did have the ability to goad him as no-one else could.

"I am sure Madame Dupont is the most popular and expensive modiste in London, but I am not your mistress and a gentleman does not buy clothes for his betrothed. Quite apart from the fact that Ella and I are still officially in mourning. It is entirely inappropriate and quite intimately forward."

He wanted to shout, "*I want you to look beautiful and I want you to feel confident when you face the elite of the ton who are not known for their kindness to young women,*" but he paused before speaking and first calmed his emotions back in control.

"The gowns you possess are not suitable for London society and I refuse to be seen with you wearing something that makes you look as though you should still be in the schoolroom. Besides, if you are dressed well, it may attract the attention of some suitable suitors," he said instead. He regretted his words the instant they were out of his mouth. Her cheeks flushed with embarrassment.

"I apologise, Your Grace, but beggars can't be choosers. My father left me with nothing as you very well know, but I did not take you for a snob, sir. I do not think I can go through with this pretence." She turned away.

"Verity, that is not what I meant at all, and as for mourning your father, mourning is what happens on the inside. Excessive wearing of black is, to my mind, just an outward show." Why anyone, even his own daughters, should mourn the old bastard he couldn't imagine. He caught her hand. "Good God, you're freezing. Why are you not wearing gloves?" he demanded.

"I forgot to bring them," She lied, not wanting him to know that they were too shabby to be seen.

He drew her hand into the crook of his arm. "You're shivering. Why did you not tell me you were cold?"

Now that he knew, she could not stop her chattering teeth any longer. "I...did...n-n-not...w-want you to....thi-think me w-weak," she stammered.

"Verity, of all the things you are, I should never consider you weak. In fact, you would give some of the soldiers in His Majesty's cavalry a run for their money. Now let's get you home."

Without hesitation, Elliott removed his coat and placed it round her shoulders and, before she had time to protest, he had scooped Verity up into his arms. "What are you doing, Elliott? I am perfectly capable of walking to the carriage on my own."

"I am sure you are, but just allow my inner knight errant to surface this once."

Verity gave up the struggle and nestled against his warmth, taking comfort from the heat of his body. When her nose grazed his cheek, he sucked in his breath. "Bloody hell, woman, the only time I have felt a nose that cold was on my dog."

"How charming, a horse, a cow, and I am now likened to a dog," Verity muttered. "You need have no fear that my head will be turned by your flowery compliments, Your Grace."

Elliott could not help but laugh. Verity was in his arms once more and it felt right, he felt whole again. The thought brought him up short, though. For all he was still attracted to her, he could not deny it, he must not forget that now he was no longer the penniless third son, and she had conspired with her late father to trap him into marriage, regardless of her professions of innocence. Although he was quite happy to go along with Govan's plan and enjoy Verity's company while this lasted, he must keep it light. He must not allow emotion to cloud his judgement. The sooner this charade was over the better.

Verity sensed by the subtle tension in his muscles that Elliott's mood had changed. "I think I may manage now, Your Grace," she said in a small voice. At the carriage, Elliott dumped her unceremoniously on the seat and drove off in silence. When they reached her aunt's house, he handed her down, but drew his hand away as quickly as possible, as though burned by her touch and did not offer to kiss her hand. "I shall see you at the Howel Ball," he said coolly, and was gone.

She entered the house alone and was relieved to see a roaring fire and tea when she entered the drawing room. Aunt Bette was already dozing, and Ella was reading a novel, but she quickly set it down. "How was the drive with Elliott?" Ella's eyes were bright with curiosity.

Verity wrinkled her nose. "Not an overwhelming success. I seem to be able to bring the worst of Elliott out and he does the same to me. We cannot seem to have a conversation without it ending in a disagreement." She helped herself to a scone. "I think that Father put this ridiculous clause in his bill of sale to punish me."

"Why should Father want to punish you?" Ella laughed as she poured tea for her sister.

"The reason he wanted to punish us all," Verity replied. "For not being beautiful enough, or accomplished enough, but mostly for not being male enough."

"Well, I think Father did love us, in his own way," Ella responded. "I have to believe that," she added quietly.

Verity smiled. "Of course, you are right. Father loved us in his way. I am just out of sorts because of my latest skirmish with Elliott."

"Well, it looks as though Mr. Govan's suggestion might work, as we have been invited to so many events." Ella indicated the plethora of new cards on the mantelpiece.

"All no doubt to satisfy the ton's curiosity regarding the fiancée of the Duke of Rydale," Verity muttered. "I hope they are not disappointed."

CHAPTER 8

The following evening, Verity took a deep breath as they waited in line to be announced. Madame Dupont had certainly worked her magic, and in surprising time having been at work less than a week. Her new gown was of white taffeta sprinkled with seed pearls and a gossamer thin overskirt, the peach sash emphasizing her narrow waist. Aunt Bette's maid had drawn her hair up, leaving a few tendrils loose about her ears. Elliott had sent a suite of pearls for her to wear which she had almost sent back, but the gown was cut much lower than she was used to, indecently low she thought, that she had worn the necklace to cover her unveiled skin. Ella also looked wonderful in pale blue silk and Aunt Bette's maid had arranged her hair so that the scar was barely visible.

Aunt Bette patted her hand. "Do try not look so nervous, my dear, it's a ball, not an execution."

"I am not sure I belong here," Verity whispered back.

"Of course, you are, for you are the daughter of an earl. Do you see that woman over there in the most sinful red dress?" She pointed her fan in the direction of a handsome woman in her thirties with a voluptuous figure, and a dress with a neckline so low that it looked as though she was in danger of falling out of it. "That is Princess Natalya Grazinsky, now married to the Earl of Bolton. Apparently, she's some Russian princess, though the rumour is that she was his housemaid and the reason she speaks with such a strong accent is to hide the fact that she was born in Liverpool."

Verity's eyes widened. "Is that true?"

Aunt Bette laughed. "Who knows my dear, and in truth no-one really cares. In this case, the ton find it most amusing and if she makes Bolton happy, who is to judge? The point I was trying to make is that nothing in the ton is entirely what it seems, and you have as much right to be here as anyone else. Now let us proceed."

As they were announced, Verity could hear the moment when conversations stopped, and glasses of champagne paused in mid-air. It seemed that the whole ton had turned its collective judgemental gaze on her. She reached for Ella's hand. If they wanted a show, that was what they would get.

Two hours later, she collapsed onto one of the small gilt chairs next to her sister. "I believe my new slippers are quite worn out." She laughed, though she knew she could not hide her disappointment from Ella. Elliott had been nowhere to be seen. His absence had, of course, been noted by the ton, and she could not help but overhear some of their remarks,

"Must be bored with her already."

"Word is she's not up to life in London. Bit of a country mouse, I believe."

"Pretty enough little thing."

"Quite plain without the help of Madame Dupont. I'd recognise her work anywhere, and she said she didn't have the time to finish my gown."

"She was most gracious when I stepped on her foot."

"Rydale could have the pick of the crop, so God knows what he sees in her."

"Women all look the same when the candles are blown out."

"Wouldn't mind a crack at her myself when Rydale tires of her."

The last three comments were from two gentlemen who were leaning against one of the columns with their backs to Verity as she returned from the ladies' retiring room. "Would you excuse me, gentlemen? I seem to be having trouble getting past your huge egos," she had said tartly as she brushed past.

In truth, Verity was both angry and disappointed that Elliott had not appeared. She had not wanted for dance partners; indeed, her card was full, but in her imagination, she had danced every waltz with Elliott, a fact that annoyed her even more. She should have known better, she knew, flashing her brightest smile at Lord Steventon, who had arrived bearing a glass of punch for her and taking a sip from the flask he continually carried.

"I am devastated to learn that your ladyship is already betrothed." He grinned as he licked his lips. "It is so unfortunate that the finest rose in the garden has been plucked before so many of us had a chance to see it."

It was all Verity could do not to roll her eyes. "I had no idea, my lord, that you were interested in horticulture. As to my betrothal, it is not entirely settled."

"Then may I request a second dance before the evening is over?" Lord Steventon's eyes lit up.

"No, you may not, Steventon," came a decidedly unfriendly voice from behind Verity, "and do not think of even looking at this particular rose in the garden," he added softly, "or I may be tempted to plant you in the ground."

"Of course not, Your Grace," Steventon stammered as he backed away, much to Verity's amusement. Quelling her confused feelings, her desire, joy, anger, and frustration, she turned to face her fiancé.

"Now, Lady Verity, if you would do me the honour, I believe this is my waltz." Elliott held out his hand, his tone was lighter, but there was no mistaking the determined look on his face.

She looked at his outstretched hand, "I believe I promised this dance to..."

He cut her off. "It's fine. Lord Hadfield was more than happy to concede to me," he snapped.

She placed her small hand in his large one and allowed herself to be led onto the dance floor. An unconvincing smile was pasted onto her face.

"It would be more convincing were you to try to look as though you are enjoying dancing with me." Elliott's voice was low, and near enough to her ear to make her shiver. "Or at least try to look as though you are not attending a funeral," he added, the harsh tone in his voice softening once she was in his arms. The false smile had not fooled him. Not when he knew her so well for so long.

"What do you care about whether I am enjoying myself?" she hissed. "Or should I get down on my knees and be thankful that the great Duke of Rydale has finally condescended to grace us with his presence? I will not be ignored and stared at only for you to pick me up at your ease like a child's plaything!"

Elliott did not reply for a moment, for his mind had wandered down an extremely pleasant alley at the thought of Verity on her knees in front of him, and it had nothing whatsoever to do with prayer. "I was detained, so I apologise," he said simply, but without explanation. "Now would you tell me what you mean by telling Steventon that nothing is entirely settled?" he went on coolly.

The truth was, he had watched Verity long before he had made his presence known to her. She had taken his breath away when he had slipped into the ballroom. He must have a word with Madame Dupont, though. The dress she had made for Verity was stunning, the cut emphasised her small waist, but it was the daringly low-cut bodice that exposed the top of her creamy breasts. He enjoyed looking at her, but he knew that every other man in the room would be doing the same. He also knew that they would be having the same thoughts as he. She had been dancing with one of the many young bucks who had clustered round her and her sister. He didn't like it; he didn't like the way that they looked at her. He didn't like the way they made her laugh, and he certainly didn't like the way they held her. Mostly, he didn't like the fact that he didn't like it.

Verity could scarcely believe her ears. "Well, it is not settled. It is not even a proper betrothal. You said that we should both use the time to look around for suitable suitors," she muttered furiously, "and I have been dancing for that purpose as well as to do your reputation a service! I have no intention of shaming you," she said bitterly.

"I did not suggest that you should flirt with all the eligible men in London and let me tell you that most of the men you have thrown yourself at tonight are far from eligible. You seem to have a remarkable talent for attracting the wrong sort of men," he shot back.

Verity could feel her temper rising. "The wrong sort of men?" She raised an eyebrow. "Like you, perchance?"

"I believe you will find that I am not only the most eligible man in this room, I am also one of the most suitable," he said quietly.

Verity was unimpressed. "Then you must have changed considerably, as several people have been kind enough to point out to me at least three of your mistresses this evening."

"I have had mistresses, I see no reason to deny it, I am not a monk, and yes, some of them are here this evening, but I would point out that I am not responsible for the guest list," he hissed. Fortunately, at that moment, the music stopped, and he was obliged to escort Verity back to her seat.

CHAPTER 9

"*S*top glowering at the poor girl and drink this." Stephen Thorne handed his brother a glass of brandy.

"I should damn well think I am glowering. She is flirting and they are lapping it up," Elliott replied as he tossed the brandy back in one. "Mara has not once looked at her face the whole time he has been dancing with her, his eyes are out on stalks." He snared another glass from a passing servant. "And as for Prince Ambrogio, I actually saw the bastard pat her behind. I am seriously thinking of calling the pair of them out."

Stephen could not keep the laugh from his voice. "Duelling is illegal, Elliott, as you very well know, and as I have no desire to spend time in prison as your second, I suggest you leave the lady to deal with them on her own. I would not say she was flirting, merely surviving the onslaught of besotted swains. She seems to have been doing so very nicely as far as I can tell."

Elliott quirked an eyebrow.

"Truly, I heard her ask Lord Mara if he had considered getting spectacles and she stamped on poor Ambrogio's foot every third beat of the waltz. I do not believe you saw what happened with the young Marquis of Sandford?"

"What the devil did he do to her?"

"I have no idea, but I know that during one of the country dances, she aimed an over enthusiastic kick and got him right in the balls." He laughed. "Sandford may well be the last of his line."

Elliott could not help but smile, in spite of himself. "That sounds like Verity. She does not suffer fools gladly, indeed, she does not suffer them at all." It was reassuring to hear that although he managed to rile her every time, he had her alone with the intention of allowing her to enjoy herself, she never had reason to attempt to harm him. That was reserved for other men. It was almost heartening, if he cared. No doubt about it; he found her feistiness refreshing. She didn't simper, and when she didn't agree she told him. In no uncertain terms. It wasn't refreshing, it was arousing, very arousing.

His smile faded as quickly as it had appeared. "However, that is beside the point. It offends my honour to have half the men in the room leering over my betrothed."

Now Stephen quirked an eyebrow. "I thought this was supposed to be a charade. Are not you and she supposed to be playing the roles of happily betrothed lovers and using the time to look for more suitable matches? If I recall it correctly, you considered her to be a scheming bi...."

"I know what I said," Elliott interrupted him. "The fact is, after due consideration, I may as well marry Lady Verity as anyone. You yourself said it," he continued, taking another glass of brandy and tossing it back. "I need to marry and produce an heir, and Verity will serve that purpose very well. She will be happy to live at Swallowfield and raise the children, and I shall be free to continue with my life. Nothing need change."

"I don't know that that's exactly what I said, Brother." Stephen took a swallow of brandy. "And I wouldn't say that I know much about Lady Verity, but I do know something of women in general, and I doubt that the lady will be too happy with that arrangement."

"I don't see why not. She will continue to live in the home that means so much to her and will want for nothing," Elliott reasoned. "She will have the all important title of duchess, but live simply in the country."

"My God," Stephen laughed, "are you thinking of putting her in a convent? Look at her, man, surrounded by adoring throngs and quite lively out there."

Elliott scowled. The only place he wanted her to be adored and lively was in his bed.

They both watched as Verity waltzed past them, laughing at something her partner said. "That is it," Elliott ground out. "I am sending her home now."

———

Five minutes later, Elliott found himself in a group which contained not only his betrothed, but Countess Natalia Waskova who was, until three weeks ago, one of his most enthusiastic lovers.

"I must congratulate you, Lady Grainger," he heard her say as he moved next to Verity, "on your betrothal to Elliott. The duke is quite a catch, is he not?"

"Thank you, Countess." Verity's tone gave nothing away. But Elliott knew that she knew exactly who Natalia was.

"We are having a little soiree, next week. Perhaps you might come, with your sister and aunt of course," Natalia purred.

"That is most kind, Countess."

"You and I will have much to talk about. I am sure of it."

"If I might claim my betrothed," Elliott stepped in, glad to interrupt a conversation between Verity and his mistress. He could kill Natalia for what she was doing to Verity. He knew he could handle Natalia's mischief, temper, and tantrums, but Verity would be like a lamb to the slaughter.

"So nice of Lord Mara to introduce me to the countess," Verity began as Elliott took her arm and led her from the ballroom. "Obviously a very old friend of yours," she continued. "I thought she looked charming in that green gown," she added conversationally. "And those emeralds were quite spectacular."

"I did not notice," Elliott grunted.

"I cannot imagine how you could possibly have missed them," Verity went on, "especially as I believe they were attracting the attention of just about every man in the room. Although I'm not certain," she mused, "whether it was the emeralds or their position, nestling between her ample...."

"As I said," Elliott cut her off, having no interest in having a conversation with Verity about his ex-lover's breasts, "I did not notice, and neither should you."

Verity skidded to a halt. "How could I not notice? The woman was thrusting them in everyone's face all evening, and do not tell me you know nothing about those emeralds. At least three people were more than happy to tell me that you bought them for her. I do not imagine for one moment that they were for her birthday." Verity's eyes flashed.

Seeing a door, Elliott opened it and shoved Verity in before turning back and locking it behind them. They had stumbled into the library, where a fire blazed in the great hearth and the many candles illuminated the hundreds of books lining the walls. Fortunately, they were alone.

"I apologise for the fact that you have had to meet up with some of my past tonight. I cannot deny that there have been women in my life, as I said, I am not a monk. I assure you that I did not know that Natalia would be here tonight."

"Or Lady Bentham or the Honourable Mrs. Coleford? Was there a woman other than myself, my sister or my aunt here this evening who has not been your mistress?" Verity challenged, her eyes like emerald fire.

Elliott felt his temper rising. "You are treading on dangerous ground, my lady, considering the way you flirted with all the men you were dancing with, they were all thinking the same thing."

Verity rolled her eyes. "I danced with the gentlemen who asked me. I laughed at their sometimes ridiculous jokes, and I was polite. As to their thoughts, I have no idea what they were thinking."

"This," he groaned hoarsely, "is what they were thinking." He hauled her into his arms and kissed her, his mouth grinding down on hers, softening and teasing as she responded to him. He hardened further when she could not stop a small sigh escaping as their tongues intertwined.

"*That* is what they all wanted to do." He spoke softly into her mouth as he caressed her waist. "And this." He tugged the bodice of her gown down, his eyes gleamed silver as he took in the perfection of her small, rounded breasts, their rosy tips already hardening under his hot gaze.

"Elliott, what are you doing?" Verity stammered, squirming slightly, sending shocks through his groin, but making no move to remove herself to refuse him of his desire.

Elliott's eyes took in the vision before him, hungrily possessive. This vision was his, his alone, and no other man would ever see or touch the mouth-watering rise and fall of the perfect breasts before him. He raised his hand and gently grazed his thumb across the peak, and Verity gasped delightfully at his touch. He lowered his head and took the other in his mouth, pleasuring both buds, stroking and teasing with his fingers, lips, and tongue. He hardened painfully as he felt sensation after sensation wash over her, as she whimpered and pressed against him. Somewhere, somehow, his brain regained some control of his senses and he straightened, stepping back and quickly adjusting Verity's gown. It took all his considerable willpower not to lie her down and take her there and then.

Now that there was some physical distance between them, he was angry with himself for allowing his control to slip. He wanted her, he could not deny it, but so did all the other men in the room. It was sheer lust, nothing else. He would not let emotion cloud the issue. Ton marriages were based on mutual convenience. He would provide her with a comfortable life, and she would provide him with an heir. The fact that they were clearly sexually attracted to each other would mean that the getting of heirs would be more of a pleasure than a duty. Entirely pleasurable, in fact.

CHAPTER 10

*V*erity's mind was in a whirl, and she blushed as she thought of what she had just done. Her breasts felt shockingly cold without his touch and her body was fairly taut with alarming sensations. Elliott had kissed her and touched her and not only had she not stopped him, she could not have stopped him. She had enjoyed it, she could not deny it. When he touched her, and she felt a new kind of excitement, she had not wanted him to stop, she had wanted him to carry on.

"You are to go home now, Verity. My carriage will take you." His words hit her like cold water, bringing her back from the sensuous web he had woven, returning her to herself. "I do not understand," she murmured. "What about Ella and Lady Bette? I came with them, so surely, I should wait for them."

"You will go now, for I refuse to watch as a parade of unsuitable men takes every opportunity to ruin your reputation. I will call on you tomorrow." His voice was implacable.

"So I am to be sent home like a naughty child because of some foolish men?" she demanded.

Elliott ignored her protest. "I will explain that you felt unwell. Now, you can either walk to the carriage on my arm in a civilised manner, or I can put you over my shoulder and carry you there. You have given me enough trouble for one evening. Make your choice."

Minutes later, Verity sat alone in the ducal carriage, fuming. Elliott Thorne was the singularly most arrogant, high-handed, pig-headed man she had ever met. How could he do those things to her one minute and change completely the next. Her breasts tingled even at the thought of his touch. She never wanted to see him again and when he came tomorrow, she would tell him so, the arrangement be damned.

As the carriage turned into Bloomsbury Square, Verity recognised the old Grainger town house. She rapped on the roof of the carriage, and it halted. She could see a candle shining in the kitchen window down the area steps. The house now belonged to Elliott, along with everything else her family had owned, but she suddenly had an urge to see the place once again.

"You may go on home, Riggs," she said to the coach driver. "I shall be perfectly able to walk from here."

"'Is Grace's orders were to ensure that you got home safely, my lady." Riggs was clearly reluctant to disobey his master.

"It is only round the corner, Riggs, and I have a desire for some fresh air. I promise you I shall be perfectly all right."

"Even so. My lady."

Verity put on her most winning smile. "I promise that His Grace will never know."

"If you're sure, my lady. If anything were to 'appen to you 'is Grace would have my ba...er, guts for garters."

Verity laughed. "This will be our little secret, Riggs. Why don't you go home and have a cup of tea before you have to go and pick up His Grace from the ball?"

"Oh, I don't have to go back my lady, 'is Grace is going with 'is Grace's brother, the other duke, to a party after the ball. At some foreign count's, I believe," he added conversationally.

"Is he indeed?" Verity fumed. She knew precisely which count and countess, and how could he? How dare he? Minutes after...being inti-mate...with her, he was already planning a liaison with his lover. "In that case, Riggs, you go home. I'm sure Mrs. Riggs will be glad to see you."

The coachman broke into a rare, toothless smile. "That she will, your ladyship, and I shall be glad to sit before a warm fire, if you're quite sure you'll be all right."

"Of course, I shall, Riggs. I have been familiar with these streets since I was a schoolgirl."

She watched as the carriage disappeared into the night before descending the area steps and tapping at the door. As a child, she had often snuck into the comfort of the warm kitchen when her father was in one of his rages. The door was opened ,and she was soon enveloped into the arms of Mrs. Clayton, the house-keeper who looked a little rounder and a little greyer, but as usual refused to stand on ceremony. Before she knew it, Verity was sitting by the fire with a cup of tea and a currant bun, just as she had on numerous occasions when she was a child.

"What's this we hear about our little Lady Verity marrying a duke, well the duke who is to be our new master, no less?" Mrs. Clayton's eyes were twinkling, but Verity knew that behind them was a keen intelligence. "Isn't he the lad you were sweet on when you were a girl?" Verity nodded as she swallowed. "The one that left you high and dry. He wasn't a duke then, I recall."

"No," Verity replied. "He made his fortune and was adopted as heir to some relation of his mother's."

"And now he's come to claim his bride."

"His prize more like."

There was a pause as Mrs. Clayton waited for Verity to continue, and in the face of warmth and kindness, it all came tumbling out, not the official version for the ton, but the truth. Verity concluded, sniffling, "I do not know what to do, Mrs. Clayton. Father seems to have trapped us both in this awful nightmare, for I doubt that I can make Elliott happy nor he me. Every time we see each other, it seems as though we are determined to fight."

Mrs. Clayton patted her hand. "All couples fight from time to time."

Verity smiled sadly. "We are not really a couple, but we have been bound together by Father's machinations. Elliott does not want me, not really."

"Then the man's a fool." Mrs. Clayton sniffed. "And you will be well rid of him. If he can't see the treasure he has, then he does not deserve you."

Verity blew her nose. "Oh, Mrs. Clayton, you always made me feel better. Now I must go, as I promised Riggs I would be safely tucked up in bed before the others come home. I don't want him to get into trouble."

"Nonsense, you can't be wandering about the streets at this time of night. London is full of ne'er do wells, quite apart from the fact that you would catch your death of cold. That cloak is all very well in a carriage, but you would freeze to death before we got to the end of the street. Apart from anything else, it's snowing."

"Oh, no!" Verity looked through the window. Large flakes were falling silently, the street already had a slight covering, and the trees were beginning to look as though they were wearing lace shawls. "This is terrible. No-one knows where I am. I shall be in the most dreadful trouble." She chewed her lip.

Mrs. Clayton smiled. "I'll make a bed for you here. Mr. Clayton will run over and give a message for your maid to make it look as though you are in your bed and early in the morning, Mr. Clayton and I will see you home. We shall be so early no-one will know you were missing. Just like the time you hid in here instead of meeting that old chap your father wanted you to marry." She laughed. "There's no need to worry my dear, everything will work out for the best, it always does."

CHAPTER 11

*E*lliott had slept little. He would normally have enjoyed the evening with Waskova, gambling and drinking with a ready supply of women of the demi-monde to attend to whatever needs the gentlemen might have. Waskova and his wife had a remarkably modern attitude to their marriage: so long as neither embarrassed the other, they were free to go their separate ways. They liked each other well enough, but there had never been any attachment between them. As he watched Natalia flirt brazenly with some of his friends, the thought struck him that he could not bear the thought of anyone other than himself with Verity. He took a large swallow of brandy. If any man looked at her as they were looking at Natalia, he would beat them to pulp.

"Well, how the mighty have fallen." Natalia had moved towards him without him noticing.

"What do you mean?"

She leaned over and brushed an imaginary speck from his neck-cloth. "Your Grace has finally succumbed to the charms of the Lady Verity." Natalia stood on tiptoe and whispered into his ear, standing so close, her breasts grazed his waistcoat. Such an action would normally have produced an instant arousal, which she knew quite well, but tonight he felt only annoyance.

"Lady Verity and I are betrothed, it is no secret," he drawled, suddenly wanting to get away from her cloying scent.

"Ah, this surprising betrothal." She laughed. "What has the little country mouse done to win the hand of a great duke, I wonder?"

"I have no intention of discussing my betrothed with you."

"Ah, the English aristocrats." She laughed seductively, throwing back her head so that he could further appreciate her magnificent breasts. "For the sake of an heir, you engage yourself to this little milksop who will not hold your interest beyond the wedding night. Still," she mused, "at least she will not interfere with our arrangements, my love. Your wife can produce the heir, I shall produce the passion. I see no reason for our arrangement to come to an end, just because you will have a wife." She wound her arms around his neck.

He stepped back and gently disentangled himself from her embrace. "I am afraid it must, Natalia," he said simply.

Natalia's eyes narrowed to slits, before she quickly adjusted her face to its brightest smile, "You know where I am, Your Grace, should marital life disappoint." Then she was gone, her silk skirts rustling as she swept towards a group of young hussars. Within minutes, he heard her laughter at something one of them said and could see the young officer blush as she leaned forward and whispered seductively in his ear.

Elliott knew this performance was for his benefit, but he couldn't summon the feelings of jealousy that she intended, he merely felt distaste. He had not considered it before, but he now knew, without a shadow of a doubt, and some measure of surprise, that he did not want a ton marriage of convenience. He did not want a mistress who would be faithful while he footed the bills for her lifestyle, nor did he want to flit from affair to affair with the vain, shallow women of the ton. He sighed as he admitted to himself that the only woman he wanted in his life and in his bed, had ever wanted, was Verity Grainger and he didn't like it—didn't like it one bit.

He shook his head. He must get a grip on his emotions. There was an insurmountable gap between what he wanted and reality. Verity would be his duchess, but he could not allow himself to form an emotional attachment. He would not give her that power over his life happiness. Once again, he forced his mind back to her father's duplicity, reminding himself that she was marrying him now only because he had a title and wealth, and he would do well to remember that. Had he really thought this sham betrothal would actually result in a meaningful marriage?

Footsteps approached him. "Why the gloomy face?" His brother passed him one of the two glasses he was carrying. "You look as though you've swallowed a tiger, tail and all." They both watched as Natalie disappeared through a different door to the young officer, both knowing that within minutes the two would be intertwined. "Ah, is it all over between you and the fragrant Natalia?"

Elliott looked at his brother. "There was never anything between us other than what happened between the sheets and I grant you that Natalia is very good at that, but out of bed there is nothing in her head beyond furs, gowns, and jewels."

Stephen returned his brother's gaze. "Come."

"Where are we going?"

"Home, where we're going to drink until we either pass out or you tell me what's eating at you. As if I could not guess," he added softly.

"I don't know what the hell you're talking about."

"I think you do, since this betrothal business began, you have been like a bear with a sore head, so I'm putting it down to Lady Verity."

Under normal circumstances, Elliott's fist would have connected, but Stephen merely side-stepped. "See, Brother, you can't even punch straight, so Lady Verity definitely has a lot to answer for."

CHAPTER 12

Two bottles of brandy later, Stephen waved his arm. "The trouble is, Brother, you've gone and fallen in love with the girl," he slurred. "It happens to us all. None of us thinks we'll fall in love, but we do. We don't ever consider that we will want to settle for just one woman for the rest of our lives, but we do. Not all marriages are like Countess Natalia's y'know, endlessly unhappy." He carefully placed his empty glass on the table and stretched his legs in front of the fire. "What's wrong with Lady Verity, anyway? She seems acceptable wife material to me."

"She is," Elliott agreed. "Very acceptable. In every way, she's spirited, intelligent, kind..."

"And beautiful," Stephen put in. "Her figure is quite....!" he gestured wildly.

"Very beautiful," Elliott agreed, as he ran his hands through his dark hair. "She would make the perfect wife. I just don't know that I can trust her, and I certainly cannot afford to fall in love with her."

Stephen leaned forward. "How so?"

Elliott closed his eyes for a moment to try and order his thoughts. "You already know that I knew Verity some years ago?"

"Before you joined the militia, yes."

"Well, she was one of the reasons I joined up. I loved her beyond distraction and wanted to marry her, but when I offered for her, her father took the greatest pleasure in telling me that I would never be good enough for his daughter and to prove it he read out a message from her, which more or less said the same thing. Then he threw me out on my arse."

"But you hadn't forgotten her?" Stephen asked softly.

Elliott glanced quickly at his brother, who no longer seemed as drunk as he appeared a few moments ago. "No, I hadn't forgotten her," he admitted. "For years I dreamed of returning rich and famous and taking my revenge."

"So that's why you were determined to buy Swallowfield." There was no mistaking the satisfaction in his brother's tone.

Elliott laughed bitterly. "I thought I might enjoy throwing the old devil out on his arse."

"So what stopped you?" Stephen prompted.

"Quite frankly, he died, and it no longer seemed important. He'd already lost everything. There was no point."

"But you still wanted to punish Lady Verity."

"I thought I did," Elliott admitted.

"And now?"

Elliott took a breath before replying. "I don't."

"What changed your mind? Because the day the announcement came out in *The Times*, you were ready to have her dressed in scarlet and dragged through London on a cart."

Elliott could not help but smile. "That ridiculous clause in the bill of sale and the announcement certainly caught my attention," he said wryly.

"Do you want to know what I think?" Stephen asked.

"No, but I'm sure you're going to tell me anyway," Elliott responded.

"I think you should marry her and make it a proper marriage while you're about it. I know, the ton is full of men who marry for money and women who marry for titles and security, and many of them are unhappy, the men take mistresses, and the women take lovers."

"Get to the point," Elliott gritted testily. Stephen was getting into emotional territory, somewhere Elliott didn't want to go.

"My point is this: they take mistresses and lovers to compensate for the barren lives they have inflicted on each other."

"Men have always taken mistresses," Elliott shot back.

"Of course, they have," Stephen agreed, "but the happiest men I know are the ones who are married and in love with their wives." He thought for a moment. "Look at Wensley, Whitney, and his brother Bainbridge; happier men you will never meet."

Elliott thought for a moment. It was true: of his married friends, those who had married for love were content in a way that others were not. Could he have that with Verity? Could he risk falling in love with her again, tie his happiness and fate to her whims again? He ruthlessly stamped the idea out, insisting to himself what he felt was lust and that was all he felt for the sublimely alluring woman. It was all he would allow himself to feel where Verity Grainger was concerned.

"For what it's worth," Stephen sighed as stood up, "I think Lady Ella and Lady Verity are diamonds of the highest quality, and you would be a fool to let Lady Verity slip through your fingers." He threaded his way carefully to the door. "You'd do well to set a date before she takes your advice and looks for someone else while you are leaving her to do the socializing."

"What about you and Lady Ella? Am I right in thinking that you are developing a tendresse for her?" Elliott asked coyly. He could not help but notice the wistful light in his brother's eyes when he spoke of Verity's elder sister.

Stephen smiled. "One sister at a time, Brother, one sister at a time. Good night."

Stephen closed the door quietly behind him, and Elliott stretched out his long legs. The fire was dying, but as he sat in the glow of the embers, he went over the conversation again. Stephen was right. He wanted Verity. He wanted to watch her as he stripped the clothes from her body, and to hear the little sounds she would make as he kissed and caressed her. He wanted to see and touch and taste every inch of her, bury himself deep inside her and hear her cry his name as he made love to her and see her face as she came apart in his arms.

Elliott shook his head to clear his mind of the images it had conjured up, unwilling to feel the pinch in his trousers this night. Stephen had turned into a romantic fool, but he most certainly was not about to become so. He didn't love Verity, he *would* not love her, he couldn't afford to love her, but he lusted after her, that he could not deny. And why should he deny himself? They would marry with a degree of haste, and he would avail himself of her body as and when he required her. It was the obvious solution. She would grace his house and his bed, while he would enjoy the getting of children and that would do, it would have to. He would marry her. He would tell her in the morning, he thought as he drifted off to sleep.

CHAPTER 13

awn was breaking when the three conspirators stole quietly
through the almost deserted streets. London was beginning
to wake up, candles still glowed in windows as servants began to go
about their duties. It had snowed all night, at least a foot had fallen.
Snow always makes anywhere look magical, Verity thought as she
passed under trees, their branches bowing over with the weight of their
white burden. Their steps were muffled as they made their way across
the square.

"'Tis cold enough to freeze the tail off a brass monkey," Mr. Clayton
grumbled, sucking his teeth.

"Then you should have stayed home," Mrs. Clayton replied. "Lady
Verity and I are quite capable of walking on our own."

"Can't let the two of you out without protection, now can I? Never
know who's lurking about."

"Lurking? Who would be foolish enough to be lurking in this
weather? Lurking indeed," Mrs. Clayton scoffed.

The two of them continued to bicker as they passed the frozen foun-
tain with its statue of a Cupid perpetually shooting his arrow, now
covered in a cloak of snow. "Mrs. Clayton, thank you for looking after
me last night, and you, Mr. Clayton, for ensuring my safe return this

morning. I feel much better, but I shall be perfectly safe now on my own," she said quietly.

Mrs. Clayton looked up at the house doubtfully. "If you're sure, my dear, Clayton and I don't mind waiting until you're safely inside."

"I shall be fine," she reassured them. "It's so early, I shall be in my room before anyone knows it." She kissed the old couple before she ran lightly up the steps.

Candles burned in some of the windows as the maids bustled about lighting fires. Far in the distance she could hear the reassuring sounds of pots and pans being banged about in the kitchen, and much to her surprise, the door to the drawing room opened and her aunt, who was not usually an early riser, rushed out in a flurry. "I am so glad that you are safe and sound!" she exclaimed. She looked nervously round, and added in a hushed tone, "Unfortunately, we have an early visitor."

The hall boy took her cloak and gloves, "Your ladyship...." he whispered nervously, but was interrupted by a familiar voice shouting angrily. "Where the hell have you been?"

Verity whirled round. The last person she expected to see was Elliott, yet there he was, standing in the hall and he was not happy at all. He fixed the hall boy with a glare, who hastily disappeared down the hall. In less than a second, he had covered the distance between them, opened the drawing room door and ushered her inside, his eyes flashed cold and steely. "I would appreciate a few moments alone with my fiancée, Lady Newsham, if you would be so kind."

His tone brooked no argument and her aunt nodded respectfully, though her eyes glanced at Verity worriedly. "I shall be in the library," she said and moved rapidly down the hall.

Elliot quietly closed to door with an air of finality. There was a pause before he spoke. "I want to know where you spent the night, because I know sure as hell that it wasn't here."

Verity looked at him; he was magnificent, she could not deny it. Even now, with his eyes a steely grey, boring into hers, she wanted to raise her hand and smooth back the dark lock of hair that had fallen over his eyes. She took a deep breath to steady her nerves. "That, Your Grace, is none of your concern," she said airily. Verity knew that she was baiting a bear, but she was still furious with him for sending her home so that he could go to his paramour.

"I should say it is very much my concern since I saw the way you were flirting with half of London last night. Could it be that you sneaked out to meet one of the rakes at whom you were boldly throwing yourself?" he demanded.

Verity's hand shot out and connected with his cheek in a resounding slap. "How dare you question my morals when you could not get rid of me quickly enough so that you could go to your mistress?"

His cheek instantly started to redden. Elliott could not deny her accusation. "I went to see Natalia to tell her that my relationship with her is over," he ground out. He knew he was being unreasonable, but the thought of her with anyone else was driving him insane.

"Am I expected to believe that?" Verity shot back, scornfully.

"Believe what you will, but I have told you the truth. Now extend me the same courtesy and explain why you were sneaking into the house like a dockside whore after I had arrived to call."

Her hand shot out again, but this time he reacted quickly, and he caught her wrist. "I would advise that you do not do that again," he growled. His voice was deceptively quiet, but there was no doubt that he was beyond angry with her.

It was quite clear that she was furious with him in return. "If you must know, I spent the night with the Claytons, a very respectable couple I have known since I was a child," she ground out angrily.

Elliott frowned, releasing her wrist. "The Claytons...I have never heard of them."

"Of course you don't know them, as they don't mix much in society," she snapped. "Now, if you have finished insulting me and my virtue, perhaps you would leave." She spun on her heel defiantly, storming toward the door.

"Verity, wait, I have something to say to you."

She paused. "I cannot think of a single thing, Your Grace, that you would say that I would wish to hear. You have said quite enough for the morning."

"Wait." He caught her hand once more, but she quickly snatched it away.

"Don't touch me. Given what you think of me, I cannot think that you would want to sully your hands."

Elliott closed his eyes briefly; this was not how he had imagined this meeting going at all. He had pictured Verity falling into his arms with gratitude after he explained the terms under which they would marry, and she would happily agree with a demure smile. The anger was unexpected, to say the least, and he had yet to even tell the blasted woman his decision! He took a breath, then said, "I apologise for my behaviour. I was frantic with worry when it emerged that you were not in your bed. It does not excuse my behaviour. I know that and once again, I am sorry."

He saw some of the tension left Verity's body as she released a breath slowly. Finally, she looked him in the eye with a pleasant look on her face. "What was it you wanted to say, Your Grace?"

"I have decided that we shall marry in accordance with your father's wishes."

There was absolute silence for a moment before Verity burst out, "You must be insane. Have you had a recent blow on the head, Your Grace?"

"Not at all. I have given the matter much consideration. I need an heir and for that I must have a wife. You need a husband, so I have decided that we shall marry in due course. In fact, as soon as possible. There is no need to delay, as notice of our engagement has already been posted, so we might as well get it over with." He paused, waiting for a response such as the one he had imagined, but with her continued silence, he continued, "We shall make Swallowfield your main residence and our children will be raised there, just as you were."

CHAPTER 14

*V*erity could scarcely comprehend how, in such a short time, her well-ordered life had been turned upside down. Since her father's death, she had learned that she had no fortune and no prospects of marriage, and then Elliott had re-appeared in her life like a whirlwind. In a matter of weeks, and quite against her wishes, she was summarily betrothed to a man she despised and was about to be married into a loveless ton marriage which she knew, from the bitter experience of her father's wives, would be a disaster for the both of them.

She raised her head and looked questioningly into his eyes to see if she could see the slightest hint that he wanted to marry her because he felt something, anything, for her. She knew that he did not love her, but she realised that, try as she had to wipe him from her heart, that she could not say with conviction that she felt nothing for him.

For seven years, she had carried the hurt and humiliation inside her when he had left her without a word. 'Gone to the army, and to the devil. A good for nothing fortune hunter. Do you think he wanted you, girl? He was just after your dowry, that's all you were to him, money, that's all you are to any man. He's gone and good riddance. You will never speak his name again,' her father had commanded. She had spent months on the verge of tears, never allowing them to fall.

Now it seemed that Elliott wanted her once more, not for money this time, for she had none. Now he wanted her for the purpose of breeding his heir, and once she had succeeded in that, what then? What if, like her mother, she couldn't provide the sons men in his position set so much store by? Sense and reason asserted itself and she knew that if she had to go through with his plan, now would be the only opportunity she had to negotiate anything. "And how pray is this arrangement going to work? Given the fact that we cannot be in each other's company for five minutes without arguing, I cannot imagine it would be remotely pleasant for either of us..."

"I doubt that it will make much difference to our lives, Once Swallowfield is ready, you will spend your time there with any child or children, until they are of an age to go to school."

"And you?" she asked.

"I shall continue as I do now, in London or wherever my business takes me."

"I see." She kept her voice even though her heart was breaking. "So you will carry on with your life in society while I am kept in isolation at Swallowfield?"

His face brightened at her acquiescence. "In essence, yes, but you will not be alone. Of course, your sisters may live there until they marry, and I shall no doubt visit from time to time. I must if we are to conceive of an heir."

"How very magnanimous of you," she murmured bitterly.

"I thought so, too." He beamed happily, either uncaring or entirely deaf to her despair. Neither of which boded well.

"And am I to be allowed out at all?" she asked.

He frowned. "Of course. Swallowfield is not a prison."

"Oh?" She feigned surprise. "So I may be permitted to go to the village perhaps once a week? And should I be expected to wear the Rydale livery to advertise who owns my life? Or am I to be trusted to even behave appropriately after being banished from society? Please,

Your Grace," she said with exaggerated formality, "I wish only to adequately fulfil your expectations for your wife."

He sighed and raised his eyes to Heaven. It seemed that he may have misunderstood her reaction. This was possibly not in fact going nearly as well as he thought. "What are you trying to say, Verity?"

She opened her eyes innocently. "I am merely trying to understand the conditions under which I am expected to live as your wife, Your Grace. Because it seems to me that my sole purpose is to provide you with an heir, if that happens, and given that you apparently intend to spend as little time as possible in my company there is some doubt as to how it might be accomplished, but if that happens, what then?"

"What do you mean, what then?" he replied testily.

"Well, am I still to be kept out of sight and out of mind while you gallivant around the place with your current paramour?" she asked. "Or perhaps when I have done my duty and borne you an heir am I permitted to take lovers as well? After all, what is sauce for the goose ought to be sauce for the gander," she said and smiled sweetly.

Elliott's temper was beginning to fray, much to his further annoyance. Verity Grainger had always been able to get under his skin. "I will make it as clear as I can, Verity. We will marry as soon as possible and once Swallowfield is habitable, you will live there. Until that time, you and your sisters may come to live at my townhouse. You will live at Swallowfield with such children as we have, and when they are of an age to go to school you will of course continue to live at Swallowfield should you so wish. There will be no lovers. I do not think I can make it any clearer. In any case," he added, "it is apparently what your late, unlamented father wanted."

"No," she replied, firmly.

Elliott quirked a ducal eyebrow. "No?"

"No, Your Grace, I will not marry you on those terms."

His eyebrow rose higher. "You believe you have some negotiating power?"

Verity laughed. "I know I have very little negotiating power. I did not see what happened to Ella's mother, but I saw what happened to my mother and Caro's when they could not deliver a living male heir. My father came to hate us all for his disappointment; his wives for not giving him sons, and his daughters because we had disappointed him by not being those sons. So, if all I am to you is a means to get an heir, then I respectfully decline."

Elliott stared. He understood that she despised him, but surely, she knew him better than this. "I am not your father," he replied.

She shook her head sadly. "I understand, but I will find some other way for my sisters and I to survive. I will not be forced into a loveless marriage."

"A marriage of convenience."

"Convenient for you," she shot back. "There is nothing you have said that suggests any benefit for me."

"God's teeth, woman. There will be gowns, jewels, a carriage, furs, a fine house. Is that not what women want? What more could you want?"

This was proving more complicated than Elliott had envisaged. In his mind, he had informed Verity of his decision and she had fallen at his feet with gratitude. He was determined never to give her power over his heart, though she seemed now just as unwilling to give him her own. He took a deep breath and said, "Let me explain again, we shall marry and soon as there is no reason to delay. We will spend some time in London together, and when Swallowfield is completed, that will be our main residence in the country. You will come to town as and when you wish and when I am in residence, I shall escort you to whatever social functions you wish to attend. You shall have what you desire in the way of gowns, jewels and whatever other fripperies you wish. All I ask is that you provide me with a living heir."

Verity did not speak for several minutes. Her greatest desire was to have Elliott, have him once more, and have him love her as he once had. She had wanted a life with him, and in a cruel twist of fate, she was being given one without the other. Eventually, she raised her eyes to his. "Do you really imagine that those things would make up for having a child, knowing that when they are seven, they will be taken from me?" she asked softly. "And when the child goes to school, will I be allowed to see him again, or do you intend to break off all contact with me?"

Elliott reared back. "Of course not! What sort of man do you think I am? The child will need to go to school, of course, but he will need the love and guidance of both his parents."

Once again, Verity remained silent knowing that she had little choice. If she made this sacrifice, perhaps Caro or Ella would have the chance of a better match. "Very well, Your Grace, I will accept your offer. Though, I cannot see how the getting of a child is going to work when we hate each other."

"Much to my surprise, I find I do not hate you, Verity," he replied. "In any case, you do not need to like me to bear my children."

She hid her surprise at his confession and haughtily replied, "But I do need to be able to countenance the thought of you touching me."

No sooner were the words out of her mouth than Elliott's arms shot out and dragged her towards him and his mouth came down on hers in a punishing kiss. She willed her body not to respond to the heat rushing through her, refusing to struggle and keep entirely calm. He gentled the kiss, while still holding her close enough for her to feel his hardness against her body. Without conscious thought, her mouth opened to his and his tongue found hers. Groaning softly, he pulled her even closer, and she felt warmth pool at her core, and she pressed her thighs together. Despite herself, she wanted to feel his hands on her skin, to enjoy the rapture of his mouth as she had in stolen moments long ago. Suddenly conscious of the tiny sounds she was making, she abruptly stepped away.

"Well, I think that proves that like it or not, and from what just happened I would say like it, we should have no difficulty in the getting of an heir," he declared airily.

Verity wiped her mouth. "You arrogant bastard. Very well, set the date. I will do my duty to my family and to you, but that is where this farce ends."

CHAPTER 15

$\mathcal{I}$n the six weeks that Elliott allowed for the planning of the wedding, Verity had seen little of him, as he had spent a few days on business in Lancashire and Yorkshire and two weeks in France. When they had been together, she had made sure that they were never alone, and he was certainly never in a situation where he could touch her.

Try as she might, she could not blot the memory of his searing kiss and the callous way in which he had stepped away from her as though she meant nothing to him, less than nothing. It was as though the young man she had fallen in love with had gone and been replaced by the harsh and cynical man, and yet, there were times when she saw a glimmer of Elliott as he used to be.

He had no need to look after her sisters, and yet he had promised to do so. One thing was certain, if he thought he was getting a demure bride who would do his bidding without question, he would be sadly mistaken. A wife promised to obey her husband, but there was nothing in the promise to say that obedience could not be creative.

The last task she had was her final fitting for her gown at Madame Dupont's. She had been standing for an hour as the final adjustments were made when she became aware of another woman standing watching the proceedings. Among the grey and black uniforms worn by Madame's staff, this woman stood out like a peacock among sparrows. Her dress was a deep crimson cut high in the waist and embroidered with black poppies along the waist and hem. She wore a jaunty red hat on jet black hair that had been carefully dressed to emphasise her elegant neck and show off the large diamond earbobs. Her pale skin was flawless and her eyes were the bluest Verity had ever seen.

"I think I 'ave all I need now, Lady Grainger, but please to lose no more weight before ze wedding, yes?" Madame and her assistants helped Verity down and she stepped carefully out of the dress. "This should no' be too 'ard, yes? Just t'ree days!"

"I can help Lady Grainger with her dress," the woman said. "Verity and I are old friends."

"Very well," Madame Dupont replied and disappeared with her assistants to the back room.

"Do I know you?" Verity asked.

The woman smiled, showing small white teeth. "I doubt it, Lady Grainger. We do not move in the same circles." She held out Verity's gown.

"Then I am afraid you have me at a disadvantage Lady..." Verity asked as she stepped into the gown.

The woman laughed. "No title. I am Mrs. Audra Kingsley," she said as she expertly fastened the small buttons on the back of the gown.

"I am afraid I am still at a loss."

The woman fastened Verity's sash. "Why should you? We have one acquaintance in common. Elliott Thorne."

"I have never heard him speak of you," Verity remarked, her mind was in a whirl. "I have met several of his mistresses, but no-one mentioned you, Mrs. Kingsley," she said coolly.

"Oh, I am much more than a mistress, my dear," Mrs. Kingsley was not fazed at all.

"I believe Elliott's latest mistress was Countess Waskova," Verity pressed on, determined not to be intimidated by her.

Mrs. Kingsley snapped her fingers, showing some emotion for the first time in the conversation. "That trollop meant nothing to Elliott, a willing partner for bed sport, that is all. Elliott's relationship with me is deeper, and few people know of it. I was still married at the time our affair began, so we were naturally discreet."

"And now?"

Mrs. Kingsley smiled. "Now I am a wealthy widow, I do not have to pander to the whims of a most disappointing husband." She leaned forward. "So this is what is going to happen, lovely young virgin. You will marry Elliott and produce the requisite heir and possibly a second. You will live with them at that ghastly pile in the country, and Elliott will live in London where I shall act as his hostess. The ton will, I assure you, forget your existence before too long."

"If you are that sure of this, why is Elliott not marrying you?" Verity shot back.

"Oh, I have no intention of ruining my figure by producing brats," Mrs. Kingsley spat as she gathered her gloves and reticule. "The wedding dress looks well on you, my dear, but remember, while Elliott is making his vows and each time he endeavours to make love to you, he will be thinking of me."

Verity's mind and heart ached with the needless cruelty of Mrs. Kingsley, despite spending each day convincing herself that this wedding and marriage would be meaningless to the both of them. That she was happy Elliott would find someone else to touch, to caress, and to work out his exertions with.

The day of the wedding dawned all too quickly. She looked at herself in the mirror. The gown was beautiful. She was a beautiful bride. She needed only to look happy, not feel it.

Ella came into the room bearing the bridal bouquet just as Madame Dupont was putting the finishing touches to her gown. She also bore a small circlet of white roses and stephanotis to place in Verity's hair. "As you refused the duke's offer of the Rydale tiara, I have fashioned this for you," she said as she held out the flowers.

Madame stepped forward and expertly pinned it into Verity's hair.

"It is ze perfect finishing touch," she announced. "Now you are ready to meet your 'andsome bridegroom, yes?"

Verity looked at the woman in the mirror. In a short time, her life would change forever. She would be a duchess and miserable, but her sisters would be secure and possibly, because she had married Elliott, when they married it would be to men who loved them. Because she knew that the man she married would never love her.

The ride to the new church, St. George's in Hanover Street, was short, and before she knew it, Verity was standing at the entrance on the arm of Govan, the family lawyer, who was to give her away. As she turned to take the bouquet of roses, stephanotis, and peonies from Ella, she had a moment of panic. "I can't..." she began.

"You must," Ella replied, "for all our sakes."

Verity nodded, throat tight, took the bouquet, and stepped forward.

As Verity made her way down the aisle, she could feel the eyes of the ton boring through her. The ones still in London had come to see who had finally enticed the most eligible man of this and previous seasons into matrimony. Some smiled encouragingly, others glowered, especially women with daughters whom they had worked so hard to throw in Elliot's path, one of whom would no doubt have been his bride had this whole debacle not been arranged by her late father. Furthermore, Elliott had compounded the situation by insisting on this 'marriage of convenience,' Well, marriage he would certainly get, whether he thought it convenient was still to be decided.

Verity took a moment to get her breath, since the sight of Elliott waiting for her at the altar had taken it away. His black superfine jacket fitted his body to perfection; his white neckcloth was secured with his favourite ruby stick pin, which matched his silk waistcoat. His height was emphasised by the tightly fitting cream trousers. As always, a stray lock of thick, dark hair curled down over his forehead. She could not help her body's response to him, but she determinedly put her thoughts to one side; he was marrying her to get an heir, and that was all, the words of Audra Kingsley still echoed in her ears.

As the organ swelled, Elliott turned to look at his bride as she made her way up the aisle. His heart thundered. Her gown was of white silk, over-laid with the finest Brussels lace shot through with silver thread. With each step, the gown shimmered, making her look like an angel gracing him with her presence. As she passed one of the windows, a shaft of sunlight caught her head, making the flowers look like a halo. He had been annoyed when she had refused the offer of the Rydale diamond tiara, but the flowers were perfect. "My God...but she is beautiful," he murmured.

His brother smiled. "All the Grainger girls are. I shall ask you once again, Brother, is this truly what you want?"

Elliott turned to Stephen. "Of course. I made my decision. Besides, I could hardly jilt her at the altar, could I? It has gone too far for that."

At last, Verity stood beside him, and the vicar began. "Dearly beloved..."

As the vicar intoned the words, he repeated his vows with a clear, firm voice, keeping his gaze on the vision of perfection before him. He released a silent breath of relief when she recited her vows as he held her left hand, joining them together in the eyes of God forever.

CHAPTER 16

*A*s she signed her maiden name for the last time in the register, Verity took a deep breath. She would not cry, she would never waste more tears on Elliott Thorne. She had made her bed and now she must lie on it. She relished in her small rebellion, crossing the fingers of her right hand when she promised to obey in her vows. She could have screamed at the injustice of it, marrying a man with whom she had been desperately in love seven years ago; a man who she thought had loved her in return but who, according to her father, had been interested only in her dowry. Now, due to her father's insanity, she was tied to this same man for the rest of her life. A man who clearly did not love her and wanted her only for breeding. In many ways, not so different to any ton marriage, and in every way nothing that she wanted. As she laid down the quill and stood, Elliott handed her the bouquet and tucked her hand in his arm. "Ready? Your Grace?"

Verity nodded.

"Then let us greet the world as husband and wife."

The walk down the aisle was punctuated by several of Elliott's friends congratulating him. Somehow, Verity was able to smile and nod in appreciation. In relative privacy at the church door, Elliott paused and turned towards her. "Look at me please, Verity."

She raised her eyes to his solemnly. "I know this is not what either of us wanted, but we must try and make it work or we shall drive each other mad," he said quietly.

"I rather think that particular horse has bolted, Your Grace," she replied.

"Then madness it is," he said softly, cupping her face and drawing her towards him in a drugging kiss which was neither proper, nor usually seen at church doors. As soon as his lips touched hers, Verity could not help but respond, her whole body felt alive at his touch, and this was just the touch of his lips on her own. *"While Elliott is making his vows and each time, he endeavours to make love to you, he will be thinking of me."* The memory of the woman who had spoken the words dowsed Verity in such a cold wave that her entire body stiffened, and she withdrew from him.

"Do not shrink from me, Verity. I vow that I will never harm you," he said quietly.

She nodded, sure that he would never intend to, but certain that he would.

Although the wedding breakfast was a small affair by ton standards, Elliott was quite grateful that only thirty or so sat down to the sumptuous meal, though as course after course appeared, he found himself watching Verity; she was hardly eating more than a bite of each plate.

"Is the food not to your liking?" Elliott asked. "You have barely touched it."

She picked up her spoon and began pushing the lemon souffle around her dish. "I am sure it is delicious, but I am afraid I have no appetite."

He took the spoon from her. "Just taste a little," he said quietly, dipping the spoon into the sweet confection. "My chef insisted on preparing the wedding breakfast and has worked hard since early morning in your aunt's kitchen, no doubt terrifying her servants. To say the least he is very temperamental. If you do not eat something he will fling down his hat and most likely storm off and work for the prince, who has been trying to steal him from me for years, and," he added, leaning close and whispering "we all know that the last thing the prince needs is the finest French chef in London."

At Verity's giggle, he felt a rush of satisfaction at raising her spirits. "I think that what you just said was, in fact, treason, Your Grace," she said as Elliott fed her.

"It most definitely was," he admitted, "but we shall not tell him shall we, and what he does not know will not harm him." He fed her another spoonful before adding, "Now that you are my wife, I should like you to use my given name, Verity. Please."

Verity looked at him with her mesmerising green eyes. "Very well, Your Grace, when we know each other a little better," she agreed.

Elliott felt the sting of disappointment. "I believe we already know each other well enough, Verity, but I will wait until you are ready. But at least stop referring to me as 'Your Grace' as though you are in some way inferior. Afterall, you are a duchess now as well."

"But I am lesser," she replied quietly. "I am the dowerless woman you married, not because you wanted to, but because it was convenient for you. And I would be wise to remember that. Your Grace."

───────

All too soon, it was time to leave her aunt's house and return with Elliott to his town house. Her trunk was already packed and had gone on before. The couple were showered with rice as they made their way to Elliott's carriage. There were tears in her eyes as she hugged Ella goodbye for the first time they had been separated that Verity could remember. "Promise me you will come and visit as soon as you can," she said.

"I will come, when you return from your honeymoon," Ella replied.

Verity stepped back in shock. "What do you mean?"

"Oh, dear," Ella bit her lip. "It was to be a surprise and I have spoiled it."

"No matter," a deep male voice interrupted, "it is still a surprise, for Verity does not know where she is going."

"Verity did not know she was going anywhere at all," she said, tartly. "A honeymoon," she huffed. "I do not even know if I have packed appropriately."

"See, huffing again," Elliott pointed out. "I merely thought that we could do with some time away from the gawking and gossiping of the ton. Unfortunately, I need to remain a few days in London to attend to some business, but once that is concluded, we shall depart. As you said, you need to get to know me better, and," he leaned forward and whispered in her ear, sending shock waves down her spine, "I intend that you shall know me intimately by the end of it."

Elliott could not help but notice that Verity's hands were clasped so tightly on her lap that her knuckles were white. She turned from the window to ask, "Where are we to take this honeymoon of yours?"

"It is our honeymoon, Verity. We are to spend a few nights here then move to one of my estates."

"And am I to be kept there until Swallowfield is made ready for me?"

He raised his eyes to heaven, took a deep breath and counted to ten before replying, "You are right. Swallowfield is not quite ready for habitation yet, but you are not a prisoner, Verity, so stop behaving like some kind of martyr. You are my wife and are to be treated with respect. I merely wanted to surprise you with something pleasant, so please do not be difficult about it."

She opened her mouth to say something and stopped. He grinned to himself as she realized that she was being quite unfair and that he had arranged to spend some time with her away from the distractions of both his work and London society. "It was a nice idea, duke, thank you."

He nodded. It was the first time their conversation had not ended with some kind of argument. It was not much, but it was a start.

The duchess' apartment at Elliott's townhouse was above and beyond anything Verity might have expected and well beyond anything she had been used to even before her father had gambled and whored his way through his money.

The walls were covered with pale pink silk wallpaper, the matching bed hangings were scattered with small roses in a dusky pink with matching coverlet and curtains. She took in a dressing table in front of one of the windows and several chairs as well as a daybed in the room. There were windows on two sides of the room, which would make it feel light and airy during the day, but the myriad of candles and the central small chandelier gave the room a cosy glow along with the fire in the white marble fireplace. The door to another room stood open to reveal a room set aside especially for bathing with a large copper bath in the centre of the room, something Verity had never seen before. She was delighted to see that the bath was already full of steaming water.

As her feet sank into the thick carpet, she noticed her clothes had already been hung in the large armoire and a nightrail and robe had been laid out on the bed. There was another door leading from the bedroom, which she assumed connected to Elliott's room. There was a quiet knock at the door and Elliott strode in.

Her breath caught. He was still quite dressed, but there was an air of intimacy in his dishevelled, more comfortable appearance. How dearly she would have loved to have used his given name as he asked, but if she was to protect herself, she could not give in to any kind of intimacy. If she was to survive this marriage, she must keep him at arms' length, though she knew that from tonight, that would be impossible.

"I hope your accommodations are to your taste," he said. "It has been a long day, so I took the liberty of arranging a bath for you. A maid will come and assist you. We shall stay here for a few nights before we begin our travels. Good night, Verity."

He turned to leave.

"Wait," Verity said, halting his step. "Are you not to take your rights?" she asked, a blush arising on her cheek.

Elliott halted himself abruptly. He had meant to leave quickly while he still had the willpower to do so. He had never imagined she would invite him. Elliott looked at her, the silence between them lengthening with every breath. The one thing he wanted to do with every fibre of his being was to remove her clothing until she stood naked before him, then he wanted to touch and kiss every part of her body and watch her face as he pleasured her in ways she could not yet imagine. But he could see easily that she was not extending an invitation. With chagrin, he saw she was...concerned.

"Not tonight, Verity. As I said, it has been a long day. You must be exhausted, and in any case, I have no intention of taking anything you are not prepared to freely give, whatever rights I may have. Law or not, whatever you believe, I am a respectable and honourable man. Rest tonight, but I assure you," he added, "when I do take you, you will be more than willing for me to make love to you. In fact, you will be begging me for release. I doubt that you will forget this conversation, but remember Verity, when the time is right, I will give us both the greatest pleasure a man and his wife can have."

He allowed himself to kiss her quickly and chastely, then stalked from the room before he did exactly the opposite of what he had just promised.

Verity knew she should feel relief that she did not have to face Elliott's attentions tonight, but her body felt nothing but disappointment. As she soaked in the rose-scented water, she came to the conclusion that Elliott's disinterest in consummating their marriage could only come from the fact that he did not want her, regardless of his words. She had seen several of his previous mistresses and it would appear that she did not have what attracted him.

When the maid had handed her a towel and left, Verity examined herself in the cheval mirror, dropping the towel and standing naked in front of it. Although she wore a corset as all women did, her narrow waist suggested no real need. Her breasts were small but pert with delicate roseate nipples. Her legs were long for a woman and shapely, and a neat triangle of golden curls lay between them. None of this mattered because Elliott clearly did not find her beguiling enough to want to make love to her. She smiled wryly as she pulled the sheer nightrail over her head. It was almost transparent and clearly made to entice a willing male, though it would seem that Elliott was anything but willing.

The huge bed was as soft and comfortable as could be, but sleep evaded her. She tossed and turned for hours and when sleep did come, it was punctuated by dreams of Elliott. In all of them, she was naked, and Elliott was kissing and touching her until she cried out. She was on the brink of something, but she knew not what. When she woke, she was heated, the sheets tangled, and one of the pillows on the floor. Although she was an innocent, she was not completely ignorant of what was supposed to happen between a man and his wife. She lay there for a while, frustration giving way to anger.

By the fifth night, Verity was beside herself. This is ridiculous. A man is supposed to want to consummate his marriage, especially when he so badly wants an heir. Suddenly, and without thinking about it too much, she jumped out of bed, marched to the connecting door and flung it open. Dawn was beginning to break and although the room was in semi-darkness, she could make out the huge bed at the end of the room. "Elliott," she whispered, not wanting to wake him with a start.

She ventured further into the room. "Elliott." This time her voice was louder. Still, there was no response. "Elliott." This time she spoke loudly, heaven knew the man could obviously sleep through cannon fire.

When she drew back the bed curtain, it was clear why there had been no response. The bed was made up, and clearly it had not been slept in. No wonder he did not want to spend the night with her; he could not wait to get back to his mistress. "So this is to be the way it is to be, Your Grace," she whispered. "Well then, two can play at that game."

CHAPTER 17

ollowing his bidding her goodnight on their wedding night, he knew he would not sleep, worse still, he also knew that in all likelihood he would open the connecting door. For five nights, his restlessness had taken him to his brother's where each night they had sunk the best part of a bottle of fine brandy. On the fifth night, Stephen said, "Far be it from me to criticise, Brother, but what is a man who should have been enjoying his wedded bliss with his charming wife, doing sitting in my library and drinking my brandy?"

Elliott tossed back another glass. "It would be a mistake," he admitted. "In fact, I begin to believe that the whole thing is a mistake. I do not know what possessed me to think otherwise."

"Rather too late to come to that conclusion don't you think?" Stephen quirked an eyebrow. "You needed to marry for an heir, she needed to marry for security, and your new duchess is quite a beauty. I cannot imagine that sharing her bed would be a chore."

"I know. I explained all this to her when I proposed this marriage of convenience. I was very clear about what her duties would be. She would provide me with an heir or two which she could raise until they are old enough to go to school, about the age of seven. She would live untroubled at her beloved Swallowfield and then we should have no need to have further contact, or minimal contact as and when necessary."

"Oh, my God." Stephen shook his head.

"I also made it clear," Elliott ploughed on, "that she could have as much in the way of material goods as she wished, money, gowns, furs, jewels, that sort of thing. I am not an ungenerous man."

"No, but you are a very stupid one."

Elliott choked. "What the hell is that supposed to mean?"

Stephen drew in a deep breath. "You have approached this marriage as though you were drawing up a business contract with a partner you do not entirely trust. I am not a married man, and I would not claim to be an expert, but if you want to have some degree of peace with Verity, you will have to gain her trust and show her that you trust her."

"Go on."

"I know there is history between you, and not all of it good."

"None of it good," Elliott ground out.

"That is not entirely true, is it? You loved her once, I was there, I saw what she meant to you."

"I was a callow, foolish youth, and I have learned better," Elliot shot back.

"What you have learned is to keep women at arm's length so that they cannot get close enough to hurt you again. That is why your mistresses are dismissed the minute you think they are getting too close," Stephen replied.

"Verity is not my mistress," Elliott said, surprising himself with the heat in his voice. "She is my wife."

Stephen leaned forward. "Precisely. She is the woman you promised to love, honour, and cherish only a few short days ago. She will be the mother of your children, if she ever lets you in her bed, which going by the debacle of the last few nights, I very much doubt."

"She is my wife, I can take my rights whenever I wish," Elliott shot back.

Stephen shook his head. "You and I know that you do not mean that Elliott, and that is why you are here instead of making sweet, energetic love to your beautiful duchess."

Elliott took another swig of brandy. "You are right. She actually stood in front of me and asked me if I was going to take my rights and I could not." He laughed ruefully. "Much as I want her, I do not want to take what she does not want to give. That is the truth of the matter."

Stephen shook his head. "I cannot believe that you, who is purported in the papers to be an intelligent man, have not yet worked out the answer to the conundrum of your relationship with Verity."

Elliott gave his brother a steely glare. "And that is?"

"I have told you once before. That you still love her."

"Do not be ridiculous."

Stephen laughed. "Deny it all you want, Brother, but the fact of the matter is that you never stopped loving Verity, and when you had the opportunity to claim her again, you took it." He held up a hand to forestall any retorts. "I know that you thought you were going into this for revenge on the old earl, and I believe that were he still alive, you would have enjoyed rubbing his face in the mud. But I believe that you never intended to exact your revenge on the daughter."

"She schemed with her late father to trap me into marriage," Elliott replied, hearing in his voice how weak his conviction was in that belief.

"Think about it, Brother. When you offered for her hand, Verity was just a young girl, she had no power or even say over who her father decided she would marry. In fact, I believe she was to marry that old goat, the Earl of Darfield who fortunately dropped dead before matters were settled. Her father arranged it, not for her happiness, but to settle his own debts."

"What?" Elliott's shout reverberated around the room. He was aghast; he'd never heard of this before.

"The old earl owed his friend a great deal of money, so he decided to pay him by selling off his daughter. Whether the girls know it or not I do not know, but it is no secret among the ton that their father saw women as a means to an end, nothing more. He married his wives for their dowries and the need to provide an heir, which none of them did. The daughters have never been treated well."

"How do you know all this?" Elliott asked.

Stephen shrugged. "I have not been absent from society as you have,

Brother. The stories of the father's cruelty are common. He openly described Lady Ella as a monster and bemoaned that he would never be able to palm her off on a man of means. And though he could barely bring himself to look at her, she would at least be useful to look after him in his old age."

"And yet, Verity could have escaped him seven years ago when I offered for her, but her note was very clear. I did not have the where-withal to keep her in a manner befitting the daughter of an earl, and she did not even have the decency to refuse me to my face," he said bitterly.

"Elliott, does it not strike you that perhaps Lady Verity had no say in refusing you? Does it not occur to you that she may have written that note under duress?" Stephen asked. "Think about it," he added. "You had yet to make your fortune, her father was already sailing close to the wind with his creditors, so he needed her to make a marriage to a wealthy man. The fact that she did not refuse you in person only adds to the argument."

Elliott's eyes widened. "My God," he said quietly. "I may have misjudged her."

"It is certainly a possibility," his brother agreed. "Though we may never know in surety."

Elliott looked at his brother. "What am I to do? This marriage of convenience will make us both insane."

"Then make it a real marriage."

"I rather think that ship has sailed," Elliott admitted.

"If you want a real wife, and a real relationship, you must trust her in truth and make her fall in love with you again."

"And how am I to do that?"

Stephen raised his eyes to heaven. "This hesitancy is not like you, and I am sure you do not need the whys and wherefores. Just do it, and quickly because I do not wish to spend evenings moping with you whilst you drink me out of house and home."

On the way home, Elliott planned what he would do. He would join Verity for breakfast and then he would take her back up to his bedroom and make love to her. That should settle it. It would make his feelings clear and when he ensured her pleasure, she would understand that he valued and trusted her.

He was just making his way to the breakfast room when his wife came down the staircase dressed in a dark emerald riding habit, her hair caught at the nape of her neck in a veil attached to a jaunty little hat. She was pulling on her gloves when she saw him. It was clear to him from her sparkling eyes and clear complexion that she, unlike him, had not spent the night unable to sleep.

"Oh, good morning, Your Grace. I had not expected you back so soon. I am sure there is still food in the breakfast room should you be hungry from your exertions last night." She smiled sweetly. "As you can see, I am about to go out for a ride in the park."

"I will join you. Just give me five minutes to change," he replied. It did not look good that he was still dressed in his evening clothes, something no doubt that Verity had noticed.

"There is no need, Your Grace," she said airily. "I shall ride with a groom until I meet with Duchess Emily and Duchess Helen in the park. Then we are to join Duchess Clara for lunch, now that she has returned to us."

He could not let her disappear for the whole of the morning when he needed to explain his revelation. "Verity, I should like to speak with you," he began.

"And so you shall, Your Grace. We are engaged to dine with Lord and Lady Caunce this evening, are we not? I shall be back in plenty of time to dress."

With that, his wife disappeared through the door leaving only the lingering scent of roses and vanilla and Elliott with three thoughts: that his wife's rear view was enticing, that she was still 'your gracing' him, and that it seemed that reconciling with his wife was going to be more difficult than he imagined.

CHAPTER 18

"*A*re you all right? Your Grace?"

The groom's voice was anxious as Verity rested her head on Velvet's neck before using the mounting block. She turned and pinned a bright smile on her face. "I am fine, thank you, Penn," she replied. "I promise you I will not fall off," she added, though it had taken all her willpower to face Elliott as though nothing was remotely wrong. The fact that he had clearly gone to his mistress on his wedding night, coming back in time for breakfast still in his wedding clothes made her feel sick to her stomach, and that he had continued to do so every night since was unbearable. The fact that he did not want her hurt more than it should, she knew he was marrying her for the purpose of an heir, but it would seem that apart from that, he had no use for her, and judging by his lack of enthusiasm for bedding her at all. It would seem that he had little use for her at all.

Within moments they had arrived at the park where Emily, Duchess of Whitney, and Helen, Duchess of Bainbridge were already present, chatting on their mounts. They waved when they saw her. Before long, they were trotting along Rotten Row.

"I am so looking forward to seeing Clara again," Helen explained, "she only arrived back from Cordavia two days ago. So," she looked closely at Verity, "how is married life?"

Much to her annoyance, Verity could feel tears pricking her eyes.

"Oh, my dear," Emily said, leaning over and patting her arm. "You were married less than a week ago. What can possibly have gone wrong?"

"It surely cannot have been your wedding night." Helen laughed. "If only half the stories I have heard of Elliott are true, he should have had no trouble in making sure you had a very pleasurable night."

"That is the trouble," Verity admitted, a tear running down her cheek. "There was no wedding night, nor any night since. Not for me at least, Elliott bids me goodnight and spends the night elsewhere. He returned this morning as I came out, still wearing his evening suit."

"I think," said Helen, "now we have completed the circuit, we need to make our way to Clara's. Further privacy is needed for this conversation."

The Hampton's house was one of the finest in London. The butler quickly showed them through to a large airy salon where Clara, Duchess of Wensley was writing letters, but she quickly laid her pen down. "Thank goodness you are here. I am starved," she said as she led the way to the small dining room. "I am so sorry I could not join you at the park this morning," she said, sitting and indicating that the others should do the same. "The crossing was rather rough and it has taken a day for my insides to recover." Once they had been served, she looked around. "Now, what has caused such glum expressions?"

"It would appear," Emily began, "that Verity's duke is not coming up to snuff in the husband department."

"And she has been married only a few days," Helen added.

Clara looked askance at Verity.

"It is true," Verity added miserably. "He has spent his wedding night and each since with his mistress."

"Are you sure?" Clara asked.

"He certainly did not spend it with me."

Clara raised an eyebrow. "Well, that will not do at all."

"But what am I to do about it? I know Elliott and I are not a love match, as hope of that died a long time ago. But I thought he would at least consummate the marriage, if only because he would be required to in order to beget an heir, which is my sole purpose in this marriage after all," Verity blurted out, embarrassed. She had not intended to be quite so honest.

"Well then, you must make him jealous," Clara declared.

"And how am I to do that? Elliott has women falling over themselves. One of his mistresses, Mrs. Audra Kingsley, actually turned up at my wedding dress fitting and told me that as soon as I had done my duty, I would be banished out of sight and she would have him back. In fact," Verity added, "it is not so different from what Elliott himself suggested."

Clara looked puzzled. "I have never heard of this Mrs. Kingsley, have either of you?" She looked at Helen and Emily. They shook their heads.

"Perhaps she is one of the demi-monde?" Emily suggested, "in which case we should not have been introduced."

"I shall see what I can find out about her," Clara replied.

"Regardless of the circumstance," Helen said, turning to Verity, "Elliott may think he does not want you, but I have to say that judging by the look he gave you at your wedding, that is very far from the truth. However, he certainly will not want other men to want you."

"So all you have to do," Emily put in, "is to ensure that you dance with other men at balls and even flirt a little."

"You know what they say," Clara added. "All's fair in love and war."

"But it is not war," Verity protested.

"And it is not love," Emily said with a grin. "Not yet."

"Now to plan your next move," Clara began. "I know you are engaged at the Caunce dinner tonight, but I have vouchers for Almack's later. Ensure you are wearing your most daring gown and that you dance with all the men who ask you."

"The last time I did that, Elliott sent me home," Verity said, remembering her anger at being treated like a naughty child.

"Ah, I sense the green-eyed god is already present, but you must ensure that you do not dance with Elliott," Emily added. Verity was very dubious about this advice, but Emily and Helen had much more experience; they had each been married several years and had engaged enough with their husbands happily that they had plenty of children between them.

Helen grinned. "That should ensure that the campaign gets off to a fine start."

Verity looked at the women around her in confused wonder. "I understand all of you are quite happy in your relationships, and there was plenty of scandal, but surely you never had to face your husband despising or scorning you, as Elliott does me."

"Oh, dear Verity, there is much you do not know." Helen laughed. "As the Bard put it, 'the course of true love never did run smooth,' and that has certainly been the case for us, but Clara and I will be glad to explain further, after you have been introduced to marital bliss."

Clara set down her cup with a clink. "On the note of marital bliss and womanhood, can any of you ladies tell me of a remedy for an ill constitution? I have been feeling quite unwell since our journey and my usual remedies have not yet been successful."

Helen and Emily exchanged a look. "Clara, dear, let us speak of this another time."

Verity closed her eyes. Clara was ever young, it seemed, but Verity had seen enough of ill women to suppose the cause. She suddenly hoped the visit passed quickly.

As they sat in the coach on the way to the Caunce house that evening, Elliott observed his wife as she kept her gaze firmly out of the window. She took his breath away in the ivory taffeta gown hugging her body until it fell in gentle folds at her feet. The pale peach sash emphasizing her narrow waist, and her neckline low enough to draw the gaze without being scandalous. Her auburn curls had been swept up and twined with peach ribbons and another encircled her slender throat, making him want to remove it and kiss her throat all the way down to the tops of her breasts and beyond. Even the thought of doing it caused him to harden, because regardless of his fine words about not taking what Verity was willing to give, all he really wanted to do was to draw her on to his lap, pull down her gown and take her breasts into his mouth. Then he would pull up her skirts and bring her to a climax before taking his own pleasure.

He crossed his legs, feeling how such thoughts were going to lead to trouble. At his sudden movement, Verity looked round and gave him a polite smile. It was the one she had given him this morning before she went out and it was the same one she gave him when she offered him tea this afternoon, as if he were an elderly distant relative or acquaintance. She was withdrawing from him, and he wanted to know why. He also wanted to know why in the devil they were going to Almack's after dinner tonight and silently cursed Clara Hampton for giving Verity the vouchers.

"Are you sure you want to go to Almack's?" he asked. "It is the place young ladies go if they are searching for a husband and as you are not on the marriage mart, it seems somewhat redundant."

She smiled brightly. "Oh, but I have never been, Your Grace. Ella and I were not wealthy enough, nor would our father pay for us to have much of a season, so I should like to go and see what it is like," she replied.

"Hot, crowded, and tedious with nothing in the way of proper drink and awful food," he said.

"Well, we shall have eaten at the Caunce's, Your Grace, and if the dancing is too much you can always join the other married men in the card room."

He grunted a reply. Something had changed in Verity, and he could not put his finger on what.

CHAPTER 19

The Caunce's were excellent hosts, the food was delicious, and wine flowed freely. Lord Caunce was well known for the cellar of fine wines he kept, though for all Elliott cared he could have been drinking ditch water. Ever since they had arrived, Verity had carefully contrived to ensure that she was always at least three guests away from him. What was worse was that during the dinner she had been laughing and flirting with Alexander, the Caunce heir. He did not like the way the young man was looking adoringly at his wife, specifically, his wife's breasts.

"So nice to meet your new wife, Rydale," Lady Caunce remarked. "She seems to be a charming little thing and certainly seems to be able to coax Alexander out of his shell. He is usually so quiet at these affairs, one has to virtually beat a conversation out of him with a stick."

"Indeed," he replied, taking a sip of wine. "Verity has always had the ability to charm."

"You are not long married, I believe," Lady Caunce pressed.

"A few days." He smiled. A few days in which his life had turned upside down and in which he had seen less of his wife than his valet. "We are due to leave for a honeymoon once I conclude some business in town."

"But you have known the duchess for some years, have you not?" she pressed.

Elliott once more dragged his eyes from young Caunce to address his hostess, wishing he could bodily remove the young man from his wife's presence. "We knew each other when we were younger, yes, but we parted when I went to seek my fortune. It was only recent events that brought us back together once more," he replied.

"Ah, from what I have heard, the old earl, whom I did not know, apparently wished for you and she to marry but was unable to bring it about during his life."

"Certainly, something along those lines," Elliott replied drily.

"The old earl should be commended for making such a happy match."

He smiled politely. He was most assuredly not happy to be forced to watch another man fantasize over his wife's breasts, especially when he had yet to enjoy them. He seethed inwardly for the duration of the visit, waiting until he and his wife were safely ensconced in the privacy of their carriage.

"Would you care to explain to me the attraction of that young pup Caunce?" he asked in as even a tone as he could muster.

Verity looked at him with innocence exuding from her every pore. "I have no idea what you are talking about."

"Really? You spent the evening flirting with him, which was nauseating to behold, and I would remind you that you are a married woman."

"I need no reminder from you that I am a married woman, but perhaps you need reminding that you are a married man, Husband," Verity replied, turning her head and pulling back the curtain to gaze out into the darkness.

"What is that supposed to mean?" he ground out.

She barely glanced at him. "You are supposed to be quite a great genius, gaining a fortune and acquiring a duchy for your efforts. I am sure one with such acumen can understand the whims of a mere woman."

Elliott's hands grasped her arms and pulled her towards him so that his face was inches away from hers, his eyes blazing. "Is this because I have declined to bed you that you are acting like some two-penny trollop?" He knew he was being unreasonable, but the sight of Alexander Caunce leering over her breasts, kissing her hand and lingering over it longer than was necessary had infuriated him more than he had thought possible. He was jealous and he did not like it.

Verity met his gaze coolly. "You are being unreasonable, Your Grace. I was merely being polite to a young man with even fewer social skills than you possess. Now, if you would be so good as to let me go."

"That is the trouble, Verity. Where you are concerned, good seems to go out of the window," he murmured as his lips touched hers, gently at first, but it was not enough. He pulled her closer until their bodies were touching. When she put her palms on his chest to push him away, his arms tightened, and his lips became demanding. He ran his tongue along her lips and when she opened them, his tongue dipped inside, touching hers. When he heard the soft moan in her throat, he deepened the kiss, one hand tracing the outline of her bodice, then dipping down to stroke the tips of her already hardening nipples. He swallowed a smile at her gasp of surprise. "I always knew there was a passionate side to your nature, Verity. Making an heir will not be so much of a chore as you thought."

He had meant his words to be seductive, to tantalize her for the coming pleasure, but she pulled away and replied, "I will not forget my place, Your Grace, nor will I shirk from my duty."

Her words cut through the sensual haze that had surrounded him like a blast of icy water. She smoothed her skirt, her breath coming in even quicker than his own.

"What the devil do you mean your place and your duty?" he demanded, the glowing silver in his eyes was replaced by steel.

She turned her cool gaze on him. "I am your servant, Your Grace, your broodmare. In return for providing you with a healthy heir, you pay for me and my sisters to live in a degree of comfort. That is what was agreed in our marriage of convenience was it not?"

"It bloody well was not expressed in those terms," he replied, the muscle in his jaw working.

"No, Your Grace, but we both know that was what was meant, and we both know that the sooner it is achieved, the sooner we will be rid of each other, which is apparently your desire. However, I find I cannot meet my side of the agreement without a little cooperation from you," Verity flung over her shoulder as she exited the carriage.

CHAPTER 20

wo hours later, Elliott would have been almost happy to see only young Alexander Caunce fawning over his wife, for now there were half a dozen of them as she sat like a queen holding court with at least one young man literally sitting at her feet.

"Verity seems to have made quite an impression this evening." His brother appeared by his side and handed him a glass. "Don't worry," he added, noticing Elliott's sceptical glance, "I managed to smuggle in a little something to make this weasel's piss taste of alcohol."

Elliott took the glass and tossed the drink down. "Good God," he gasped, "What in hell is in there?"

"Best you don't know." Stephen grinned, raising his own glass. "Here's to your lovely bride."

"Who seems to have forgotten that she is married," Elliott said, sardonically.

"Then you need to remind her," his brother replied.

"Perhaps I will take her home and do just that," Elliott snarled.

"I would suggest that what you do is go and ask her to dance, she has danced with every other man, I imagine she has reached the bottom of the barrel so to speak, in other words, you." Stephen grinned.

Elliott gave his brother a look that caused others to quail, but which caused his brother's grin merely to widen. He strode across the ball-room purposefully. He had indeed watched as Verity had floated past in the arms of a parade of young men, laughing and smiling at them in a way she had never done to him. It was exactly as it had been at the previous ball; wherever Verity went it seemed, she attracted the unwanted attention of predatory males.

His eyes narrowed as his wife laughed and tapped a young man on the arm with her fan; perhaps their attention was not unwanted. He did not like that idea. This was the second time that Verity had attracted the attentions of predatory males at a ball, but when he thought about the way her eyes sparkled and heard her musical laugh, perhaps their attentions were not so unwanted as he thought. In the seven years since they had been separated, Verity had done a lot of growing up, and perhaps there had been other men he did not know about.

He shifted uneasily. Perhaps the innocent she claimed to be was just an act. Perhaps, regardless of what his brother said, she had played him for a fool from the start. The more he thought about it, the more he warmed to the idea. Despite her initial rejection of the notion, she had been eager enough to marry him when she realised that she could live in comfort with her sisters at her beloved Swallowfield, especially when he had mentioned gowns and jewels. God, she had even agreed to give up any children they might have. What normal woman did that? He could cheerfully strangle her, at the very least haul her over his shoulders and take her home where she would be locked in her room if need be until she learned to be a dutiful and obedient wife. His patience was wearing more than a little thin, both with Verity and himself for allowing himself to be duped.

"Ah, Your Grace." Verity looked up as he approached. "Perhaps you may settle a dispute. Lord Formby here suggests that I should always wear diamonds, while Sir Rogan is convinced that emeralds are more to my colour."

"I assure you, gentlemen, that rubies, diamonds, emeralds, or pearls, my wife will not be happy until she has them all," he replied with a sardonic smile. "So if you are considering taking a wife, I suggest you consider first the cost of gowns and jewels. Now, my dear duchess," he added, and held out his hand, "I believe we have time for one dance before we must depart."

Verity put her hand in his, wincing at the vice-like grip on her fingers. "What was that all about?" she hissed.

"I just thought the young pups should know the true cost of taking a wife," he replied.

"I have never asked for jewels of any kind," she protested. "Moreover, I should not want any from you."

He looked down as he took her in his arms. "Indeed? And why not, pray? Surely it is the jewels that are important, not their donors."

"You are so wrong, duke. When a man gives his wife jewels it is a token of his love for her, and as you have none for me, I shall neither expect nor want anything from you. Please," she went on, "you are holding me much too closely. Even for a married couple it is not proper."

"Propriety be damned," he replied. Even though he had convinced himself that she was a ruthless gold digger, he could not help how his body instantly responded to her. "You do not, I think, subscribe to society's demands regarding proper behaviour if your own behaviour at the only two balls and one dinner I have witnessed are anything to go by."

"I have not the slightest inkling of what you are talking about. Why would you have any idea of what I think about anything seeing as you have never bothered to ask?" she shot back. "You neglect much of the telling and listening husbands and wives do together," she added for good measure.

"In which case," he replied smoothly, "I will speak, and you will listen. When this dance is over, we are going home and when we arrive, we are going to consummate this cursed marriage and you are going to start to behave like a wife, an obedient wife, as you vowed to do."

Verity's eyes flashed with angry green fire. "And what has brought about this change pray? Are all your mistresses otherwise engaged this evening?"

"What do you mean? Mistresses?" he hissed.

"As you have not deigned to come to my bed since we married, I can only assume that you have taken your pleasure elsewhere," she shot back.

Elliott saw the flush of anger colour her cheeks, pleased with himself that he had ignited at least one of her passions. It was a start. "If you only knew," he replied smoothly, bowing to kiss her hand. "Now let us get your cloak, it is time to leave. And Verity," he added softly, "Tonight I intend to teach you the meaning of pleasure."

"I doubt it, duke," she replied. "There will be little pleasure in anything with someone whom one hates."

As they walked together across the ballroom with his hand on her back, he leaned to whisper, "Oh yes, there will be pleasure, Verity. You may be unwilling to believe it, but I intend to pleasure you to the point at which you are begging me for release."

"I will never beg you for anything," she said, coldly.

"Two points, you do not hate me and beg you will," he promised.

CHAPTER 21

When he walked through the connecting doorway and took in the empty bed, Elliott was convinced that his errant wife had run from him. A soft sigh gave her away, as he paused for a moment drinking in the sight of her as she sat on the window seat gazing at the night sky. It was a clear night, and the moon was full, illuminating her hair which was caught in a neat plait, almost to her waist. The nightgown and peignoir were of the finest material, so sheer that he could clearly see the outline of her body through them. His body tightened immediately, there was no denying it, Verity had the same effect on him today as she had all those years ago.

"Why the sigh, duchess?" he asked, moving towards her. Verity jumped at the sound of his voice. He frowned. "Are you afraid of me, Verity?"

She held his gaze a moment before slowly shaking her head.

"Are you afraid of what we are about to do?"

Another pause before once again, she shook her head before raising her shoulders. "No, duke, I know what is to be done," she replied. She met his gaze. "I know that you will take your rights and I must submit to it," she added.

His chest tightened at her words, he stepped forwards so that he was standing behind her, "Let us forget this idea of taking and submitting," he whispered into her hair. "What we are about to do should give us both the greatest pleasure." He gently slid the sheer fabric from one shoulder and kissed it before kissing softly behind her ear, noticing with satisfaction the pulse beating wildly at the base of her throat.

Placing both hands on her shoulders, he turned her towards him. "Come, Verity, it is time. Long past time." he whispered as he drew her to her feet and bent his head to take her lips in a long drugging kiss whilst gently easing the silky robe and nightrail from her shoulders and running his fingers lightly down her arms. It took little more than a tug for it to fall in a puddle at her feet and she was naked before him, as he had imagined so many times in both his waking and sleeping dreams. He took a step back to look at her, holding her arms out so that she couldn't cover herself from his gaze. She was as perfect as a woman could be, through all the layers of stays, petticoats and skirts nothing he imagined had prepared him for this, her breasts were small and pert with roseate tips already beginning to harden under his gaze, her waist was narrow, his eyes drifted lower to the neat tangle of curls, and he knew that what they covered held the promise of delightful satisfaction. Her legs were long and shapely.

He drew in a ragged breath, and was so hard he had to remind himself firmly that his wife was as yet an innocent, given her obvious embarrassment at her own nakedness. He would take care with her regardless of how much he wanted to bury himself deep inside her again and again until they were both slick with sweat and exhausted. But first, he must ensure that any fear or tension or reluctance she still possessed was washed away.

He picked her up and laid her gently on the bed. "Beautiful," he whispered, his finger reaching out and tracing her nipple, "so beautiful." And for him alone. No other man will ever see, touch or pleasure this woman.

Verity remained frozen as he slowly lifted her in his arms and laid her onto the marital bed. She was terrified of losing her heart to him again when he clearly had no desire for her other than carnal pleasure to beget an heir.

Yet his kisses did something to her and when he began to touch her, Verity gasped aloud at the sensation. She looked down at the large, male hands which were now cupping and stroking her breasts.

He smiled down at her. "You like that Verity?" he asked softly. She nodded, unable to speak, "Then I think you will like this," he murmured as he bent his head and took one nipple in his mouth, swirling his tongue around it. "Oh," she sighed as tremors of excitement began to course through her body, centring on her most female essence.

"Must not neglect this one," he whispered, transferring his mouth to her other nipple whilst caressing the first one with his fingertips. Verity could not contain the restlessness that overtook her, and every inch of her body came alive under his touch. She wanted to feel his hands all over her, and did not know how this would end. She just knew that she did not want Elliott to stop. Her body twitched under his hands and his mouth, her hands grasping at nothing, not knowing what to do.

He chuckled. "Soon, my sweet, I'll give you what you want, but first I want to savour your luscious body." His fingers trailed a lazy line between her breasts to her navel and were quickly replaced by his mouth as he kissed and licked along the line his fingers had taken. "Don't think, Verity, just allow yourself to feel," he murmured as his head dipped lower and lower.

Her eyes shot open in alarm. "Duke, what are you doing?" she gasped.

"Pleasuring you," he whispered. "You are enjoying this, I think?"

She nodded silently.

"Then give yourself up to it."

He gently parted her folds with his fingers and kissed and laved her until she could not stop the sighs and moans. "Open your eyes," he commanded as first one and then two fingers replaced his tongue, "I want to see you come."

"You want to see...oh, that is....please..." She could not finish; all she could concentrate on was the magical feeling at what his fingers and mouth were doing to her. She tensed suddenly at how wanton she must look, how basely she was behaving. Somehow, he could tell. "Don't think Verity, just feel," he murmured once again, this time commandingly. Her eyes widened as pulses of pleasure consumed her whole body.

"Elliott!" she cried as he continued his ministrations.

"Finally," he sighed, but she could not ask of what before his mouth found hers in a drugging kiss.

When her breathing returned to normal, Elliott gathered her in his arms and held her close. "What just happened to me?" she asked. "I have never felt anything like that before."

"That was your first orgasm, my sweet. The first of many I intend to give you." He grinned at her. "Whatever our differences, it would seem that we are entirely compatible in bed, and I intend to pleasure you whenever I am faced with the opportunity."

She could hardly believe his words. Surely, he meant only until she was with child. She could not begin to hope that he wanted her. "But what about you?" she asked tentatively. "It was quite pleasurable for me, but I cannot see how it could have been the same for you."

He laughed at her naivete. He had very much enjoyed pleasuring her body, lavishing his full attentions on her mouth, her breasts, her womanhood. "Oh, I shall have my own pleasure very shortly," he assured her. he was so hard it was taking all his self-control not to take her now, but he knew he had to take things slowly.

"And will what you do result in me having a babe?"

He shrugged. "It may, but we may have to do this many times before a babe is conceived."

She leaned on one elbow. "Whilst I have a degree of theoretical knowledge about what must happen, I really do not see how the practicalities work," she confessed.

He rolled her onto her back and rose. "Then I think it is time you found out," he said, quickly divesting himself of his clothing.

"Is it normal for married couples to be naked in bed together?" she asked.

He could not suppress the laugh; how had he thought she was anything but an innocent? "As far as I know, some couples are never naked in bed together," he replied with as much solemnity as he could muster, "but for us it is both natural and desirable and I intend that we shall do it often."

Once again, his lips covered hers in a drugging kiss and his fingers sought and found her already sensitized nipples making her writhe once more, bucking into his hands, before trailing down her body. When he was sure she was ready, he raised himself over her, his cock nudging her wet, warm entrance. "I know this is going to hurt you a little, Verity, and if I could take the pain for you I would, but believe me, I only want to give you and myself the greatest pleasure."

He entered her slowly and retreated. God she was tight! Each time he eased a little further so slowly he thought he was going to explode. Sweat broke out on his forehead, "Are you all right?" he gritted.

"Please do not stop now," she whispered, "I think we must be getting to the good part."

Her words lit the fuse, and with one last push, he was fully inside her. He heard her sharp intake of breath and paused once more to allow her to adjust to him. Slowly he began to move, pushing and withdrawing, desperate not to cause her discomfort but once he began to move, she instinctively began to move with him, her little cries and gasps urged him on. He quickened and deepened his thrusts, pounding into her until she cried out her release and he joined her with a gasp. For several moments all he could hear was the sound of their breathing, then he looked into her eyes and what he saw there almost undid him. He rolled onto his side, taking her with him so that they were still intimately joined.

"That was...I don't know what that was," Verity whispered. "Is it always like that? The getting of heirs?"

He laughed softly against her mouth before kissing it. "No, Verity," he said solemnly. "It is not always like that. It is rarely like that."

In fact, it was the first time he had ever felt like that bedding a woman, it was always pleasurable, or he would not have spent so much of his time doing it, but he had never felt so attuned to a woman. It felt different; he felt different, as though something profound had happened. She shifted against him, brushing his still semi-hard member, causing him to inhale sharply.

"I'm sorry Elliott, did I hurt you?" she whispered against his ear, sending a shiver down his body and setting his aflame once more for the naked, willing wife beside him.

"Bloody hell, Verity," he gasped as his cock roared into life once more. He rolled her onto her back once again and this time his control shattered as he thrust into her while reaching between their joined bodies and finding the small bud he knew would increase her pleasure. She moved with him, thrust for thrust, her nails digging into his back as she tossed her head from side to side. "Elliott! Elliott!" she cried as she came apart in his arms. He felt her inner muscles clench against him as he came with one final thrust.

"Verity. My God, Verity," he gasped hoarsely.

He remained against her, feeling the tips of her breasts rub against him with each heaving breath she took. When their breathing returned to normal, he rolled onto his side and gathered her to him, tucking her head on his shoulder. He did not want to lose contact with her now that he finally had her against him, not even to bathe. Before long, he heard her breathing slow. He watched her for a while, her eyelashes like fans against her cheek in her sleep.

He never wanted to lose contact with her. This was the woman to whom he was tied for life and yet, there was still a part of him that could not trust her entirely. There was still a part of him, irrationally that blamed her for rejecting him so brutally and there was still a part of him that believed she had colluded with her bastard of a father to trap him into marriage. The rational part of him warned him that he could not trust Verity to break his heart again. He could not, would not give her that power over him. Somehow, he would find a way to have a marriage filled with love and respect but without trust.

CHAPTER 22

$\mathcal{W}$hen Verity awoke, the sun was streaming through the window and her new maid, Daisy, was just entering from the bathing room. Mercifully, she was alone in the bed, and judging by the cool sheets, she had been for some time.

"Ah, you're awake, Your Grace," the maid said with a smile. "I took the liberty of drawing a bath for you."

"Thank you," Verity responded, hoping that Daisy couldn't see the blush she could feel, convinced her whole body was red with embarrassment. No doubt all the servants by now knew that the marriage was finally consummated, as no doubt they had also known that previously, it was not.

"I'll just pop down and fetch your tea while you get into the bath," Daisy said, heading towards the door.

Verity had no doubt that Daisy knew beneath the sheets, she was naked, especially as her nightrail and robe were neatly folded on the chair. She padded to the bathing room and sank into the rose scented bath, wincing a little as she sat down. There was no surprise that parts of her body felt tender. She smiled at the thought. It had been a wonderful night. She had not imagined that she could feel so much pleasure, and he seemed to know exactly when and how to touch her to bring her to a shattering climax. Of course, it occurred to her bitterly, he had, no doubt, had a lot of practice. She dunked her head under the water. She didn't want to think about the countess or Mrs. Audra Kingsley or any of the others. Even the thought of Mrs. Kinglsey brought back her threatening words. Would Elliott truly send her away after she bore him a son? Did he truly want to enjoy her, pleasure her, be together intimately with her, or was his performance last night just something he had to do in order to get the all-important heir?

The morning suddenly lost its bright glow, as if a cloud covered the sun.

Once she had dressed in a mint green muslin dress and Daisy had fashioned her hair into a chignon from which a few tendrils were allowed to escape, she made her way down to the breakfast room. On the sideboard was a huge arrangement of bacon, sausages, eggs, tomatoes, and mushrooms, along with a plentiful supply of toast and several jars of marmalade. The only thing that was missing was Elliott.

"His Grace has already partaken of breakfast and is at work in the library, Your Grace," Fry, the butler, intoned.

She gave him a bright smile. "Thank you, Fry," and helped herself to eggs and mushrooms. She sat alone at the table and began to push them around her plate, her appetite suddenly gone.

"Is everything to Your Grace's satisfaction?" Fry asked.

"Of course." She smiled again. "I am just not very hungry, thank you. In fact, I think I shall just pop along and see his grace." She rose from the table.

"His Grace does not wish to be disturbed when he is working," Fry informed her.

"Well, he will just have to get used to it," she replied and strode towards the door.

"His Grace did leave you a note, Your Grace," the butler held out a piece of paper.

"Thank you."

Verity,

 Thank you for last night. I have arranged for an appointment at the

modiste this morning. Now that you are a duchess you will need far more in
the way of apparel. Madame knows what, so you must allow yourself to be
guided by her. Tonight, we shall attend the opera, be ready at seven.
    Elliott

Clutching the note, Verity strode down the corridor. At the library door, she paused briefly, wondering whether she should knock, but decided that a surprise attack would be best, and flung open the door. Elliott was standing by the window, a sheet of paper in his hand, and an older man was seated at a desk writing down what Elliott dictated. At the opening of the door, he looked up and smiled the polite smile she had seen him give to her aunt.

"Good morning, Verity. I trust you have taken breakfast, though Fry should have given you a note and informed you that I am not to be disturbed when I am working."

"Oh, I have the note, Your Grace." She brandished it, coming further into the room.

Elliott saw the determined look on her face and turned to Burton. "Would you leave us for a moment Burton? Perhaps you could look through the new shipping contract."

Burton stood and bowed. "Certainly, Your Grace."

When the door had closed Elliott turned to Verity. "What was it you wanted?" he asked patiently, with a contrived neutral expression that grated on her nerves.

Verity took a deep breath, his patiently indulgent attitude eroded her own patience. "Several things," she began. "Firstly, I do not appreciate you telling me where I am to go and what I am to do with my day. Secondly, I am not a child, so I shall decide on my own clothes, not Madame, though why you want to waste money on more clothes when I am to be sent away as soon as possible, I cannot imagine. Finally, if you wish to thank me for bedding me, then do it to my face, though of course you do not need to thank me at all. I was merely doing my duty."

Within seconds, he had rounded the desk and had his hands on her shoulders. "Duty, was it?" he growled as one arm went around her and the other hand went under her chin and tipped her face towards his.

She glared back at him. "Of course it was a duty, that's why you married me isn't it?" she shot back, knowing it was a lie. The marital bed was a required duty, but it had been a pleasure, a great deal of pleasure, to partake in it with him.

"I don't believe you," he said as he lowered his head and caught her lips in a demanding kiss which, try as she might, she could not help but return. He pulled back and said quietly, "I can already feel your nipples tightening through the material of your gown, and if I were to reach beneath it, I believe I would find you already hot and wet for me. In fact, I have a good mind to do that and prove to you right here and now that making love with me is far from a duty."

Her eyes rounded with fear and the nervous passion the image ignited. "You wouldn't," she stammered.

He laughed softly. "Believe me, I would."

"What about Mr. Burton? He might come back at any minute."

He laughed again, his hand cupping her breast through the cloth, causing her breath to come out in soft gasps. "Burton will come when I call for him. In any case, the contract I asked him to look over will take him at least an hour."

"No, Your Grace." Her breathing had returned to normal, and she found the strength to step back, though she knew that had he wanted to continue, she would have been powerless to refuse. In any case, she was only able to step back from him because he released her. "As you so kindly arranged the appointment, I must get ready to visit Madame Dupont."

"As it happens, I do have another appointment this morning, but do not be late for the opera, I am not fond of being kept waiting," he reminded her.

"I am never late," she replied over her shoulder. "Nor do I enjoy being kept waiting, though you kept me waiting for seven years for your proposal, so I consider I have a great deal of time in hand."

She shut the door behind her, leaving him staring at the door.

She leaned against the wall once she had escaped him. After calming herself, she straightened herself and set out to make her appointment.

Verity was still annoyed as the carriage arrived at the modiste's and was not looking forward to being poked and pinned as various styles and fabrics were tried against her. She had rarely had gowns made to measure and found the process tedious and boring. Much as it galled her to admit it, she would be more than happy to allow Madame to make the choices. It was not long before she was surrounded by bolts of silks and satins, velvets and brocades, ribbons and lace while Madame and her assistants tried first one and then another against her. "With your colouring, I suggest ze blues and ze greens," Madame announced, turning and ordering one assistant, "Take these pinks and oranges away, zay will clash with 'er Grace's unfortunate hair. This colour of hair is not at all fashionable," she admonished Verity.

"I'm sorry," Verity heard herself say. She rarely thought about her hair, though she had noticed that the acknowledged beauties of the season were either cool blondes or raven-haired. On the other hand, she could do nothing about her russet locks, so it was not something she was going to worry about. In any case, now she was a married woman, no doubt no-one would care a jot what colour her hair was.

Several hours later, Madame Dupont had worked through the list of clothes Verity apparently needed for her role as duchess: morning and afternoon gowns, tea gowns, ball gowns, walking gowns, and riding habits, as well as spencers and pelisses. Madame would also supply bonnets and gloves to match and send colour swatches to the shoe-maker for matching boots and shoes.

It was with some relief that Verity finally escaped Madame's clutches and headed towards the Hatchards. Buying clothes was oblig-atory, buying books was a pleasure, and she dearly wished her sister was there to share it with her. She had just begun to browse the shelves when she became aware of another person standing nearby.

"Ah, duchess," a familiar unpleasant voice greeted her. "I hear that Elliott has finally steeled himself to consummate the marriage," Mrs. Audra Kingsley sneered.

"Mrs. Kingsley," Verity said, acknowledging the other woman. She was determined not to engage in conversation with her, every word of their previous conversation was burned on her memory.

"Poor Elliott. Apparently, he couldn't face the thought of bedding you at first. Fortunately, I was able to, shall we say, fulfil his needs while you were sleeping alone. I reminded him that all he had to do was think of me and imagine he was making love to me. He told me that he hopes his seed took, so that he does not have to go through this ridiculous charade again."

"I have no intention of discussing my marriage with you, Mrs. Kingsley. Good day," Verity said shortly and left the shop. She was still shaking when the carriage brought her home.

CHAPTER 23

There was a note from Elliott when she returned. He would be delayed by business but would see her at Covent Garden. Well, she would see about that, no doubt his 'business' involved Mrs. Kingsley and her long shopping trip had allowed them plenty of time for an assignation. She had the same intention of obeying his commands as he clearly had of obeying his marriage vows. She would cry no more tears for Elliott Thorne, though her heart was breaking. Last night, she had foolishly thought she had meant something to him, now she knew she was merely another body to sink himself into but conveniently the only one whose loins he could seed for a legitimate heir.

Dismissing Daisy for the evening, she dashed off a quick note to Elliott, donned her simplest gown and cloak, and stole out of the house without anyone seeing her. She made her way to the old Grainger house, for had she gone to her aunt's she would have been sent straight back home, but she knew there would be a welcome for her below stairs with Mr. and Mrs. Clayton. As she ran down the area steps, the door opened and there stood Mrs. Clayton herself, and at the sight of the warm woman, despite her earlier promise not to cry for the man, Verity burst into tears.

"Come in, come in, child," Mrs. Clayton said, her arm's arms coming around her as they had so many times as a child. "Now," she said when Verity's tears subsided, "Tell me about it."

Before she knew it, Verity was sitting in the Windsor chair and telling the old housekeeper the whole story in a flood of handkerchiefs and emotions.

"Every time I think Elliott might feel something for me, he reminds me that my only place in his life is to warm his bed until I produce his heir." Verity took the cup of tea Mrs. Clayton held out to her and sipped, taking comfort in the hot liquid. "And if that were not enough, his mistress sought me out to tell me the same." She stopped at that, unable to face the humiliation of admitting that Elliott was thinking of his mistress when he made love to her.

"Well, dearie, it seems to me that you have to either get an annulment which, judging by the red face I see is not an option, or you have to make him fall in love with you again if you are to have any kind of happy relationship in your life."

"My friends said much the same, but I do not think there is any chance of that. Elliott has hated me for so long now I do not think I can change his mind. It seems that all I can have is the worst kind of ton marriage which is no kind of marriage at all," Verity replied sadly, thinking of the disastrous marriages she had witnessed first-hand. Her father had married women for their money and their breeding potential with no consideration for their happiness and had made their lives miserable as well as his own. She had been determined that she would have something better, a real marriage, and her father had ensured that she made exactly the same mistake.

"Are you truly going to let him break your heart for a second time?" the older woman asked.

"Break my heart? What do you mean?"

Mrs. Clayton leaned forward and patted her hand. "You're still in love with him my dear. That's why this hurts so much."

Verity sucked in a breath. As much as she had been endeavouring to convince herself otherwise, it was true, she was in love with Elliott. She shook her head. It could not be true—she could not allow it to be true.

"Why? Why would I still love a man who rejected me and broke my heart so cruelly? Mrs. Clayton, why must I love a man who does not love me? Is it something in me? My father could not love me either, is there perhaps something in me that is unlovable?"

The older woman reached out and gathered Verity to her ample bosom, holding her as she shook. "Of course not, my little love. As for your father, well, I don't like to speak ill of the dead, but the only person the earl ever loved was himself and that's the truth. But this duke of yours is different and ask yourself this, my dear. If he truly didn't want to marry you, did he not have enough wealth and power to refuse?"

"But there was the threat of a scandalous court case," Verity replied, sniffling.

"I doubt the young man cared a jot about that. He's a duke and rich as Midas! No, he chose to go through with the wedding out of concern for you, if you want my opinion."

The door was flung open, and Mr. Clayton came in, declaring, "Your opinion is the gift you give most freely, particularly to me," but he chuckled as he kissed his wife's cheek.

"Oh, get along with you," Mrs. Clayton laughed.

"It looks like the little miss here needs cheering up." Mr. Clayton called her by the name he had used since she was a small child. "Here, I think an evening of cards will do the trick."

Before long, the three of them were sitting at the scrubbed table playing Vingt-et-Un for the little cowrie shells Mr. Clayton kept in a wooden box on the mantelpiece, which Verity had learned to count with as a little girl. "It is a good thing I am not playing for money," Verity admitted, as she looked at her diminishing pile of shells, "or I should bankrupt my husband within the month."

"That would get his attention," Mrs. Clayton remarked.

Verity glanced at the clock on the mantel. "I should think I shall get enough attention for being so late." She reached for her cloak. "I really must be going, as I want to get back before Elliott arrives from the opera."

"I'll see you home, lass," Mr. Clayton offered.

Verity smiled. "There's really no need but thank you. No-one will think twice about me dressed like this."

"'Tis true," Mrs. Clayton agreed. "Young women of quality are not allowed any freedom, they must always be treated as though they don't have a spot of sense. A maid going about her business has more freedom than her mistress."

"Well, in this dress," Verity replied, fastening her cloak, "that is exactly what people will think I am. Thank you both for cheering me up." She kissed both of them before opening the door and running lightly up the area steps.

Verity crept in through the kitchen door and made her way up the backstairs without a sound. She had not seen any lights in the windows and did not want to run the risk of someone waking. She had just closed the door to the backstairs quietly behind her when a cold voice said, "Would you care to explain, duchess, why you are sneaking in like a thief in the night?"

Elliott stood in the hallway, a candle on the table next to him, still dressed in his evening clothes, though his neck cloth was untied, he had removed his jacket, and his shirt sleeves were rolled up, displaying his crossed arms. His every feature expressed that he was less than pleased. "Your note said that you would not be attending the opera because you were unwell," he prompted, "though it would seem that you have made a remarkable recovery."

"I am tired, Your Grace, and I am not having this conversation with you now," she replied, walking towards the staircase.

"Oh, I think now is quite the best time to have it," he replied, his hand reaching out and circling her arm. "I should like to do so without a scene for the servants," he went on, "but that is your choice."

"Kindly let go of me, Your Grace," she hissed.

"Certainly, just step into the library." He released her arm and waited for her to move.

Verity huffed and sat herself on the sofa in front of the fire while Elliott lit several candles giving the room a warm glow, though it did nothing to soften the hard planes of his face. He had spoken quietly, too quietly, and Verity had learned that Elliott was at his most dangerous and angry when he spoke in that tone. She folded her hands tightly on her lap.

"Imagine my surprise," he began mildly, "when, having received your note, I determined it best to stop by to see how you fared only to find that you were not here. I thought perhaps you had recovered sufficiently to go to the theatre after all, so I went, only to find that you were not there, either. In fact, no-one, not the people with whom we were supposed to spend the evening, nor the servants, had in fact seen you for several hours. So, I should very much like to know Verity, where the hell you have been?"

"Why, Your Grace? Why should you care?" she shot back. "You have been spending plenty of time out without reporting your whereabouts to me."

"What are you talking about? Of course I care. You are my wife." He had been distraught when Verity had seemed to have disappeared into thin air, nearly frantic that she could have been kidnapped or attacked by footpads. She could have had an accident and was injured, alone, and in danger. He had spent several hours searching the streets, and then pacing the carpet as he tried to think what to do to find her.

"Ah, yes, your wife. The wife you do not want, keeping only for the purpose of breeding," she said, her voice rising. "You have made it abundantly clear that my role is only in the bedroom and that my presence in any other part of your life is entirely redundant, so frankly what I do with the rest of my time is of no concern to you."

"On the contrary, wife. I find I am extremely concerned to know where you have been, with whom and what you have been doing." His eyes glittered dangerously. "And why you feel the need not only to skulk about but to do so dressed as some sort of maid," his glance raked over her.

"As I am little more than a servant here, this gown is entirely appropriate. When you bought Swallowfield, you gained me as your broodmare!"

He could see the tears gather in her eyes, knowing that her pride would never let them fall. Despite what he wished, he could feel his heart-strings pulled taut. She truly believed that he cared nothing for her; that he purchased her for short-termed use of her body. He softened his tone and his form. "Whatever you think, I do not think of you in that way, Verity. Truly," he said quietly, sitting beside her and taking her hands in his. That was her undoing, although she had vowed not to shed more tears, she could not stop them.

Elliott could have sat all night with Verity in his arms, but eventually her sobs subsided, and she pulled away from him. "I am sorry, your shirt is all wet," she mumbled.

"It is of no consequence," he whispered into her hair. To tell the truth, he just wanted to sit and hold her in his arms; he hated to see her cry, and he hated himself because he knew that he was the reason that she was crying.

"Come," he said, gently pulling her to her feet. "It is late, we will talk further in the morning."

In her bedroom, Verity made no protest as he undressed her and drew a nightrail over her head and tenderly carried her to the bed.

"Sleep now, Verity," he whispered, kissing her forehead.

"Don't go," she murmured, "Please." Her eyes were huge, deep pools.

He stilled, suddenly she looked young and vulnerable, and he could not resist her. He quickly divested himself of his clothing and climbed in beside her, gently pulling her towards the shelter of his arms and taking in a sharp breath as she snuggled close. He listened as her breathing became regular and strangely, he too felt a peace he had not felt in a long time.

He allowed himself this night to believe that she loved him.

He kissed her hair and whispered, "You are more to me than you will ever know."

CHAPTER 24

*V*erity awoke with the realisation that she was trapped beneath a large muscular arm across her midriff and an even larger muscular leg across her legs. Tentatively, she began to try to extricate herself from Elliott's grasp.

"And where do you think you are going, duchess?" a deep voice whispered in her ear as his grip on her tightened.

"I, ah, thought I might get up," she said brightly. "Face the morning and do what needs doing."

"No," Elliott replied firmly. "I think not." He rolled her onto her back in a smooth movement and began to kiss her, slowly at first, then with mounting passion which she could not help but return. After the way he had comforted her last night, she was able to at least imagine that she was in the arms of a man she loved and loved her.

"Now, duchess, are you sure you want to get up?" he asked. She looked into his eyes and saw with budding joy that his eyes were pleading with her to stay beside him. She realized that he truly would not take what she was not prepared to give.

"I want to stay," she replied quietly. "Here. With you." If only for now, this day, she would be wholly with him and have him wholly with her.

"Good," he said simply, drawing her nightrail over her head and feasting his gaze on her nude body. "Because for some reason," he punctuated his words with kisses as he worked his way down her body, "I cannot seem to get enough of you."

He plunged his tongue inside her and smiled against her as she bucked suddenly, pushing her body against his mouth. "I do not think I will ever be able to get enough of you," he whispered and replaced his tongue with his fingers as he turned the attention of his mouth to her breasts.

Verity could not help responding to his touch, gasping as his fingers teased and caressed her. "Oh, Elliott," she moaned, as he moved inside her, each shift of his fingers within her causing new sensation and energy surging through her. Instinctively, she moved with him causing a moan deep in his throat, which she felt against her wet, swollen nipple still within his mouth. He parted her folds and pressed his cock at her entrance, "Yes, Elliott, Yes," she moaned. With a single thrust he buried himself in her and she moved with him, matching him thrust for thrust.

"Open your eyes, Verity," he whispered. "I want to see your eyes when you come for me." She opened her eyes and was overwhelmed by the intensity of his gaze. His movements did not stop, but when he placed one hand between them to stroke her wet nub of pleasure, she could not help but cry out as wave after wave of sensation crashed over her entire body. With a final thrust, he, too, cried out as he took his own release, then expertly rolled them onto their sides, still intimately joined.

"I am sorry if you were worried last night," Verity began, once their breath had calmed and she felt his member slowly dropping onto her thigh. "It was wrong of me to disappear like that."

Her apology surprised him. Her raw honesty was palpable, and he barely believed she would feel that way. "I was beyond worried," he admitted tentatively. "I was frantic with worry. I thought you might have been abducted or set upon by footpads. All manner of possible scenarios went through my mind and none of them good."

"Well, as you can see, I am perfectly well," she said with a soft, sensual smile.

"May I ask where you were?"

"I went to see my old friends, the Claytons," she replied.

"The ones you stayed with on the night of the snow?"

She nodded, her hair brushing against his cheek in such a casually intimate way that he felt his member begin to stir. "They are the couple who used to work for my father in the townhouse. I suppose technically they work for you now, assuming you bought the townhouse along with everything else."

"You were visiting with servants?" he asked, raising an eyebrow.

"Mr. and Mrs. Clayton are much more than servants to me," she explained softly into his chest. "I spent much of my time in the kitchen with Mrs. Clayton, hiding from Father when he was in one of his rages. Mr. Clayton would fashion wooden dolls for Ella, Caro, and me for birthdays and Christmas when Father had forgotten to buy us presents, which was not uncommon," she admitted.

"I see," he said softly. Elliott stared down at the woman he held in his arms. He had learned more about Verity's life in the last few minutes than he had in the time he had known her. The old earl had been a drinker and a gambler, that much was common knowledge among the ton, but not only did he neglect his daughters, Elliott had no doubt that he bullied and abused them as well.

"I think I had better get up," Verity said, beginning to shift her body away from his embrace.

"Oh no you don't, duchess, I have not finished with you yet," he whispered, his cock already beginning to harden. He pulled her against him, thumbing her nipples that pressed against his chest, causing her to writhe and wriggle appealingly against his cock. It was another hour before he released her and took great liberty in watching her hips sway and her breasts bounce as she fled to her bath.

He cleaned himself quickly, seeing with no small degree of satisfaction the wet, glistening proof on his bed that she had thoroughly enjoyed herself and been lavished with joyful attention in return.

He dressed quietly while she soaked and resolved to meet her in the breakfast room when we were ready.

Elliott was tucking into ham, eggs and hot rolls when Verity entered. He stood as she entered. "Come and sit, Verity, I shall prepare a plate for you," he said, moving to the sideboard where a number of silver salvers displayed a variety of foods.

"There's really no need," she replied, pouring herself a cup of tea and adding a splash of milk. "I find I am not very hungry."

"Nonsense," he replied with a gleam in his eye. "After your exertions last night, this morning, and all that I intend to subject you to tonight, you need to keep up your strength." He set a plate of eggs and rolls before her.

She took up her fork. "I was thinking...." she began.

"I wanted to..." he said at the same time.

"Please," she said, "go on."

Elliott took a breath. "I wanted to tell you that we shall be departing for the country the day after tomorrow. The business I needed to complete will be finished today so we shall leave London for the country."

"Is Swallowfield ready?" she asked, voice tinged with anticipation.

He shook his head. "Not yet, though by the time we return it may well be. I have a very good and large team of men working on it. No, we shall travel down to my estate in Hampshire, Orlando Court, named I believe because a previous incumbent of this title was fond of the works of Shakespeare."

"I had not realised you owned other estates," Verity replied with thinly veiled surprise."

"The main ducal estate is in Yorkshire, but there is also a Scottish castle, and a manor in Norfolk, as well as various other smaller manors and hunting lodges," he replied. "When I inherited the dukedom, it came with estates and other responsibilities." He was quite pleased she was ignorant of the extent of his wealth. Had she truly been after his money as he had once thought, she would have known down to the last brick and blade of grass, the extent of his holdings, and been quite eager to take part in them.

"It must mean a great deal of work," she responded. "I had not realized how many responsibilities you maintained since inheriting."

"I enjoy work," he replied easily. "Work, the right kind of work, gives a man's life purpose. Knowing that I have responsibility for the livelihoods of many people is a responsibility and knowing that it is my duty to ensure that they have a roof over their heads, food on their tables, and clothes for their children as well as a little extra with which to have some kind of leisure time, is not only a duty, but a privilege."

Elliott watched Verity as she listened. She remained silent for a few moments, clearly considering the new development. He only hoped she could see and trust in him as honourable.

"You may not have been born with a title," she finally said, "but I can think of no-one who is better deserving of it, Your Grace."

He smiled. "Thank-you," he said simply. "I have one final meeting with Burton, but I wondered whether you would like to call on your sister before we depart, I can have the carriage brought round directly."

She pinned a bright smile on her face. "Of course," she responded cheerfully, "I shall leave directly after breakfast."

CHAPTER 25

"*V*erity," Ella squealed with delight, flinging herself at her sister almost before Verity had removed her cloak and bonnet. "Aunt Bette said I must leave you newlyweds alone until after you returned from your honeymoon, but I am so glad to see you. Come, there's a fire in the small drawing room, I will ring for tea."

Within ten minutes they were sitting by the fire, sipping tea. "So, tell me everything," Ella asked with a smile, "is marriage to Elliott all you hoped it might be? Has he fallen in love with you again?"

Verity took a deep breath. She had never lied to Ella, there had never been a reason to before, she knew that above all Ella wished for her happiness, but she could not in all conscience give Ella the answer she clearly wanted to hear.

"My marriage to Elliott is a business contract, that is all," she replied, quietly. "I am to provide Elliott with a living heir, or perhaps two, and in return for that we will be able to return to Swallowfield and live in comfort, all of us, you, I and Caro. Elliott will provide for us and if and when you and Caro marry, he will provide dowries. That is what was agreed between us."

Ella's face fell. "But Elliott loves you," she said.

"No, Ella, he does not. Once I have done my duty, he will have little to do with me. That is the truth of the matter."

"I can't believe this of Elliott, I know this marriage was somewhat forced on you both," Ella murmured, "but he does love you still, I know it. I saw the look he gave you at the wedding."

"Elliott will play the part of the loving husband in public," Verity replied, "but he has never given up his mistress. I have even met her since the wedding."

Ella put her cup down with a clatter. "But the talk of the ton is that the countess is seen everywhere with her latest lover, an officer in the Hussars."

"Apparently, the countess was not the only lover Elliott had. The one I met, Mrs. Audra Kingsley, is his true love."

Ella wrinkled her brow in thought. "Mrs. Kingsley? I have never heard of her. She certainly has not been to any of the balls, or any social event that I know of."

"She is a widow," Verity explained, "not long out of mourning, well out of mourning dress, I should say. From the way she spoke of her late husband I doubt there was much actual mourning involved. But she seems to know Elliott very well. In fact," her voice wobbled, "she made quite the point of telling me that when Elliott is making love to me, he will be thinking of her. So as to your question about whether Elliott loves me, now you know."

Ella rushed to sit beside Verity and put her arms about her, Verity could no longer hold in the hurt and pain as she sobbed into her sister's arms. "Mrs. Kingsley said that when I have had a child, Elliott will leave me at Swallowfield and she will be the one on his arm," Verity said quietly. "And, given the way Elliott has been behaving, I have no doubt that she is right."

"But surely, Elliott has not neglected you in the bedroom." Ella blushed as she spoke. "I know as an unmarried female I am not supposed to know about such things, but I am not a complete ninny and Father had, as you know, many interesting books on the subject which he thought he had hidden."

Verity could not help but chuckle. "They were most educative," she replied. "Since you ask, to begin with, Elliott showed no interest in me at all. In fact, for the first few nights of our marriage he did not come home until the morning, still dressed in his evening attire. I can only think he spent the nights with Mrs. Kingsley. Recently, however, he has been, shall we say attentive, and I am ashamed to admit that I got quite caught up in it and dared believe that he cared for me again. But I can only imagine it is that Mrs. Kingsley reminded him of his obligation for an heir and he is keen to get the whole thing over and done with. Why, he dismissed me first thing this morning, just after breakfast. The sooner I am with child, the sooner he is free."

"Oh, Verity, I am so sorry, I know that I pushed you into this marriage."

"It was Father, and the ridiculous clause in his blasted bill of sale," Verity interjected with sudden fury in her voice. "How like Father to make it seem like we finally had a solution to the troubles *he* placed on us only to find that our lives are all the more wretched because of it! So please, dear Ella," she added, "you must not blame yourself. We had little choice, in the matter but at least this way we have a roof over our heads and Caro, and you should be able to make good marriages and be provided for properly."

"I have no intention of marrying," Ella declared. "As Father said, no man will want to marry me looking as I do. I shall enjoy being your companion and being an aunt to your children. If I was to be a governess, I shall take great joy in helping you to care for your children."

"And you will be a marvellous, beloved aunt," Verity replied, one hand unconsciously shifting to her belly where, even now, she may be holding a child. She could not face telling Ella about Elliott's plan to remove her children from her care once they were old enough to go to school.

"In any case," Verity took a sip of her tea, anxious to change the subject, "Elliott has announced that we are to spend two weeks away from London at one of his estates in Hampshire, Orlando Court."

Ella's eyes widened. "I had not realised that Elliott owned Orlando Court."

Verity looked up. "You have heard of it, then? I had not known he had any other holdings."

Ella nodded. "You remember Elizabeth Frankworth? She was in my class at school, not a particularly pleasant girl if you recall, but she frequently boasted about the fact that her family were often invited to spend Christmas with the old duke who was, I believe, a distant relation. Apparently, there is some story that Shakespeare actually visited there in his youth. If Elizabeth was to be believed, Orlando Court is the size of a small palace and quite as luxurious."

"Well," Verity replied, "I begin to feel that I know as little about Elliott now as I did seven years ago."

"Perhaps some time with Elliott, away from the distractions of society will give you the opportunity to get to know each other better," Ella suggested. "Even," she added, "find some common ground upon which to stand."

"Perhaps," Verity agreed, though wherever they were, the spectre of Mrs. Kingsley seemed to hover.

She passed her time with Ella simply after that, reading the letters Caro had sent from school and writing responses. She wished with all her heart she would be able to return to Swallowfield to spend the holidays with her sisters.

When she returned home, her maid was already packing her clothes in large trunks ready for the journey to Hampshire.

"I am not sure I shall need all those gowns," Verity protested. "I doubt we shall see many people in the country."

"His Grace's orders. Your Grace," Daisy said. "There will be some visiting to the local families and there's talk of a ball."

"A ball? That is the first I have heard of it," Verity said, raising her eyebrows. Why would Elliott want to throw a ball with his wife when he intended to leave her at Swallowfield to be forgotten? Surely the less exposure she had to any kind of society, the better. There was no doubt that Elliott Thorne was an enigma.

The luggage carts set off at dawn the following day, followed after breakfast by the coach bearing the servants who were to accompany them on their journey. Verity was just coming down the stairs when Elliott came out of the library. "Ah, there you are," he said with a smile. "I've just sent for the coach to come round from the mews."

"Are you travelling in the coach with me?" Verity asked.

"Of course. Why would you think otherwise?" he replied.

"Because the thought of us travelling in a confined space together for a day without a referee seems to be a recipe for disaster," she said, crisply.

To her surprise, Elliott threw back his head and laughed. "Oh, I think I can manage to keep my temper under control, if you can keep that sharp tongue of yours from cutting a slice off my hide."

Clearly in spite of herself, she could not help but smile. "Are you suggesting a truce?"

"I believe I am, not just for the duration of the journey, but for the whole of the trip. I propose that we try to be cordial towards each other for the next two weeks," he said, suddenly serious. "I want us to enjoy some time together, Verity, to get to know each other again. Who knows? We might even find we actually like each other?" he added with a grin.

She regarded him coolly. "I think that might be a bit of a stretch."

"Cordiality it is," he countered. At least she had not reverted to 'Your Graceing' him.

The arrival of the coach curtailed any further conversation. Verity turned away, adorably flustered. He grinned behind her. She could never resist him when he was being charming. He knew it, she knew it, and what's more, he knew that she knew it.

Elliott handed her into the coach and settled himself in the opposite seat. Coach travel was rarely comfortable, but Elliott's coach was equipped with the latest steel springs and had been built with comfort in mind. The soft velvet squabs and metal springs absorbed the jolts as they bounced along the cobbles of London, through Wandsworth and Putney Heath, to Kingston, Esher, Cobham and Ripley to Guildford where they made a stop at The Angel.

"Come in, come in Your Grace," the landlord beamed as Elliott stepped down from the coach. "And is this delightful young lady your new wife?" he asked, bowing as Verity stepped from the coach. "She is indeed," Elliott replied, "delightful," he added with a wink.

"It is indeed an honour to meet you, Your Grace," the landlord continued, "now come in, I've kept the private parlour for you, there's a fire in the grate and Bessie will be through with your food as soon as you're ready."

The parlour was clean and cosy and as they sat down, a plump woman who Verity thought must be the landlord's wife came through bearing two plates of steaming beef stew and a jug of ale.

"My goodness," Verity murmured, "I had not realised I was hungry until it arrived."

"Bessie is indeed a good cook," Elliott replied, picking up his knife and fork. "It is why I always break my journey here."

Hungry as she was, Verity could only manage barely half of the food on her plate.

"Was there something the matter with the stew?" Bessie asked as she cleared Elliott's empty plate and Verity's half-full one.

"Not at all," Verity replied, "indeed I would say without a doubt that it is the finest stew I have ever tasted, there was just too much for me."

Bessie nodded, satisfied with Verity's explanation.

Verity looked up, aware that Elliott was looking at her. "Are you quite well, Verity?" he asked. "I have noticed, of late, that you rarely finish your meals."

"I am as fit as a fiddle," she replied firmly. "Ladies are trained not to eat too much. We are supposed to have the appetite of a sparrow."

"I am glad to hear it, not the part about the sparrow. I just wondered whether there was something causing your loss of appetite."

Despite the warmth of the fire, Verity felt chilled "I am not with child if that is what you were thinking." Of course, that was what he was thinking, the sooner he got her with child, the sooner he would be able to dispense with her and return to his lover. Possibly even cancel this trip, as it would be evident he could fulfil his duty without needing to be apart from his mistress.

His next words surprised her. "I am glad that you are not carrying a babe just yet. I think we need some time together, Verity, to get to know each other as husband and wife and have a strong sense of trust before we become a family."

"I will remind Your Grace that you do not want a *family*, you want an heir," she said, standing abruptly. She could not sit and listen to him mock her. "Now is it not time for us to be on our way?" She turned and headed towards the door, averting her head so that Elliott could not see her tears. talk of a family was the last thing she wanted to hear because it would make her dream and dreams of happiness and families were dangerous.

CHAPTER 26

Orlando Court was far bigger than Verity had been expecting. Although Elliott had made it sound like a small manor house, she remembered Ella's words and kept her expectations tempered. But even as they traveled down the long drive, she could not see the house for several minutes, passing first one gatehouse then another with the two parts of the gatehouse attached together by a bridge room. Through the arch Verity got her first view of Orlando Court.

"The original building was Tudor," Elliott explained. "I have just finished making some additions and improvements. As a matter of fact, this is the first time I have seen it since it has been finished and furnished."

"It looks very imposing," Verity replied.

"I hope it is more comfortable than imposing," Elliott said as the carriage drew to a halt between the two staircases flanking the front door, where the servants stood on either side to greet them. "I was thinking of using it as a retreat from society, one I can share with my family and close friends."

Verity tried to catch his eye, but his gaze was fixed on the building. She could only presume that he meant his brother and his mistress would keep him company here in the future.

Although dusk was falling rapidly, Verity could see that the house was huge. Two wings were built on either side of the huge entrance which boasted a triangular pediment on top of the columns. Verity counted at least forty windows along the frontage, each one ablaze with light. "I shall never be able to find my way about," she murmured, adding, "Swallowfield seems like a miniature in comparison."

"It is ridiculously large," Elliott agreed.

"Then let us go inside," Verity replied, "the servants will be getting cold waiting for us."

Elliott seemed to know the names of most of the servants and greeted them personally as they made their way down the line. It seemed that his profession that he saw as his duty to care for this land and those who worked it was a privilege rather than a duty held true. Elliott had never known true poverty, nor had she, but they were both acutely familiar with what it was like not to have money and power. The fact that now he was in a position to improve the lives of others and wanted to do so, moved her almost to tears. She had never before witnessed a man in his position give the slightest thought to the lives of those who served them, let alone the lives of the poor they either chose not to see, or blamed them for being born into poverty. Elliott, she realised, was truly an honourable man, far more honourable than she had given him credit for.

"How do you do that?" Verity asked once they were sitting in a small, cosy drawing room.

"Do what?" Elliot asked.

"Remember everyone's name," she replied. "From what you said, I guess that you have only met the servants here once or twice and yet you could name them all."

He looked embarrassed, as if she had caught him in an embarrassing predicament. "I just seem to have been blessed with a good memory."

She shook her head. "A good memory is remembering what day one is to go to the theatre, or to be able to tell a good anecdote. Your gift is far more than that."

He sighed and ran a hand through his hair. "Very well, I have an almost freakishly good memory. Once I have read or learned something, I find it impossible to forget it. I am also able to read and write at what I know is a far faster rate than others."

"Elliott, that is quite the most extraordinary thing I have heard."

He smiled, but it did not reach his eyes. "Then you do not think I am some sort of oddity?"

Verity took his large hands in hers. "Of course not, it is a great blessing. If I possessed such a skill, I should be shouting it from the rooftops."

He looked down at their joined hands. "Believe me it is as much a curse as a blessing," he said quietly.

"How so?" She could only imagine how a perfect memory could ease many difficulties, for business, opportunities, socializing, and records.

Elliott looked into the distance. "At school... Boys are not always the kindest of humans and if they sense something different about another child it gives them a stick with which to beat them. I was roundly considered a freak and seen as cursed."

"What did you do?" she asked, softly.

"I learned quickly to hide it and often pretended that I did not know the answer to the masters' questions. I found it was easier to take a beating from the masters than to lose every friend I had."

"But what about later, when you were in the army?"

He took a deep breath as his eyes clouded over. "There are sights, sounds and smells from the battlefield I can never forget, try as I might."

"Oh, Elliott, I had not thought of the full implications of your gift. It is indeed a mixed blessing."

He suddenly cupped her head and looked deep into her eyes. "And you of course, I could never forget you. I remember the day we met, you were kneeling in your father's garden grubbing in the dirt and talking to a clump of violets. There was a streak of mud across your cheek, and I thought you were the most beautiful thing I had ever seen." He paused and added, "I still do."

"And I thought you quite the most handsome man I had ever seen,"

Verity replied, adding, "but there again, I had really only seen my father and his friends and believe me, none of them were worth an oil painting."

Elliott laughed. "Ouch, how to pierce a man's ego."

"Come, Your Grace, please show me around this beautiful house," she said, breaking away from him and willing her heart to slow down. Surely, he had been about to kiss her, Elliott was becoming some sort of drug that she was beginning to rely on, and she knew that down that road lay ruin. Her heart was going to be broken by this man again, but she had to put it off for as long as possible, because she did not know if she could recover from it a second time.

She could not understand why he was telling her this at all. She felt that in the past day or two she had learned more about Elliott than she had when she had loved him with all her heart.

"Very well," he replied, holding out his arm, "We shall begin in what is called the grand salon. Not my term, but that is what I was told it was called the first time I came here."

***

The room took her breath away: there were four arched windows from floor to ceiling, which would flood the room with light during the day. Four large chandeliers provided light during the evening, their flames reflected from the large mirrors on the walls. A blaze burned in the white marble fireplace, in front of which were two cream sofas and throughout the room were more sofas, chairs and occasional tables each with a small candelabra, giving the room a warmth, which was unexpected in such a large space. The cream-and-gold colour scheme was beyond anything that Verity had beheld either at Swallowfield or in the London townhouses she had visited.

"It is quite the most magnificent room I have seen," she breathed.

"It has turned out rather well," Elliott agreed. "Now let us see the dining room. I believe we should give a dinner for the local families as soon as possible."

"But why?"

"So that you can get to know them, of course." He looked surprised at her question.

Verity laughed. "Although I shall be happy to play hostess for a dinner, please feel no obligation on my account."

Elliott raised an eyebrow. "I do not follow."

Verity shrugged. "As I shall be living at Swallowfield and unlikely to visit Orlando Court again, there would seem to be little point in me getting to know the neighbours."

Elliott took a breath before saying carefully, "I should still like to give a dinner and get to know our neighbours while we are here. Let us not concern ourselves with the future whilst we are here."

Verity inclined her head tersely. "As you wish, Your Grace."

"In fact," Elliott went on, "It has been in my mind to throw a ball whilst we are here, a grand ball so that I can show off my new wife."

Verity turned towards him, so Daisy had been right! "Why are you doing this, Elliott? Why are you being so cruel?"

Elliott reared back. "What do you mean, Verity? Cruel?"

"This play-acting, pretending that I am to be a real wife, that I shall see this place again, that it is important that I get to know the neighbours when we both know that you cannot wait to be rid of me once I have provided what it is you paid for."

He moved towards her, his hands resting on her arms. "Verity, look at me," he commanded softly.

She raised her tear-filled eyes to his. "Our marriage has been far from conventional, I agree," he said softly, tucking and errant curl behind her ear, "but for these two weeks or so, I would very much like us to try to live with like something approaching a normal couple. The constant battle between us is wearing to say the least. We agreed to a truce before we set off, shall we try to keep to it?"

Verity swallowed. "Very well," she agreed with a soft sob.

"I have an idea." His eyes sparkled as he spoke. "If we are to get through the next fortnight without killing each other, for the next two weeks we shall play the roles of a happily married couple. I shall be an attentive husband and you shall be an adoring wife. We may even convince ourselves that we are not star-crossed lovers."

"Very well," she replied softly.

"Good," he said softly, lowering his face to hers. He could barely convince himself that he did not love her, that he felt much more than lust or desire. He needed only to convince her that they could have a life together, find peace and love once more. Two pleasant weeks should prove to her once and for all that he would remain by her side and honour his vows, despite her continued insistence that he was eager to set her aside. "I believe this bargain should be sealed in the traditional way," he murmured as his lips sought hers. Within seconds, what had started as a gentle exploration became deeper as Elliott drew her into his arms, moulding her body to his so that he could feel her breasts through his shirt.

Breathing heavily, he broke the kiss, but kept her in the circle of his arms. "I think it is time for me to show you the ducal bedroom," he whispered into her ear, smiling as he saw her shiver. He had not been the only one moved by the kiss.

"What...about the d-dining room?" Verity stammered.

"The dining room be damned," he replied. "We shall see it in the morning when we break our fast, but for now I have other appetites that need attending to."

"But what about..." she began.

"Verity, there is nothing, literally nothing in the world at this moment in time that is more important than me making love to my wife. We have wasted seven long years when you could have been in my bed."

"And five nights of our marriage when you went to ..."

"I have already explained that that part of my life is over, Verity," he interrupted. "It is over and done with, and from now on, there is only you." He swept her up in his arms. "I shall do my best to finally convince you of that right now."

"As you wish," she replied. For the moment at least, she was his.

He just needed to keep her that way.

CHAPTER 27

Once they had entered his chamber, Elliott set Verity down on her feet and shut the door behind them, clicking the lock to ensure they would remain undisturbed even after sunrise. The room was decorated masculinely with pale green silk wallcovering, darker green drapes on the windows had been drawn, and a marble fireplace blazed with a warm glow illuminated two armchairs. The bed on a dais at one end of the room looked as large as Verity's entire bed chamber at Swallowfield. There were no bed curtains, but someone had already turned down the watered-silk coverlet revealing snowy white sheets and pillows. There were several tallboys and a huge wardrobe fit to accommodate a man of high calibre. A decanter of sherry and glasses sat on a small side table.

Verity suddenly became aware of Elliott's gaze as she took in the beauty of their surroundings. "It is truly beautiful," she said. "Are you responsible for all the design throughout the house?"

He smiled. "Much as I should like to claim credit for it, I have employed a designer who deals with it all. I merely indicated what I wanted, and he interpreted it, rather well, I think."

"Indeed," she replied, running her fingers along the back of one of the chairs.

"Perhaps a sherry?" he asked, moving towards the table. "You seem a little overwhelmed. Is it the setting or your husband?"

Verity sank into the armchair and accepted the glass Elliott offered, taking a small sip before wrinkling her nose. "I have never tried sherry before," she admitted. "Although Father kept a fine cellar, we were never permitted to taste any, he said there was no point in wasting good wine on silly girls."

"It seems that we know little about each other, which is surprising, given our history, but I should like to know more of your life, Verity, if you would care to tell me." Elliott took a sip from his own glass and settled himself in the seat opposite her. "I would like you to be comfortable here, and with me."

"Well," she began, taking a second sip, this time carefully savouring the warmth as it slipped down her throat, "Ella, as you know is the eldest of us three girls, her mother was the daughter of a duke and came with a handsome dowry, which Father used to shore up some of the more crumbling wings of Swallowfield and buy himself a fine stable of racehorses. She was greatly weakened after Ella's birth and although she went on to conceive two more babes, she lost them before she could bring them to term, though I believe they would have been boys. It is said that she was overtaken by great melancholy, fell down the stairs in the old tower, and died from her injuries."

"What was she doing in the old tower?" Elliott asked.

"I believe Father had her moved there because he could not bear the sound of her constant weeping, or so Mrs. Clayton told me."

"Bastard," Elliott said quietly. "A man should look after his wife, in sickness and in health, not shut her away when she is grieving. Vows and honour do not cease due to inconvenience or struggle."

"Father could never abide sickness or weeping," she whispered harshly. "If we were ill, he did not come to see us and left us to our nurses. If we fell or were injured, we were told to get up and on no account were we to cry. He forbade our nurses to come to us if we were crying, so we just stopped." After a pause, she added thoughtfully, "No-one would come, so there was no point. My sisters and I looked after each other when we could, in the privacy of our rooms."

"Good God."

Verity stared into the flames. "In what was considered at the time to be a scandalously short amount of time after Ella's mother's death, he married my mother. She was only the daughter of a mere lord but had a healthy dowry which my father used to increase his racehorse stable. I was born within the year, but mother was unable to bear further children, something for which my father could not forgive either her or me. We were both summarily ignored whenever possible as punishment for disappointing him. She died when I was small, a riding accident. Something spooked her horse, and she was thrown, she never recovered consciousness."

"Verity, I had no idea." He reached over and took her hand in his, gently stroking the palm. "Please do not go on if this distresses you."

She returned his gaze. "No, you asked, and I find I want to tell you," she replied. If only to have greater understanding between them, to have a foundation of truth between them.

"Father quickly married again, rather like Henry the Eighth, his desperation for a son dominated his every thought. Caro's mother came from trade, her father was a grocer, but her dowry was generous, and Father was prepared to hold his nose at the thought of tainting his old and noble bloodline and marry someone from trade at the thought of her money, because by this time his horses were losing him more than they were worth.

It took Caro's mother longer to conceive a child, which infuriated Father. Caro's birth was long and difficult and soon after, her mother caught a fever and died. From that point on we saw very little of Father. Ella's mother had left money for any children to be educated, so Ella and I were taught by governesses and tutors, but by the time Caro was only seven, as far as Father was concerned, she was old enough to go to school. Father sent her away, which was actually for the best. Ella and I had become used to dealing with his rages and drunkenness, but Caro was only young."

Verity stopped, thinking of the summer she had spent with Elliott and his betrayal as well as the betrothal her father had forced her into was too painful to relate after all she had just told him. "There you have it," she murmured, "not much of a life, really."

He rose and gently drew her into his arms, before sitting down and settling her on his lap, needing to feel her close, wanting to take away her pain. "I am sorry if dragging this up has distressed you," he whispered into her hair, "it was not my intention to upset you. I had no idea seven years ago of the life you were leading." He stroked her back as she leaned her head against his shoulder, safe and protected in the circle of his arms.

"It is strange," she mused. "I believed that I would never be loved. That there was something about me that was unlovable and disappointing, as Father had made so clear. I never really knew love until that summer..."

"That wonderful, golden summer, when we met, and the world was alive with possibilities?" Elliott finished with a smile. "I had not expected to fall in love," he admitted. "Yet, when I met you, all sensible thoughts left my head, until all I could think of, all I could dream of was you."

Verity laughed softly. "Every waking moment, all I could think of was when I should next see you." She sat up. "What young, romantic fools we both were."

Elliott pulled her back against his long body. "Young, yes, and romantic too, but fools? Never."

He drew her close and his lips found hers in a long, drugging kiss that stemmed from his heart and his soul. He rose with her in his arms, walked towards the bed, and gently laid her on it, revelling in the fulfilment of the desire to finally—finally—having her in a large, comfortable bed where he could enjoy entangling himself with her. He slowly lay himself beside her and reached for the tiny, silk covered buttons at the front of her bodice, patiently sliding each one out of the buttonhole and easing the bodice from her shoulders, luxuriating in kissing every inch of her flesh as he uncovered it. She squirmed and blushed with the attention but was clearly making efforts not to show embarrassment or modesty.

"You are the most beautiful and desirable woman I have ever

encountered," he said softly, as her bodice drifted to the floor, and he concentrated his efforts on unlacing her corset. When the tip of her tongue slid out to wet her lips, in nervousness or uncontrolled lust, he was almost undone, but he wanted to take his time and love Verity as she deserved to be loved.

When her skirts and petticoats joined her other clothes on the floor, she lay before him clad only in her chemise which did little to hide her body from his hungry gaze. He could already see her hardened nipples through the thin, delicate fabric, which also did nothing to hide the shadow of dark curls at her core.

"I feel like a child unwrapping the most beautiful and exciting gift," he said, salivating at the prospect of uncovering and tasting her. He reached a hand under her chemise and slid it slowly up her body, dragging the cloth up until he was able to pull it over her head. He paused for a moment, taking in the sight of her. "And the gift is more beautiful and exquisite than I imagined," he said as he lowered his head and kissed each breast in turn. He ran his hands gently over every inch of her satiny skin. "So beautiful," he whispered, kissing his way down her body until he reached her most intimate part.

"Open for me, Verity."

Her hands twisted the sheets nervously at her sides, but she slowly parted her thighs, turning her head away as if ashamed.

He settled himself between her legs, his tongue gently grazing her entrance before he plunged inside, swirling his tongue around, revelling in the scent and taste of her and the frantic sounds she was making as her hands gripped the sheets. He did not, could not, stop until she screamed his name and her whole body trembled. He held her as the tremors subsided. "Elliott," she whispered, her eyes still glazed. "What must I do to please you as you pleased me?" she whispered.

"If you please me anymore, Verity, I may not survive," he laughed softly.

She took a breath. "I want to touch you," she said quietly, her embarrassment evident in her blush. Elliott would enjoy this time of their relationship where she was still hesitant and unsure but was enjoying the hints of the vixen beneath that as yet remained leashed.

"Then who am I to refuse?" He laughed. She clearly had no experience with male garments, so he quickly divested himself of clothing until he lay naked next to her, allowing her to tentatively explore his body at her ease.

She hesitated but propped herself up on one arm and reached out a hand cautiously. He drew in a sharp breath as her narrow fingers brushed across his flat nipple. She instantly drew back, "Is that not pleasurable?" she asked.

"Oh, it is pleasurable all right," he replied, feeling his cock jump at her touch.

"Good," she said, her fingers gently caressing the whorls of dark hair on his chest, stroking his chest and feeling his nipples as if familiarizing herself with his body. Minutes passed before she began tracing the narrow line down his stomach.

He groaned as her fingers brushed his rigid cock, "Jesus," he ground out through gritted teeth. If she touched him much more he would explode.

Once again, she quickly drew her hand back. "Should I not touch you there?" she asked.

"Touch me," he gasped, "please, Verity." He could not help groaning as her slender hand closed around him, hesitantly teasing and caressing until he felt himself begin to twitch and buck into her hand and could stand it no longer.

"I need to be inside you, Verity. Now," he said as he rolled her onto her back and entered her with a quick thrust. Nothing, nothing had ever felt like this. She matched him thrust for thrust until they were both panting, each other's pleasure driving them to new heights. Too soon, eternally too soon, they found their release together and he felt whole as he felt himself merge fully with her.

When he awoke later, he drew up the coverlet and looked at the woman sleeping in his arms. "Never think you are unlovable, sweeting," he whispered into her ear. "You deserve to be loved and cherished and that is what I shall do for the rest of our lives," he promised, before falling into a deep, peaceful sleep.

CHAPTER 28

*V*erity smiled as she saw the single red rose placed on the pillow beside her. She reached out and ran her fingers over its velvety softness and raised it to her nose to take in its scent. She was still holding it when the door opened and Elliott walked in wearing only his breeches, his hair still wet from his bath.

"Ah, you're awake, duchess. A rose for a rose; I must be getting romantic in my old age as I went to the hothouse myself to pick it," he said with a smile. "Your maid has drawn you a bath and much as I should like nothing more than to spend the day in bed with you, we need to ride to our neighbours and issue invitations."

"Invitations?" she asked.

"Invitations," he confirmed. "We shall hold a dinner in a week's time and a ball in a fortnight."

"Do we have to do it so soon? Or at all?" she asked.

He sat down on the bed, "Of course, we talked about this. If you are to be a great London hostess, which I know you will be, you must practise. This will be the first of many triumphs."

"But I won't be..." she began, as Mrs. Kingsley's words echoed once more in her mind.

"You will be magnificent as you always are," he interrupted. "Now

—" he mimed a swat at her bottom, "—go to your bath and wear clothes for riding."

As she sat in her bath, enjoying the hot, rose scented water, she went over the events of the last few days. Elliott had been the epitomizing playing the role of a loving husband. They had talked together, they had listened to each other, he had made love to her, and it had all felt so real, but was it? The night she had just spent had been magical, and if she did not know better, she could have convinced herself that Elliott loved her. Still loved her? Loved her...again?

She shook her head sadly, anything he said in the throes of passion or even in the afterglow was not something she could rely on. He desired her and wanted her, that much she knew. Beyond that, as his wife and the mother of his child, he might come to respect her, but that was all she could hope for. He would use her body when and as desired, even pleasuring himself and her, but when she gave birth to his heir, he would have no further interest or use for her.

Still, trying to make peace with her thoughts and feelings, his thoughts and feelings, and his behaviour in seclusion was nigh on impossible.

Did he feel something for her? Did he want to make this a proper marriage? Or was he just employing a different tactic to get what he wanted as quickly as possible? She felt more confused than ever, but she knew instinctively that she had to remain guarded. Although she wanted to trust him, to believe his words, she could not afford herself to do so, because when he left her at Swallowfield, her heart would break.

With a smile pinned on her face, she swept into the breakfast room dressed in her green velvet riding habit, holding the little hat and gloves which she placed on the side table.

Elliott rose as she entered. "You are so beautiful, at times you take my breath away," he said, going towards her and drawing her into his arms. "I am beginning to regret saying that we would go visiting already," he whispered, dropping a kiss on the tip of her nose before capturing her lips. When he raised his head, they were both breathing heavily. "Well, Your Grace, you rather missed the opportunity for *that* sort of behavior when you demanded that we go riding." She laughed.

"I know the kind of riding I prefer." He leered outrageously. Then he laughed when her face scrunched up in confusion. It was strongly implied that this "riding" was intimate, but she could not imagine how riding would come up in the bedroom.

"However," he continued, "I had sent messages to say that we would be calling so I shall have to content myself with the thought of what we shall do when we return."

"You are extremely forward," she said.

"Insatiable is the word I might have used," he countered, "though I find myself that way only with you."

When they had finished breakfast, they walked to the stables where two horses were saddled and waiting, a large black stallion and a smaller, brown mare. "This is Ladybird," Elliott said as he boosted her into the saddle. "She's a placid little thing and should give you no trouble."

"What is your mount called?" she asked, watching him effortlessly hoist himself aloft.

"Collier, and I shall hope that today he behaves like a gentleman."

"'E needs a firm 'and Yer Grace and e'll do as 'e's bid," the groom said as he handed Elliott the reins.

Before long, they had left the gardens and rode out into the park. For all that Ladybird was smaller than Collier, she seemed determined to keep up with him. They trotted across parkland and walked through the woods that separated Orlando Court from its nearest neighbour. Lord and Lady Dean were delighted to meet the new duke and his duchess and accept his dinner invitation, as were Sir Harry and Lady Schofield and Lord and Lady Graham.

"I did not think they would all accept our invitation," Verity remarked as they rode towards the meadow adjoining the park.

"Of course they accepted," Elliott replied. "They are all curious to see the renovations at the house, and they are all dying of curiosity about the new duchess. They all want to be able to boast that they were there when you gave your first dinner." He laughed.

"Just to be clear," she said with a grin, "if they are expecting me to cook, they may well be in for disappointment. I once helped Mrs. Clayton to make bread and it could have been used to shore up a wall."

"Of course not." Elliott chuckled. "Our guests have no wish to risk life and any remaining teeth."

"Wretch." She smiled as she tapped her heels into Ladybird's side. "The last one home has to arrange the menu with Cook," she said over her shoulder as Ladybird broke into a gallop.

They were almost home when Verity took the small fence at the edge of the woodland. Elliott's heart was in his mouth as he saw her saddle slide to the side as Ladybird sailed over and Verity lost her seat. For several heart-stopping moments she hung on until her foot slipped from the stirrup then hit the ground with a thud and did not get up. He pulled up Collier and was off his horse and at her side. "Verity, Verity," he asked frantically, his voice hoarse, "are you all right? Where does it hurt?"

He did not know what to do. Shake her? Keep her still? She had not yet opened her eyes. This was how her mother had died. Was she even breathing? "Verity, please open your eyes, my love," he pleaded. He almost cried out with relief when she took in a shaky breath and opened her eyes.

"I fell off," she said groggily.

"I know," he replied softly, "I saw. Are you all right, where does it hurt?" he asked, beginning to run his hands over her body to check for broken bones. He had seen men take lesser falls than the one he had just seen who had broken several bones, and he knew that if infection set in there was little that could be done. Injuries were not always apparent from the outside.

"I shall be fine, Elliott," Verity said, trying to sit up and wincing as she did so.

"You are not fine," he replied sternly. "You took a hell of a tumble. I do not think any bones are broken, but once we are back to the house, I shall send for a physician to perform a thorough examination to make sure."

"Really, there is no need to make a fuss," she said. As if to prove her point, she attempted to stand but promptly swayed, nearly sending him back into a panic.

"Verity, we need to get back to the house, so I am going to lift you onto Collier. We'll ride together and Ladybird will follow," he said, not knowing if she could hear him or not.

"Get back on," she murmured, though her eyes remained closed. "Got to get back on horse when you fall, or Father will be so angry. Weak...weak to be hurt."

"Verity, you are in no fit state to ride a horse. Just trust me," he ground out as he lifted her up, settled her on his horse, then leapt up beside her.

The journey across the park was tortuously slow, but he dared not try to go faster, the weight of his wife against him told him she was barely conscious. Fry was at the door as he rode up. "Send for Dr. Lamb," he said over his shoulder as he ran up the stairs with Verity in his arms. With Daisy's help, he got her undressed and into bed and remained sitting by her side until Dr. Lamb arrived.

"Well," the doctor began when he had thoroughly examined her, "her Grace has taken quite a fall, but as far as I can see, there will be no lasting damage."

"When will she awake?"

"That is a question I cannot answer with any degree of accuracy, though I should venture to suggest within an hour or so. She has a large bump on the back of her head which is a good sign."

"A good sign?" Elliott almost shouted. "She is injured! How could a large bump possibly be a good sign, sir?"

"Indeed, were we looking at a dent, the situation would be far more serious, in fact, I should go so far as to say dire," the doctor replied calmly. "However, the duchess is young and strong, and she'll be right as rain in a day or so. I shall return in two days."

"I hope you are right," Elliott replied, looking at his prone wife.

"I shall be, you will see," the doctor said as he packed his bag. He paused at the door. "Your Grace, if I may, I have seen many a distraught husband, and I understand your feelings, but you must remain calm for your wife's sake. Excess emotion will only disturb her recovery." With that, he bowed and left the room.

It was dark when Elliott finally heard a voice croak out, "Elliot?"

"Thank God," he said quietly. Never before had his name sounded so sweet from a woman's lips.

"Please...may I have some water?"

He poured some from the carafe on the nightstand and held the glass carefully while Verity sipped slowly.

"How do you feel?" he asked, taking her hand.

"I feel as though every bone in my body is aching," she said softly.

"You fell from Ladybird, so it is not surprising," he replied, stroking her hand.

She wrinkled her brow. "I...we were racing back before setting the menu with Cook. I was winning. I went to take the last fence, as it is so small to jump, but then..." She shook her head. "What happened?"

"The saddle started to slip because the buckle on the girth gave way," he replied. "Something that should not have happened. Something that Jackson, my head groom, says has never happened before."

Her eyes grew wide. "What are you saying Elliott?"

"Either the buckle was faulty, and it was new so that is a distinct possibility, or..." he hesitated, should he be honest and tell her the groom's opinion, or should he protect her from unnecessary worry?

"Or?" she prompted.

"Or someone tampered with the buckle so that at some point, during one of our rides, it would come under pressure as it did, and give way."

Verity stared at him. "Are you saying that someone deliberately tried to injure me?" she could scarcely believe her own words.

He nodded. "I think we have to consider it a distinct possibility."

"But who? Who could possibly want to do that?" she asked. "I barely know anyone. I cannot think that I have offended someone so much that they would want to do me harm."

"We should know more when Jackson has completed his investigation," he said. "In the meantime, you are to rest and let your body recover."

"I am not staying in bed," Verity announced. "Other than a few bruises, mostly to my pride, I am quite capable of going downstairs, and in any case, I have much to do to prepare for our dinner guests."

"We can cancel the dinner..." Elliott began.

"Certainly not," she interrupted. "A dinner has been promised, and a dinner there shall be," she added determinedly.

"Very well." He sighed. "I know there is no arguing with you when you are in one of your moods."

She raised an eyebrow. "For your information, this dinner is your idea to launch me as a hostess and for your further information, I do not have moods."

"Of course, you do not." He grinned.

Despite her protests, when she was dressed, Elliott insisted on carrying her to the library so that she could meet with the cook and housekeeper to discuss the menu and arrangements for the dinner, but where he could do some of his own work at the same time. She did not object as, despite her protests, her head did rather hurt, and she had some difficulty focusing.

Elliott kept an eye on Verity as she met with the staff. He was impressed not only by the clear communication of her ideas, but with her manner with the servants. She respected them and he could see that they already respected her. Verity was taking to the role of duchess as though she was born to it. What had he been thinking when he considered his initial plan of leaving her at Swallowfield and continuing his life without Verity by his side? She was everything any man could want in a wife: a fiery temptress in bed, a great manager of people, and he had no doubt that she would make a great hostess, not just here in the country, but she would be among the great hostesses in London.

It occurred to him then that he did not want her to leave his side. He wanted her in his bed and by his side. He wanted to be able to share his thoughts with her and listen to hers every night. He wanted a real life together with children and all that a family entailed. He didn't need to give her his heart for she already had it. Elliott paused in his thoughts, his pen hovering over the document he had been signing. Was it true? Had he done what he had sworn not to do? Had he fallen back in love with Verity Grainger?

Elliott carefully put down his pen and considered Verity as she discussed the seating arrangements with Fry. He lusted after her, that he could not deny, had done so since she had fallen back into his life, but this was something else. His heart had nearly stopped when he saw her fall from her horse. He had felt fear for the first time in a long time, fear for her safety. If he lost her now, having only just found her again, he did not know how he would survive. Somehow, she had worked her way back into his life and his heart, and he now knew for certain that what he wanted with Verity was a real marriage. They were compatible sexually—extremely compatible—but he was unsure of what Verity felt towards him.

These days at Orlando Court had reduced some of the tension between them, but he had the feeling that she was holding something back, that she did not entirely trust him and how could he blame her? She had agreed to this marriage of convenience because frankly, she had little choice. He had given her little choice. His stomach clenched when he recalled the way in which he had explained that she would be left at Swallowfield after she had borne his children. No wonder she kept referring to herself as a broodmare. Was that what she was thinking when he made love to her, that he wanted to get her with child as quickly as possible and then abandon her?

He needed to rectify this as soon as he could. If he wanted to have a real life with his wife, to make her know that he was committed to her, he needed to assure her that she was more than a convenient mother to his children. He resolved to discuss this with her that very night.

Or perhaps, he considered, he would wait until the doctor returned. He did not want to overwhelm her and disrupt her recovery.

The door to the library clicked shut as Fry left and Verity continued to make a few notes before looking up and smiling. "Who would have thought a dinner for so few could have the facility to turn into some kind of battleground?" she laughed.

"Battleground?" he asked, attempting to clear his mind.

"According to Fry, the Grahams and the Schofields need to be kept apart at the dinner table, something to do with the Schofields less-than-pedigree bull getting into the field with the Govan's prize herd of cows."

"The result being?"

"A rather unattractive mixture of two breeds apparently, though according to Fry, they produce fine milk."

"Well, it should be possible to achieve."

"Ah, you simple man, that is not the only issue. Fry, who is, incidentally a mine of information, tells me that Lady Dean was once pursued by Sir Harry but threw him over when she was offered the prospect of becoming Lady Dean, as a lord is of course a far finer catch than a mere sir. Should I succeed this evening without swords being drawn I shall consider it a triumph."

"I shall put your name forward for a post in the diplomatic service." He grinned. "I doubt that the Duke of Wellington had this trouble seating guests the night before the Battle of Waterloo."

CHAPTER 29

Daisy was putting the finishing touches to Verity's hair for the dinner when Elliott walked in. There was no doubt that he was a handsome man, and his evening jacket of midnight blue emphasised the width of his shoulders, his shirt was snow white as was his neckcloth, held in place by a sapphire pin above a silver waistcoat. His long, muscular legs were encased in silver grey trousers. He was intending to take her breath away.

"You look very handsome," she said, as Daisy pinned the last of her curls into place.

"Thank you," he replied, "when one is escorting the most beautiful woman one has to make an effort."

"Such flattery," she said with a smile, standing and smoothing out her skirts.

Standing in front of him was a goddess, her pale green silk gown with its gossamer-like overskirt was shot through with pearls, which gleamed in the candlelight. The neckline and high waistline showed off her delightful decolletage to perfection and emphasised her slender frame.

He cleared his throat. "I bought these for you," he said, holding out a velvet box, "as they remind me of your eyes." Verity took the box and carefully opened it revealing the shining emeralds he had chosen.

The stunning necklace of square cut emeralds had a long drop in its centre as well as matching ear bobs.

"They are beautiful," she said quietly. "Thank you."

"May I?" he asked, taking the necklace out of the box and opening the clasp.

Verity stood still as his hands reached around her to fasten the necklace, then rested on her shoulders and turned her so that they were both standing in the mirror. The emeralds did indeed add the finishing touch, contrasting with her hair and making her eyes dark, green pools.

"I cannot believe you are real," he murmured, breathing in the rose scent of her hair. "You are like a beautiful sea nymph."

"Beware then," she said, "they are the ones who lure sailors onto the rocks. The emeralds are beautiful, thank you for allowing me to borrow them. I shall return them to you in the morning."

Elliott frowned. Borrow? His gift had not received the response he had hoped for. He had imagined that later, when the guests had departed, he would have Verity in his bed wearing only the emeralds, the lust shining in her eyes reflected in the gems. "Are you sure you like them?" he asked. Jewels had always been accepted with delight in his experience with other women.

"Of course," she said evenly, "what woman does not like beautiful jewels?"

He nodded, unconvinced. There was a wariness about her he had not seen since they had arrived at Orlando Court. "I have no experience with earbobs," he said, "so I shall leave you to put them in yourself. I believe I heard a carriage drawing up," he added. "I shall go and greet the first arrivals."

When she heard the door quietly click behind him, Verity sank down onto the stool in front of the mirror. Verity did not know much about jewels, having only ever owned a single strand of pearls from her mother, but she knew instinctively that these were of high quality. Of course, he would purchase nothing else. But why did he have to bring emeralds? Did he not remember the ball where his mistress, the countess, had flaunted his gift for all to see? Did he give emeralds to all the women he entertained? Were these the very jewels a mistress had rejected?

She began to put the earbobs in like an automaton. Whatever his motive, he was right, the emeralds did add the finishing touch. If only she could get the image of his other women wearing emeralds out of her mind. Countess Waskova and Mrs. Kingsley were her mind's constant companions, both of them residing in her head and relentlessly eating through her confidence like a knife through butter. Both of them telling her that she was not beautiful enough, not wanton enough to satisfy Elliott's needs, not intelligent enough, just not enough of anything, something she had been told all her life.

"But, for good or ill, he married me," she said to her reflexion, before picking up her silk shawl, "and now it is time to be the duchess he has bought."

From the moment she stepped into the drawing room, Verity had acted as though she had been born to the role of duchess, though he had been right about the emeralds which had put her in such a strange mood: she looked magnificent. Elliott observed her from his position in front of the marble fireplace. She had greeted each guest with charm and grace, engaged the women in conversation and laughed at the men's ridiculous jokes. During dinner, the sound of conversation and laughter coming from her end of the table made him envious that he was sitting so far away. She had sent almost invisible signals to the servants so that everyone's wine glass never ran dry and course after course arrived, not only on time, but hot, something Elliott had noticed did not always happen in the grandest of houses.

While the men had enjoyed their port and cigars, he had heard shrieks of unladylike laughter coming from the nearby room where the ladies were taking tea, which had made him suggest that the men cut down their time at the table. Several of the men had complimented him on his fine choice of a duchess, and now she was sitting at the piano playing a piece which enabled conversation to continue, though, as he looked around the room, most of their guests had paused their conversations and were listening to the beautiful rise and flow of the notes. There was an appreciative round of applause when the piece ended, and he strolled over towards her.

"It would appear that the practise your aunt insisted on, has paid off," he said as he sat beside her on the piano stool.

She leaned towards him. "I think it is because the people here are probably all worse at this sort of thing than I," she whispered. "I made up that last piece as I went along so that no-one would know what it was supposed to sound like." She grinned.

He raised an eyebrow. "What, you're a composer as well?"

"I do not think I shall be troubling Mozart or Haydn any time soon," she replied, "unless it is to make them turn in their graves."

"I very much doubt that." He smiled down at her. "Now I believe we must return to our guests as Sir Harry and Lady Schofield and Lord and Lady Graham are making up a four for whist. Would you mind showing Lady Dean the library? Lord Dean has asked my opinion on some land he proposes to purchase in the north."

"Of course, Lady Dean has already asked about your books. She is, I believe, an avid reader."

Elliott watched her go and, with a sigh, resigned himself to unpleasant conversations with Lord Dean rather the pleasurable pleasure with his wife.

Upon entering the library, Lady Dean exclaimed that she had never seen such a fine collection of books. "Lord Dean is not at all interested in reading, unless it is books about some kind of sport, and he absolutely thinks novels should be banned."

"I am sure that the duke would be happy for you to borrow any of his books," Verity replied.

"That is most kind, my dear duchess, thank you," the older woman said, adding, "I believe you were a Grainger before you married?"

The question came as something of a surprise. "Yes," Verity answered.

"I believe I knew your mother. She was the earl's second wife I seem to recall."

"My mother?"

"We were at school together, though I was a little older. She was such a talented girl, musical and quite the scholar as I remember, though she was told quite firmly to concentrate on her embroidery and sketching in order to attract a husband. Why women should have to hide their intelligence is beyond me."

"Please, Lady Dean, would you tell me something of my mother? She died when I was quite small and Father almost forbade us from talking about her, then he married soon after, so I have very little in the way of memories," Verity implored.

Lady Dean patted her arm. "Of course, my dear, come, shall we sit for a moment, and I will tell you what I remember."

The two women sat on the leather chesterfield in front of the fire. "You bear such a remarkable similarity to your mother, for she also had that very same auburn hair and those clear green eyes. When I knew her, she had a great deal of trouble taming her hair into the plaits we were expected to have as there was always an errant curl here or there, much to the annoyance of Miss Timmins, one of our less sympathetic educators." The older woman grinned as her eyes misted over at the memories.

"Our school uniform was not the most flattering, simply a brown dress and it had to be covered with a pinafore. On one occasion, we made a raft and your mother decided that her pinafore would make an excellent sail." Lady Dean laughed gleefully. "The journey across the lake was not an overwhelming success, the raft capsized, and your mother and I were covered in mud and weeds. We were just returning to the dormitory, dripping wet, when Miss Timmins appeared, showing around the parents of a prospective student. You can imagine that she was less than amused."

"Oh, no. What happened?" Verity asked.

"Well, we were put on bread and water for a few days and given kitchen chores, but apparently the girl whose parents were being shown around thought the school sounded such fun that she demanded to go there. I think Miss Timmins was less than pleased at the thought of another one like us in attendance." Lady Dean laughed.

"Thank you for sharing that story, since I have so few memories of my mother," Verity said, catching hold of the other woman's hand and pressing it. "I would love dearly to spend more time with you when we visit Orlando Court."

Lady Dean smiled gently and patted Verity's hand. "I very much regret that I lost contact with Alexandra, but it seemed that she had no sooner left school than she was out and married to your father." Lady Dean looked at their entwined hands before returning her gaze to Verity. "I have to say I do not think Alex was entirely happy with the arrangement. I believe your grandfather arranged the match with your father and in those days, one did as one's father bid."

"One still does," Verity replied wryly.

When they returned from the library with Lady Dean clutching an armful of books, the party was beginning to break up, carriages had been called for, and guests were donning their travelling cloaks. As they stood on the steps to wave their guests off, Verity found that Elliott kept his arm firmly around her waist.

"Well, duchess, your first engagement as a society hostess has been an undoubted success."

She smiled up at him as they returned indoors. "I think our guests enjoyed themselves."

"Thanks to you," he said, taking her hand and raising it to his lips. "But now I think it is time for bed."

After being assured of her wellbeing, he chose to convey his change of feelings as he best knew how rather than using words that so often became misunderstood. When he made love to her that night, he lingered over her, bringing her to the peak of ecstasy several times before taking his own pleasure. Although he knew he had satisfied her physically, there was something missing. As was she when he awoke the following morning, and his bed was empty and cold. Sitting on the nightstand was the jewel box with a note:

Thank you for the opportunity to wear these lovely jewels, Elliott.
I return them to you for safe-keeping.
Verity

"What the devil?" he said, getting out of bed and stalking to his bathing room, furious that the gift he had so lovingly chosen for her had been rejected. When he entered the dining room, Verity was standing by the window, a cup of tea in her hand. There was little sign that she had eaten anything, and the set of her shoulders told him that something was clearly bothering her.

"Are you ill, Verity?" he asked, coming to stand behind her, his anger instantly replaced with worry.

She turned and pasted a smile on her face, but he could see it did not reach her eyes. "No, of course not," she replied.

"Are you sure? You are rather pale," he said, searching her face.

"I am quite well, I assure you," she replied. "I am not with child, if that is what you were wondering," she said quietly.

"I was worried when I found you had gone this morning," he ground out. "Your head is still yet sore."

"I could not sleep," she said.

"And why was that? I would have thought my efforts last night ensured that you were exhausted." His hands on her shoulders stroked downward toward her breasts. She caught them before they could descend.

"What if..." she began, biting her lip. "What if I am unable to give you a child?"

He stood still for a moment, then dropped his hands to his side. "Then we shall live our lives without them."

"But that is why you married me, so that you would have an heir," she said quietly, a single tear making its way down her cheek.

He brushed away the tear with his thumb before enfolding her in his arms. "If children are meant to be then they are meant to be," he said, softly.

"But I saw how my father despised the wives who could only bear female children, let alone their inability to provide him with an heir," she choked. "I could not bear living through that once more, or having my daughters know that..." she broke down into wracking sobs.

He turned her to face him and placed his finger under her chin so that she had to look at him through the tears streaming down her face. "I find I do not despise you, Verity, and I never shall, nor," he said, looking into her troubled eyes, "have I ever despised you. I give you my word. But it is early days in our marriage, there is time for babes to come if they will."

"Thank you," she said, giving him a watery smile.

Elliott enfolded her in a chaste embrace. Although it was not how he had anticipated explaining his love to her, he felt relieved that she now understood. What he would still like to know is why she had returned the emeralds, but that question could wait for another time.

CHAPTER 30

Once news had got out that the duke and duchess were ensconced in Orlando Court and were receiving guests, neighbours from the depths of Hampshire began to arrive to pay their respects. The silver salver in the hall had to be emptied of visiting cards twice a day and Verity had to order extra cakes to be available for their guests. The invitations for the ball had arrived and Verity was sitting in the small drawing room writing them when Elliott strode in.

"I think it fair to say that the ball will be well attended," he said as he dropped a kiss on the top of her head, made his way to the table and helped himself to one of the shortbread biscuits left over from the last wave of visitors.

"It will, if I ever get all these invitations sent in time," she replied, indicating the pile at her side.

"Burton will be coming tomorrow, no doubt with his assistant, and I am sure they will be happy to lend a hand."

Verity looked up in alarm. "Mr. Burton is coming here?"

Elliott nodded. "Unfortunately, business does not always wait as there are some documents I need to sign and Burton has some information I have been waiting for. It will mean that, for a few days at least, I shall have to spend time ensconced with Burton."

Verity pasted a smile on her face. "Do not worry, I shall have enough to occupy my time with the arrangements."

Elliott sighed wistfully. "I am sure that I am not the first man who would rather spent time with a beautiful woman than an old man."

Verity nodded in agreement, but kept her head down, stoically focusing on her work.

With the assistance of Burton's man, the invitations were completed and sent before dinner the following day. Kendal was a young man who was clearly keen to impress his employer, following the debacle of the Latin codicil to the Swallowfield contract, and approached the planning of the ball as though it were a military exercise. He quickly engaged a small orchestra to provide the music for dancing and, when Verity told him of her ideas for decor, liaised with the gardeners for flowers of the appropriate colour and sent to Guildford for fabric for the swags Verity wanted to hang in the ballroom. The house became a hive of activity, with the housemaids cleaning the ballroom from top to bottom. The four chandeliers were lowered and each crystal polished until it shone like a diamond. The kitchen was a source of heat and noise as the chef and kitchen servants planned and began to prepare.

Kendal was so efficient Verity found herself with nothing to do two full days before the ball, so she decided to walk to the village and meet the villagers. It was not a long walk, and the paths and fields were, for the most part, mud and puddle free. Once Elliott had disappeared to the library with Burton immediately after breakfast, she donned her stoutest boots, bonnet, and pelisse and set off with Daisy for company. The walk was quite pleasant and enjoyable. The leaves were just beginning to unfurl on the oak trees and the hawthorn was well and truly out, making the hedgerows look as though they were covered with lace. The daffodils nodded on their slender stems, and they heard a cuckoo in the distance.

The village looked prosperous, each house had been newly thatched and caused Verity to remember Elliot's words that it was a privilege as well as a duty to look after the people who lived on the estate, and the High Street boasted an inn at either end of the village, a butcher, a candlemaker, a haberdasher, and a baker. It being market day, there were stalls along the street selling all manner of goods from vegetables to ribbons to pots and pans. Verity and Daisy spent a pleasant hour or so wandering among the stalls before deciding to visit the bakery, drawn in by the delicious aroma of freshly baked bread and the sight of pastries and cakes after a morning's exertion.

"May I please purchase two of those?" Verity asked the jovial baker.

"They be lardy cakes, Yer Grace," he replied with a smile and a bow "the best in 'ampshire, if I says so meself."

"They look delicious," Verity replied, "but how did you know I am the duchess?"

The man's smile grew broader. "You can't far...break wind in this village, Yer Grace, without someone knowin', then it don't take more'n five minutes for the news to get from one end of 'igh Street to t'other'."

"I shall have to remember that." Verity laughed.

"We're that glad to 'ave the new duke 'ere," the baker said as he wrapped the lardy cake in brown paper and expertly folded it so that it could not fall out of its wrapping. "By the time the ol' duke passed, God rest 'is soul, 'e 'ad neither the money nor the interest to see to the village and 'is estate manager wasn't interested in anything other than lining 'is own pockets. The new duke is a fine man ye can be sure, an' we're all glad of it."

"Thank you," Verity replied, taking the package and handing over two coins. She was surprised that the lives of the commoners' lives had been so drastically impacted by Elliott.

"There ain't no need for that, Yer Grace," the baker responded. "Pleased to serve you I am."

"Then take the coins and use them to pay for bread for one of the more needy families," Verity said, "as you will know better than I who they are, and if you could let me have a list of who is in need, I shall make sure that their needs are provided for. I am sure that His Grace would like all of his people to be well and able."

"Thank 'ee Yer Grace," he smiled again, "'Tis good to know the duke and 'is duchess are goin' to take an interest in us folk once again. I'll send the list to 'ee directly."

Verity continued along High Street with Daisy, looking at the town and eating the lardy cake, when they were suddenly aware of shouts and a commotion. Verity turned, shocked to see a cart out of control careering towards them. The terrified horse was overturning stalls, spilling goods onto the street.

"Quick, Your Grace," Daisy said as she pushed Verity into the narrow alley between the apothecary and The Blue Star Inn just as the cart scraped the bricks as it flew past, knocking off one of its wheels which went spinning down the road on its own.

"My goodness," Verity exclaimed as they watched the cart disappear down the lane. "I wonder what happened to spook the poor horse like that!"

"I don't know milady," Daisy replied, "the horse was definitely frightened, but did you see the driver?"

"I imagine the poor man was also frightened out of his wits," Verity replied, turning and looking at the carnage the horse and cart had left behind. "To be honest, I really didn't see much of him, my attention was on the horse."

"Well, let's hope he has that poor beast under control now," Daisy replied, "and I think we should make our way back now. If His Grace hears about this before we're back safe and sound, he'll no doubt be driven wild with worry about your safety."

"I suppose so," Verity said, doubting so very much, "but let us just help these poor people put their goods to rights before we go."

It did not take long before the High Street was looking as it had before the incident, and apart from a few squashed vegetables and an upturned barrel of ale, no-one would have been any the wiser.

They walked back through the woods and park easily, though the sun was quite warmer now, and were fortunate to approach the house without anyone the wiser. Verity hoped to be able to change quickly and pray that none of the villagers would alarm Elliott as to her involvement in the village. Unfortunately, just as they entered the house, Elliott was just emerging from the library and drew up short.

"What on earth happened?" he asked in alarm, taking in the dust and stains on their gowns.

"There was a little incident in the High Street," Verity replied lightly.

"It caused quite a stir, a horse was spooked and ran out of control, but thankfully apart from my gown and a few cabbages, no real harm was done, although the men might be a little short of ale at the inn tonight."

"Ale?" he asked, puzzled.

"A barrel of ale was one of the casualties of the incident." Verity laughed. "At one point I thought some of the young lads were going to lap it up from the street, such was their distress. Now," she added, looking down at her gown, "I think I had best take a bath, I do not think that 'eau de cabbage' is a perfume that will catch on with the ton."

She left Elliott behind her, pleased that she had put him off any concern. Within half an hour, Verity was soaking in a rose scented bath, the incident with the horse apart, she had enjoyed her foray into the village. She felt she could have some purpose in improving the lives of the people on Elliott's estates if she was given a chance to do something useful. Once she was ensconced at Swallowfield, she would ensure that she engaged with the people who lived and worked on the estate. It was something her father had little time for, and she was determined that she would try to make up for his neglect. Elliott would probably be content for her to do so, she rather got the impression that she would be able to do whatever she liked so long as he did not have to see her, though the thought made her rather melancholy.

Unfortunately, she could no longer deny to herself that she would miss him when he was in London, or wherever he intended to live with Mrs. Kingsley. She would miss his laughter and his ability to make her laugh. She would miss him in her bed and, she would even miss their disagreements.

Her reverie was interrupted by Daisy apologizing for forgetting the towels and excusing herself to fetch them.

"Of course," Verity replied calmly, sinking further into the water, "I am quite happy here, so take your time."

CHAPTER 31

*E*lliott was feeling far from calm when he emerged from a conversation with Daisy while Verity was in her bath. Her words struck fear into his heart.

"That weren't no accident, Your Grace. My lady didn't see the driver, but I did. It's true the cart was swinging from side to side, but when he saw the duchess, he drove straight towards us, and if we hadn't been standing by the alley, he would have run us down, I'm certain of it."

Someone was trying to kill his wife, but the question was who and why. He was determined to ensure Verity's protection at all costs. Though it would need to be discrete, as Verity would no doubt protest.

"Someone is to watch over the duchess at all times, from the time our guests begin to arrive until the last one departs." Elliott spoke to Jones, the man Burton had quickly engaged in order to ensure that Verity was safe.

"Certainly, Your Grace," Jones replied.

"They are to be as unobtrusive as possible, you understand. I would rather my wife did not know of the extra measures we are taking."

"Of course, Your Grace. My men and women are used to this sort of assignment. They will be disguised as footmen, servants, guests, and lady's maids, all persons who have a legitimate reason to be at the ball and who will be able to move freely around your house without raising suspicion," he reassured, adding, "my people are carefully recruited and trained. Should a situation arise, they will be able to deal with it swiftly and effectively, often to the point that guests do not realise anything untoward has happened."

"Thank you, Jones," Elliott replied. "Your presence and that of your team is a great reassurance."

"We shall also be listening to see if we can glean who is behind the attacks, Your Grace," Jones said. "They have failed in their attempt on two occasions, but they may not be so unlucky in the future."

"You believe this person will try again?" Elliott asked.

The other man nodded. "In my experience, if a person does not give up after the first failed attempt, they will invariably continue. It becomes an obsession with some. However, protecting the duchess at a ball where there is a limited guest list is a relatively easy assignment. Have no fear on this occasion sir, however, bear in mind that this madman for that is surely what he is, will try again. My investigators in London are searching for anyone who may have cause to harm your bride."

"That is what I am afraid of," Elliott murmured, nodding as Jones bowed and took his leave.

For this, her first ball as hostess, Verity had chosen a cream watered silk gown with a gossamer thin overskirt shot through with diamantes so that her skirts glimmered as she moved. The neckline was lower than she would have chosen, but in London she had seen respectable women with even lower. Roses in gold thread were embroidered at the waist and hem. She grimaced as Daisy adjusted the tiara of diamonds which had been delivered to her room earlier. It had arrived along with a stunning necklace, earbobs and bracelet earlier in the day, with a note from Elliott.

'To my duchess,
  A diamond of the first water.
  E.'

The jewels were beautiful and expensive, there was no doubt, but Elliott's gifts were confusing. He had already attained her, there was no need for him to give her expensive gifts and frankly, the more he tried to act as a proper husband the more difficult and painful it would be when he left her for someone else. She was just drawing on her long, white gloves when Elliott appeared in the doorway. His black tailcoat and trousers fitted him to perfection and were set off by the gold brocade waistcoat, his snow-white neckcloth held in place by a diamond pin that perfectly matched her gift.

"I am sure our guests will think we have coordinated our clothes," Verity said, as she did her best to unobtrusively feast her eyes on the handsome man who was, for the time being, hers alone.

He stepped further into the room and stood behind her as they both looked into the cheval mirror. "You are truly beautiful," he whispered into her ear, sending shivers down her back. "I want to send all our guests home and take you to bed," he went on, kissing the delicate skin below her ear. "I want to take off that delightful gown and everything else slowly, so that I might savour every moment, before laying you on the bed and making sweet, vigorous love to you until you melt. Except for the diamonds," he added, playfully nipping her earlobe. "You may keep them on to reflect the light in your eyes as you come for me."

"You are incorrigible." She giggled, picked up her silk fan and swatted him with it. "I would remind you that I am a respectable married woman and respectable married women do not do that sort of thing."

"They do if they are married to less than respectable men," he replied with a lustful smile, "and being less than respectable is far more fun. Now come, duchess, we must be on hand to greet our guests." He held out his arm but could not resist gently pinching her bottom as they made their way to the ballroom.

It took more than an hour to greet their guests, so by the time the ducal couple entered the ballroom, footmen were already circulating with trays of champagne and the small orchestra were beginning to tune up on the dais that had been erected at the far end of the ballroom. Verity set herself at the edge of the ballroom and watched as the dancers moved around the room like clockwork dolls, each woman adorned with heirloom family jewels glittering in the candlelight. Their gowns were all the height of fashion as though Hampshire was proving that fashion was not just seen in London. The younger women were in pastels while the older women wore bolder colours. She noticed Elliott dancing with several of the young women who had been standing at the side of the room tapping their feet to the music as they no doubt wished for someone to ask them to dance.

"Champagne, Your Grace?" a young footman asked as he appeared at her side.

"Thank you." she said and took the glass from his tray. She had barely raised it to her lips when Elliott stood in front of her, declaring, "I believe this is my dance," and quickly took the glass from her and placed it on the table before holding out his hand.

"I have waited all evening for this," he said, as they took their places on the ballroom floor. "I have done my duty and danced with any number of women, both young and old, and now it is time for my reward."

"A waltz?" She smiled up at him as he took her in his arms.

"A waltz with you," he replied, his eyes blazing into hers.

As they danced, Verity could not help but notice the approving looks of some of the older ladies as well as some of the blatantly jealous looks of the younger ones. "You seem to have made quite a hit with the local females, Elliott," she grinned. "The olders seem to think we are a great love story, whilst the younger ones look as though they would gladly do away with me," she teased.

"Do not say that, for God's sake. Do not say that," he said, before forcing his face to relax. "None of them can hold a candle to you."

Verity laughed, "Thank you, Your Grace." She curtsied as the dance drew to a close. "And now I must talk with the Dowager Countess of Whernside, as she was very kind to Ella and me when they were small girls." She curtseyed again and went in search of the old lady.

Elliott stood at the edge of the ballroom, his shoulder propped against a marble column nodding and smiling to his guests as they danced past him when he heard a discreet cough behind him.

"Excuse me, Your Grace, but I need to speak to you," Jones said. "In private," he added.

Elliott led the way to the library. Too on edge to sit down, he perched a hip on the edge of his desk.

"What is it?" he demanded.

"I have reason to believe, Your Grace, that someone tonight tried to poison the duchess," Jones said.

"What the hell? How and how do you know?"

"One of my men saw a footman he did not recognise offer the duchess a glass of champagne, just before you and she went onto the dance floor."

"I took that glass from her hand myself just as she was about to take a sip," Elliott responded. "My God, had I not..."

"Fortunately, so, sir. My man retrieved the glass immediately, and from the slight scent of almonds, he determined that the glass contained some arsenic. Possibly not enough to kill your lady wife, but certainly enough to make her very ill."

"My God," Elliott repeated, running his hand through his hair. "What about this footman, has he been apprehended?"

Jones shook his head ruefully. "I am afraid not, sir, by the time my man ascertained what was in the glass, he was nowhere to be seen. I can only apologise, sir. However, there should now be no doubt that whoever wishes to do the duchess harm will stop at nothing to achieve his ends."

"Indeed," Elliott replied, "and has had the audacity to make an attempt in my very home."

"My advice would be to take the duchess to another location, sir, which would at least make the perpetrator change his plans and give us time to investigate further."

"I agree."

"I would suggest one of your smaller estates, sir, possibly remote, where newcomers are easier to detect."

"Then we shall go to Swallowfield. I received a message that the work on it is complete. I had hoped to stay here a little longer, but Swallowfield has the advantage that the duchess grew up there and not only knows the locality, but the people as well. Furthermore, they know her and would be alert to any stranger in their midst. I shall also send for her sister, so that the duchess is never alone."

"That sounds like a very good idea, sir," Jones said, "though given his audacity in making an attempt tonight in full view, we must be ever vigilant. In the meantime, we will strain every sinew to find out who this scoundrel is and bring him to justice."

Elliott nodded. "We shall leave the day after tomorrow."

CHAPTER 32

*V*erity was sitting in the morning room attending to some letters when Elliott found her the following morning. Dressed in a cream gown of sprigged muslin, her hair loosely tied with a matching green ribbon, she took Elliott's breath away. Dressed in a ball gown with jewels, she was magnificent, but there was something about seeing her dressed simply that reminded him of the innocence of their love seven years ago. The intervening years had made him rougher, harder. He knew that life had not been easy for Verity, he knew that now, but who, other than a madman, could possibly want to harm her? Verity was all that was good in his life, had never caused anyone harm, and he would be damned if someone thought they could take her away from him. He feared very little in life, but the thought of living it without Verity terrified him. He would do anything to protect her.

He paused at the door, arranging a smile on his face as he entered the room. "I have good news, duchess, Swallowfield is ready sooner than expected. We shall depart tomorrow."

"That is wonderful news," Verity replied with a smile that did not quite reach her eyes.

"I thought you would be pleased," he said, coming to stand at her escritoire.

"Oh, I am, of course I am," she assured him. "It is just that I have grown to love Orlando Court, too," she admitted. "I find that I enjoyed being your hostess, and perhaps we could give a ball to celebrate the renaissance of Swallowfield."

"I am afraid there will be no balls at Swallowfield for the foreseeable future," Elliott said, firmly. He could not and would not risk another attempt on her life like the one she was blissfully unaware of last night.

Her face fell. "Of course, I understand," she replied stiffly.

"I am quite sure you do not," he responded tightly, frustrated at her sudden anger.

"Of course, I do," she snapped. "I remember our arrangement very clearly. I am to live at Swallowfield, and you return to your life in London or wherever you choose with your paramour."

Elliott recoiled. "Paramour? What the devil are you talking about?" He had had no lover almost since his engagement began and he could not imagine she was still upset about lovers from his past.

Verity rolled her eyes, angry tears beginning to appear. "Oh, for heaven's sake, Elliot, do not play games with me. I know exactly what you intend to do, your lover told me so herself."

"Then I wish I had been told of my intentions as well, so that we might at least be in an understanding!" he replied, carefully curbing his temper. He took a deep breath. "Verity, who is this alleged lover who spoke to you?"

"This is ridiculous. You are being ridiculous. You know very well of whom I speak. Mrs. Audra Kingsley," Verity shot back, rising and taking a step towards the door before Elliott's hands clamped on her arms and turned her to face him. "She has sought me out many times to make your intentions very clear!"

"Who?" he demanded, his face set in frowned puzzlement.

Verity met his gaze, eyes glistening. "Mrs. Audra Kingsley, widow of the late Mr. Kingsley who told me herself that once I am installed at Swallowfield and have produced your necessary heir, which I believe she refuses to do or you would no doubt have married her, she will be the one on your arm and in your bed."

"I have no idea who you are talking about. I admit I have had mistresses, I never took a vow of celibacy, but I swear to you that I know no Audra Kingsley." His eyes blazed into hers. "When did she seek you out? How many times has she approached you?"

"Well, she certainly seems to know you and has twice sought me out to tell me in detail your plans. Now," she added, trying to pull away, "if you would excuse me, Your Grace, I need to pack."

His grip tightened. "When? When did this woman claiming to be my mistress approach you?"

"Does it really matter?" she cried, but quieted when she saw his face. "With irony worthy of Shakespeare, she actually told me of your plans whilst I was being fitted for my wedding gown, and she was at Hatchards when I visited and told me of your relief that you had finally bedded me and your hope that your seed had taken so that you did not need to bed me again. There! Are you satisfied?" She wrenched herself from his slack grip and fled.

When she had gone, Elliott was left staring at the door in bewilderment. Who the devil was this Audra Kingsley and why would she want Verity to believe she was his mistress? And Verity did believe it, he could not blame her for that, she had indeed met at least two of his former mistresses at their very first ball. He had not, however, even considered the prospect of taking a mistress since before he had married, the very idea was an anathema to him. He did not want a mistress, he did not want another woman, he wanted Verity. He wanted his wife!

He ran a hand through his hair, this whole notion made no sense, but he had to find out who this woman was and what her motives were, given the risk to Verity's life he could not presume that the two things were not related. He strode off to find Jones.

At last, in her room, Verity let her tears fall silently. She would never allow him to know how humiliated she felt. How dare he force her to discuss his mistress, mocking her that he did not know of her? How dare he stand grimly as she had to announce that she was aware that his bedding her was a chore and a lie? She threw herself into packing her belongings. It should be a joyous moment, after all, she was going to Swallowfield, her future was secure, that was what she wanted was it not?

She paused, a shawl in her hand. No, it was not enough; Swallowfield was a house, and she wanted a home, a true home and family with Elliott. Somehow, she had done what she had promised herself she would not do and allowed him into her heart. She sat on the edge of her bed. In truth, she loved Elliott, even through the difficult years when he had abandoned her, she had never stopped, which was why it had never stopped hurting. She was a fool to have allowed herself to begin to hope that they might have a future together, to have a real marriage and be a family. She carefully folded the shawl and placed it in the trunk before straightening her spine. Elliott Thorne had broken her heart once, but she was damned if she was going to give him the power to do it again.

She was careful to avoid him the rest of the day and the whole of the next. A woman claiming illness was not to be disturbed, nor doubted. She took small meals in her room and passed time alone, attempting to write her thoughts into letters that were only burned.

Then the time came to depart to Swallowfield, the journey was slow. There had been an unusual amount of rain and the roads were pitted and muddy, even with Elliott's luxurious carriage, travel was uncomfortable, made worse by the fact that Elliott chose to ride alongside the coach, leaving Verity and Daisy to travel together. They stopped once again at The Angel in Guildford, but this time Elliott barely sat to eat his meal before leaving the dining room and consulting with the coachmen and other outriders in the yard as the horses were attended to. As soon as they were harnessed to the coach, he returned to hurry Verity back into the coach. "We need to make haste if we are to reach Swallowfield by dark," he explained, handing her into the coach.

"Perhaps if we had a smaller entourage, we might make quicker progress." Verity nodded to the four or so men who were riding with her husband.

"There have been reports of highwaymen along the route," he lied.

"His Grace certainly seems eager for us to get to Swallowfield," Daisy ventured as the coach set off with a lurch.

"Indeed," Verity replied. The sooner they arrived, the sooner she could be discarded like an old gown or piece of furniture that is no longer of use. The rain had stopped, and it seemed that the road dried as they approached Swallowfield, and their progress was faster. At last, Verity recognised the tall poplars, planted by a previous ancestor, which bounded the south drive. She gasped as Swallowfield came into view. Even in the twilight she could see that the roof had been replaced and candles were lit in almost every room, giving an air of welcome to weary travellers.

The coach had barely drawn up before the front door opened and a voice called out, "You are here at last," and Ella bounded down the gleaming, newly-restored steps and hugged her sister almost before her feet touched the ground.

"Ella, I had no idea you would be here," Verity exclaimed, smiling broadly.

"I received word two days ago from Elliott that Swallowfield was ready, and he sent a coach to bring me here. He is so thoughtful, Verity! He wanted me to be a surprise so that you could be welcomed home properly!" Ella laughed. "And you will not believe the improvements he has made here," she went on, taking Verity by the arm and practically dragging her through the threshold, leaving Elliott to oversee the baggage. "Swallowfield has not looked so well for generations I should think! Even the village is also much improved, you know Father barely cared for it. I believe he must have employed an army to get it done, and in so short a time! The man is marvellous, indeed!"

"He is indeed a marvel," Verity replied drily.

"Come, Sister, hot baths and a meal have been prepared," Ella said, taking her sister by the arm.

As she luxuriated in the rose scented water, Verity looked around at the room that had been constructed especially for bathing just next door to what had been her mother's suite. What would be her suite now, as the duke's wife, she supposed. The copper tub was highly polished and the large gilt mirrors on two of the walls made the room look huge. Dark rose drapes hung at the windows and a marble-topped table full of interesting-looking coloured glass bottles and jars completed the room. It was clear that Elliott had spared no expense in the renovation from the little she had seen of Swallowfield so far. Her suite had been completely renovated. Gone were the dreary, dark green drapes and bed hangings which had always seemed to be covered in dust. The walls were covered with the palest of pink watered silk wall-paper with drapes and hangings in a deeper, dusky pink. A vase of pink roses stood on a rosewood table in front of the window, giving the room a delicate scent. A door, opposite the large bed led to what she remembered as her father's and would now be Elliot's suite of rooms.

The thought of spending a night in her father's chambers made her deeply uncomfortable. She could only hope, when the time came for Elliott to summon her, that the room had been entirely redone. By the time she emerged from her bath, Daisy had hung her gowns in the spacious armoire and was folding the last of her under things into the drawers in the matching tallboy.

"His Grace and Lady Ella wanted to know if you would join them for dinner in the dining room, or would you prefer to have a tray sent up."

"I find I am too tired, Daisy. Please have a light tray sent up," she replied, slipping on her nightgown and climbing into bed. Much as she was excited to see her sister, she could not face the questions she knew Ella would ask. She would face the both of them tomorrow.

CHAPTER 33

*I*t took a few moments for Verity to orient herself when she awoke, Daisy was just opening the drapes and had placed a cup of tea on her bedside table.

"It's a lovely day, Your Grace," she said. "Perhaps the pale green muslin with the leaves embroidered on it today?"

"Whatever you think, Daisy," Verity replied, taking a sip of tea as she accustomed herself to her surroundings.

"His Grace is already in the breakfast room, Your Grace," Daisy went on, opening the armoire and taking out the gown. "He asked that you join him as soon as you are dressed."

"Then I suppose we should not keep him waiting," Verity said. She had slept better than she had been expecting following their rather rushed departure from Orlando Court.

Half an hour later, wearing the green muslin, matching slippers, and with her hair tied back from her face with a dark green velvet ribbon, she walked into the breakfast room to find Elliott tucking into eggs, bacon, mushrooms, and toast. He rose as she entered.

"Good morning, Verity," he said evenly. "Let me bring you a plate."

Verity arrived with such grace and vitality, finally fully at comfort in her own home and surroundings, that he felt as if he had been transported to the past. She looked as beautiful this morning in the simple gown as she had at the ball, and as she had when he had looked in to find her sleeping last night. She had not stirred as he dropped a soft kiss on her brow, nor had she heard his solemn vow to protect her.

"Just some tea and toast please," she replied with a smile, wondering if this would be the last breakfast they would share together, but determined that Elliott would never know how much his parting would hurt.

"Your sister has gone to the stables—something to do with going to see some newborn kittens," Elliott announced as he gathered her food.

Verity smiled again. "Ella could never resist animals, kittens, puppies, lambs, she would make pets of them all. Much to Father's fury."

"What did your father do?"

Her smile faded. "All were banished from the house. The final time, when she was nine, I think, to teach Ella a lesson for taking in a cat and keeping her and the kittens in her room, he made her watch as he drowned them."

Elliott choked as he flinched in horror, almost dropping her plate. "My God. What sort of a man does that? And to his own daughter no less!"

"My father was, as you surely must know from your own dealings with him, the sort of man who should never have been a father," she replied, quietly. "None of us could find it within ourselves to mourn his passing, not really as daughters should, and in fact his death was a great relief to us all, even though he left us with nothing."

Elliott set her tea down so hard that it splashed onto the table. He took her hands in his, desperate to assure her that he was nothing like her father had been, that she deserved all the happiness he could provide for her. "I swear to you, Verity, that neither you, your sisters, nor any children we produce, shall want for anything I have in my power to grant you. I promised to take care of you, and it is both my honour and duty to do so," he said, his eyes holding hers.

"Thank you, Elliott," she replied, her eyes filling with tears.

He gently brushed one away with his thumb as it slid down her cheek. "Please do not cry, Verity. I never want to make you cry." He bent and softly kissed her cheek.

"I am crying," she gave a watery smile, "because you have already done so much for my family."

"Our family," he corrected. "Your sisters are mine now and our children will have as many pets as we can handle." He stood up. "Now, if you have finished that pathetic excuse for a breakfast that would not keep a sparrow alive, shall we go and see the improvements?"

"May we go into the gardens first? I caught a glimpse of them from my chamber and it looks as though your men have been as busy outdoors as in."

He was loath to admit it, but he was eager to see what she thought of the gardens. They had spent much time there in their youth, and he knew she had always enjoyed them. He had put particular attention and time into the areas he knew she would enjoy, like her private bathing room and the garden. She could not know it, but it had been designed so that each season would bring its own delights. When the gardener had shown him the old plans for the lake and canal for boating, he had been unable to resist adding them. And, true to his word, the gardener had made them look as though they had always been part of the landscape.

The sun was beginning to have some warmth as they walked through the parterre in front of the house which led to what had been Ella's mother's rose garden and would be glorious again in a few weeks when the buds opened.

Verity gasped as they walked through the new wrought iron gate. "You have restored the maze," she gasped, and turned to Elliott, her eyes shining. "I thought it was neglected for so long that it was beyond repair."

"Your father had a very good gardener whom I have re-employed. His grandfather planted the maze apparently, and he took a great deal of pride in restoring his grandfather's work. Shall we test it?" he asked, taking her hand.

"Of course!" She laughed. "However, I should point out that I have played in this maze since I was in leading strings. I wager I shall beat you to its centre." With that, she picked up her skirts and ran, quickly disappearing from his view. Elliott could hear her giggling as he closed in on her in the centre of the maze. He found her sitting demurely on the new bench as he rounded the last corner. "Why, Your Grace, I could have walked to London and back in the time it took for you to get here."

"Impertinent chit," he grumped, then laughed as he sat and pulled her onto his lap, kissing her soundly. Her breath hitched as he deepened the kiss, then his fingers found her breasts as he trailed a stream of kisses along her jawline and down her throat to the neckline of her bodice.

He settled her on his lap so that she straddled him and pulled up her skirts so that he could explore her with his fingers while kissing her breasts through the thin fabric of her gown, smiling as her nipples hardened. "I have to see you," he said, tugging the bodice of her gown down with his teeth so that her breasts were exposed to his hungry gaze.

"God, you are so beautiful, Verity, and I want you. I never stopped wanting you," he murmured as his fingers teased and stroked her. "Not once since I met you, even in the time we were apart, I have always wanted you." Verity's head fell back as she revelled in the sensual web he wove around them. "Do you want me, Verity?" he asked. "I need to hear you say it."

"I want you," she breathed. "You must know how I want you."

He groaned as she shot her hips forward, rubbing against him.

"Then you shall have me," he murmured against her mouth as he unfastened the fall of his breeches and entered her in one swift motion. "Ride me, Verity."

Verity's eyes widened as he filled her, instinctively beginning to move with him. The lust in her eyes drove him wild. He held her waist and growled, "Take me deeper, Verity," then succumbed to the vision before him and took first one of her breasts into his mouth, then the other. Sweat began to bead on his brow as he held back, refusing to find release for himself before Verity had reached the pinnacle. "Come for me my sweet, reach for it, and I will give it to you." He swallowed her cries with a kiss as he felt her whole body tense and her internal muscles pulse against him, and he could not supress his own orgasm, mixing their bodies together.

"Dear God," he said several seconds later, when he was able to speak, drawing her towards him, refusing to let her break their intimacy.

"That was..." she began.

"Earth shattering? The most moving experience of your life?" he suggested.

"I was going to say unexpected," she replied, primly.

Elliott threw back his head with a shout of laughter. He had never laughed after sex before and found he liked it. That she could maintain a prim expression of propriety even as he could feel her moisture dripping onto him as his member began to retreat from her core delighted him. *She* delighted him. "I think," he said, in mock severity, "that you are going to be the death of me, duchess."

"And I think, Elliott, that you are going to be the ruination of me," she replied, climbing off his lap and straightening her skirts. "What would people think if they saw or indeed heard what we have just been doing? And outside where anyone might have happened upon us?"

"Firstly, I do not give a flying fu...fig for what people think. Secondly, I am a duke so people generally let us get away with anything, and thirdly, you are a married woman, so you cannot be ruined."

"Oh, believe you me, women are held to an entirely different standard to men," she shot back. "I know that before we were wed, you had considerable practise at..." she broke off, gesturing to the bench and his still-exposed prick, blushing vividly, "what we have just done."

"Making love?" he provided, helpfully he thought.

"Exactly so," she replied, a delightful blush coming to her cheeks. "However, as a single woman, had I even been caught in the same room alone with a man, any man, I should have had to marry him, no matter how repulsive an individual he might be."

Elliott raised his eyebrows. "Are you saying that you would have wanted the freedom to be with other men, to gain greater sexual experience as men are encouraged to do before marriage?"

Verity rolled her eyes. "Of course not. I am just pointing out to you that the life and expectations of a gentleman are completely different to those of a lady. Our lives are determined by our fathers and husbands, and although we are permitted to go to school, we are not permitted to go to university. If we are found to possess even a shred of wit or intelligence, we are told to hide it because gentlemen do not like women with their own ideas. Ladies are not permitted to earn our own livings beyond being governesses or companions. We are not permitted to go anywhere alone without a chaperone as though we are small children who must be protected. Any money we may have is usually under the control of our fathers, brothers, or husbands. In short, our lives are made small and never in our own hands."

Elliott remained silent as she spoke, her passion evident. He had never truly considered the lot of women. Between the expectations of society and the pressures from her father, it was no wonder that Verity chafed at any hint of obligation or duty to him. She had never been given any freedom, not even as a child. Finally, he spoke. "I suppose I have never really considered the lot of young women," he admitted honestly, straightening his clothes, "as I have had no need, having no sisters of my own. All the gentlewomen I have come across seem to be happy with their accomplishments, embroidery and the like. Whilst, from what you have just said, it would seem that beneath the placid exterior, there is a boiling volcano."

"I am sure some ladies are quite happy with their lot, either because they are naturally inclined or have accepted it. I just feel that there is so much more we could accomplish if we were able to do so. The only one I am aware of is Helen, Duchess of Bainbridge who has managed to overcome all odds to become a celebrated authoress," Verity replied.

Elliott took her hands. "Then let me make this promise: whatever it is you wish to accomplish, I shall never stand in your way and I shall assist you in any way I can. If anyone attempts to disparage you, I shall support you stalwartly. And if we are blessed with a daughter, I shall ensure that she knows that her wisdom comes from her mother and she shall have the ability to follow her dreams, whatever they may be." He paused. "There is, however, one condition attached."

"And that is?" Verity asked, hesitantly assured of his character.

"I want to see that boiling volcano of passion, such as I saw today, every time we make love."

As she gasped, he thrust his tongue into her mouth and kissed her passionately before she could object. She squealed gleefully as he pressed her against him once more, anyone listening by the hedges be damned.

CHAPTER 34

*E*lla had promised to visit the new vicar and his wife, Elliott had disappeared to work, so Verity decided to inspect the old east wing which had been derelict ever since she could remember. Ella would surely not be interested, and Elliott would demand she take a troop of guards along with her, so she was content to go alone.

The old east wing had once been a castle and some remnants of that form remained in the cut of the stone steps leading to a turret room which, according to legend, had once been some sort of prison from where the lady of the manor looked out when she had been imprisoned by her husband. If the legend was true, her father had clearly not been the first earl with little affection for his wife.

Verity paused at the top of the steps. She and Ella had only once been to the turret out of curiosity as girls. There had been no glass in the window and dry leaves had swirled around the room, accumulating in the corners with other detritus and animal leavings. The stone fireplace and chimney had provided nesting for birds and probably mice. A few broken sticks of furniture had littered the cracked floor and it had taken little imagination on their parts to conjure up the ghost of the white lady who haunted the tower.

The turret room was now anything but a cold, damp prison. Verity stared in wonder at the drastic transformation. The walls had been freshly plastered and painted in pale gold which was reflected in the tones of the Aubusson carpet and heavy, velvet drapes. A white marble fireplace stood in place of the smoke-blackened stone one she remembered from her youth and a new bed with gold hangings stood at one end. She looked out of the window, there was indeed an excellent view of the estate and parkland beyond; she could see as far as the village.

"I thought this would make a good guest suite," Elliot's voice interrupted her musings.

She turned and smiled. "What you have achieved here is quite wonderful," she replied.

He shrugged. "I know how much this house means to you, even though I now know that not all your memories of it are happy ones."

"The few memories I have of my mother are here," she said, looking out of the window again. "Though the surroundings are much more peaceful now."

He came further into the room. "Then we must ensure that we make happy memories."

She shot him a puzzled look. How could they make memories in the day or so he would be here with her before he took his leave to return only as and when he felt the whim. "Of course, Your Grace," she replied, still not turning to face him.

She felt his hands on her shoulders. He did not turn her to face him, but remained behind her, close enough for her to feel the warmth of his body through her own clothing. "I have been thinking that I might stay here a while," he said, his voice low and rough. "I have no business that demands my return to London for the moment, and I should like to ensure that you are fully settled here as well as get to know the workings of the estate. There is much to be done to modernise it so that it begins to show a profit. The land is fertile, and the workers are willing, there is no reason why, with a little investment, it should not be extremely productive. I have spoken to some of the tenants who spoke highly of your grandfather, but as to your father..."

"My father was interested only in himself," she responded, doing her best to ignore the heat of his hands. "He cared for nothing other than his own pleasure and the greatest pleasure was gambling. He cared nothing for his family, and he cared nothing for his inheritance, seeing it only as the means to indulge his great love. It is a terrible thing to be ashamed of one's father, but there it is."

He turned her around and held her close. "I swear to you that will not happen with any children we have," he said quietly.

Her eyes blazed into his. "How, Your Grace?" she exclaimed. "How is that going to be possible when you plan on being absent for most of their lives? How is it possible that you shall be the father they want and need when you are in London or God knows where with God knows whom, when they will be here?"

She fled before he could see her tears. How dare he sully the memories of her mother's room with the pain of knowing that she would be just as alone.

Elliott stood, dumbfounded, as she ran from the room leaving him looking after her and catching the hint of her rose scent. His plan of marrying for convenience had long been abandoned in his mind though he had somehow still not managed to communicate it to his wife, whom he was beginning to doubt would ever believe him in any case.

He leaned his arm against the window with a sigh. He had made a hell of a mess of everything. He had thought that each time he made love to Verity she would understand that things had changed between them. The notion that he wanted her just to beget an heir was a nonsense and had been from the beginning, he realised that now. He wanted her as his wife in every sense of the word, a true partner, but he was afraid; afraid that she did not want him, afraid that before he could tell her he loved her, that the lunatic who had twice tried to kill her would try again. The thing that made him most afraid was that he did not know who, how, when, or why, all he knew was that they would try. He briefly considered telling Verity about the danger but rejected the idea, there was no point in worrying her and making her afraid. He would deal with this, and God help the man when he did find him, he would rip the man apart with his bare hands if a single hair on her head was harmed.

His mind went back to the meeting he had just had with Jones, one of his men had been checking the woods and discovered a thin wire strung between two trees along the bridle path.

"Had the duchess not seen it strung at head height for a rider," Jones had explained, "she would have been decapitated, and that's what was meant to happen. Whoever is doing this is a determined bugger."

Elliott took in a breath. If he lost Verity, he lost everything, but someone clearly wanted her dead, although he would do anything to protect her, he hesitated, he could and possibly should tell her the truth, but he did not want to frighten her. Hopefully he could deal with the matter, and she need never know and if she thought he was being ridiculous then it was a small price to pay. What terrified him was both the relentless nature of the attacks, their frequency and the fact that the madman seemed to know exactly where they were. He was getting closer and their luck in holding off the attacks would not last forever.

For the next few days, Verity threw herself into settling into her role as chatelaine. She was delighted to welcome the Claytons back in their old roles as housekeeper and butler, though she knew there would be some competition with Elliott's man, Fry. As she explored the renovated rooms with her sister, deciding which should be used on a daily basis, she was touched to see that not only had Elliott had them refurbished, he had recovered many of the items they had been forced to sell after their father's death.

"What is the matter?" Ella asked as Verity failed to answer her question on a Limoges vase for the third time.

"I was just thinking," Verity replied, "Elliott has gone to considerable expense to restore the house to its former glory, that it will be a shame that for most of the time at least half of the rooms will be closed and shuttered."

"Why dearest? Surely, we shall be able to give balls and parties. I believe Grandfather used to give a Christmas Ball and a May and Harvest Dance for the villagers, it would be lovely to revive those old traditions, let alone whatever society events the duke wants to host," Ella replied.

"Elliott has made it very clear that there will be no balls or dinners and once he has the desired number of children to secure his heirs, we shall see precious little of him as I told you once before."

Ella led her to the leather chesterfield in front of the fire and they sat together. "I do not understand," Ella said, "I know your marriage had a stormy start, but I had begun to think that you and the duke had settled your differences."

"Alas, I believe our differences are a chasm too wide to bridge." Verity looked into the flames. "Every time I begin to believe our marriage could be a real one, something happens to set it back."

"Elliott loves you, of that I am sure," Ella declared.

"He has shown little evidence of it," Verity huffed.

"It is there in his eyes every time he looks at you. Last night at dinner he looked as though he wanted to devour you."

"Ah, yes," Verity replied, thinking of the stormy lovemaking of last night in which he had reached for her three very enjoyable times. "We seem to be extremely well suited if we do not actually talk to each other," she said wryly.

Ella leaned forward and took Verity's hand. "Things will turn out. Elliott loved you once and I believe he still does."

Verity looked at her sister. "I want to believe you, but Elliott is a proud man. I had not known how much our parting hurt him. I thought only of my own heartache."

"Then give him time," Ella replied. She stood up abruptly. "Now, I feel our moods would be greatly improved by some fresh air. What say you to a ride into the village to see the improvements Elliott has made?"

"An excellent idea," Verity declared, pasting a large, false smile on her face. "I certainly feel in need of some fresh air, and we might see what is needed to improve things further. I will meet you at the stables in half an hour as I believe Elliott has had Ladybird brought for me."

"And in this you cannot fault his generosity. There is another mare for me, and I believe her name is Beautiful, though I have seen her and can only surmise that the name is ironic," Ella laughed.

Verity could not help but laugh aloud when she approached the stables where both horses were saddled and waiting by the mounting blocks. Beautiful was indeed an interestingly mismatched horse with a chestnut coat, a grey muzzle, and large brown eyes, but the thing that caught the attention was the addition of a blonde mane.

"I rather think she reminds me of young Lady Hearst," Ella said, "though in all honesty I think Beautiful's mane is slightly fuller and definitely more natural."

"Do not be unkind, Lady Hearst, after all, does have to suffer the company of Lord Hearst, a man who can speak of nothing but hunting, shooting, and fishing. I doubt he even notices Lady Hearst is in the room, let alone the colour of her hair," Verity replied, stepping up to the mounting block.

"I find I have little sympathy for her, given that she was so horrendous to all of us at school. To think that at school she boasted of the advantageous marriage her father was planning for her. Pride certainly cometh before a fall," Ella laughed.

"Well, just ensure that you do not fall from Beautiful," Verity said, giving Ladybird a gentle nudge with her foot. "Lanes or woods?" she asked.

"Lanes I think, it's such a lovely day, we can ride through the woods on the way back if you wish."

"Lanes it is," Verity said over her shoulder, setting off at a trot.

"Do not even think of making this into a race, Sister!" Ella called after her. "You have never won a race against me."

"Ah, but I have practised in the time since," Verity replied and nudged Ladybird once again into a canter.

"A race it is," Ella responded.

By the time they had reached the end of the drive, the riders were side by side commenting on the trees Elliott had planted and looking forward to seeing the village, all thoughts of a race forgotten.

CHAPTER 35

*A*s they approached the village, they could see that many of the roofs had been re-thatched, and the stone walls repaired. Many had been freshly whitewashed and even the road running through the middle had been cobbled, replacing the dirt track they remembered from childhood. The shops on either side of the road looked well-stocked and welcoming. The green at the centre of the village had been tended and several children were chasing each other through the willow trees and around the pond where a few ducks sounded to be laughing at their antics.

"Ducks are the most amusing creatures," Ella said, looking at them, "they always sound to be having a wonderful time, laughing at some duck jest or other."

Verity smiled back, the fresh air and ride had done her good and she was grateful Ella had suggested it.

There was no doubt that Swallowfield, as at Orlando Court, would benefit from having Elliott as a landlord. He was proving to be dutiful to the needs of the villagers, and she could see that the improvements he had made were appreciated. She recalled that her visits as a child were met with sullen villagers, and she had kept close to her governess and father. Fortunately, none of the villagers seemed to bear a grudge for her father's actions and she and Ella were welcomed. They spent a little money in each of the shops before turning their mounts back to the lane towards the house.

When they returned, Ella remained in the stables to play with the kittens while Verity returned to the house. She was startled to find Elliott was waiting in the hall. "Where the devil have you been?" he immediately demanded.

"Just to the village," Verity replied, taken aback. "You were busy, so Ella and I decided on an outing. What you have achieved there is...."

Elliott took her by the shoulders, cutting off her words, his eyes blazing into hers, "You are not to leave the grounds without an escort, do you understand? I will not be disobeyed in this, Verity."

"It was just a trip to the village," she began, unwillingly feeling cowed by a man's temper burning in this house again.

"You are not to go anywhere without telling me where you are going and you will have an escort," he repeated insistently.

"So I am to be a prisoner here after all?" she asked.

"I am trying to ensure your safety."

"You are being ridiculous," she shot back.

"You will obey me in this matter," he repeated. "I will have your word on it, Verity," he added, "or I will instruct the servants to restrict you to your rooms."

"As ever, Your Grace, your word is my command," she replied coolly, before dropping a deep curtsey then walking away.

Verity spent the rest of the morning in the small salon writing letters to Caro, Emily, Clara, and her aunt. She met with Mrs. Clayton and discussed the weekly menus before taking a book and heading out to the garden. The weather had turned warmer, and she could see the buds beginning to form on the rose bushes the spring flowers in the beds were almost gone and the summer flowers were not yet ready to raise their heads, but the sun was warm, so she decided to take her book to a secluded corner of the sunken garden.

It was there Elliott found her, so engrossed in her book that she had no idea he was there. She looked like a wood nymph sitting on a rug in her pale green gown with dark green ribbons in her hair. She had taken off her shoes and stockings and he could see her dainty toes peeking out from beneath her gown. Their marriage had not got off to a fine start due, largely to his deliberately asinine behaviour. Although he had long abandoned the idea of a marriage of convenience, every time they had a disagreement, Verity was reminded of the reason why she had agreed to marry him and now, for some reason he found unfathomable, someone was trying to kill his wife. In the years when they had been apart, it had never occurred to him to seriously pursue another woman because he now realised that the only woman he had ever wanted as a wife was Verity. The wife he had waited for seven years to marry, the wife he loved deeply, without whom his life would be only half a life. Verity brought challenge, vitality, and laughter to his life and without her his life would be ashes. He made a silent vow that they would get through this nightmare, he would protect Verity—with his own life if necessary—and they would live a long and happy life together, they would have children that they would raise together, and, God willing, they would grow old together.

Verity looked up as he cleared his throat. "I thought I might find you here," he said quietly.

"I felt in need of some air," she replied. "Truth be told, I have not felt quite myself since we returned."

"I apologise for my behaviour earlier," he said, hunkering down beside her. "I may have been a little..."

"Overbearing?" she suggested. "Ducal?"

"Overprotective," he finished. "There have been reports of highwaymen, footpads, and poachers," he lied. "It is not that I do not trust you to look after yourself, I am just concerned that you are safe when there is danger around." If it took a lie to convince her that his demands for her safety were met, it was a small price to pay. The reality was that the risk was far greater.

"Highwaymen, footpads, and poachers," she replied in a sceptical tone. "My goodness, Swallowfield must have increased in wealth greatly to attract such a wide range of criminals."

"I have it on good authority," he persisted. "In fact, the day after tomorrow, I shall be riding to see Sir William Hastings, the local magistrate to discuss what may be done."

"Ah, Sir William has been the magistrate since I was a small girl. Please give him my regards and ask Lady Hastings about her orchids, but try to avoid her small dogs, as they tend to be ankle biters," she said, smiling in happy memory, and it was as though the sun had suddenly come out from behind a cloud and warmed his body.

Elliott could not help himself, so taken was he by seeing her fully enjoy herself in this Eden he had created for her. He leaned over, brushed his palm against her cheek, and caught her lips in a kiss. He had intended it to be a gentle kiss, but her gentle sigh against his lips quickened his senses. He drew her towards him, wrapping an arm around her shoulders while the other crept around her waist, pulling her to him until their bodies were pressed together. He slipped his hand lower so that he cupped her pert derriere.

"Verity," he breathed as his tongue traced her delicate ear, "I want you. I want to make love to you now."

"Elliott," she gasped, "We cannot, not here. Anyone might come across us."

His response was another drugging kiss, hearing her gasp as his hand slid around her arse until it touched her womanhood. "You want me too," he said. "I can feel your heat and moisture calling to me. Your breasts," he lowered his head, nipping at her nipple through her dress, "are calling to me. You want me, Verity. This garden is out of the way," he murmured, shifting his hand so that his fingers could stroke her sex under her skirt. "Your sister is in the ring training Beautiful to do tricks. The gardeners are pruning the maze, and the indoor servants do not come down here."

Her breath hitched as he began to tease the sensitive bud that was quickly becoming slick with her need. "I want..." she began.

"What? What do you want?" His voice was a low growl, his fingers insistent. "Tell me and it shall be yours."

"I want...you," she moaned shakily, moving unsteadily against his hand, "you...to make love to me," she whispered.

"Do you want me, Verity?" he asked silkily, wanting to hear her say it, to revel in her desire and need. "Do you want me to carry you to my bed?"

"I want you...Elliott." She gasped, mewling with need. "I want you to take me. Here, Elliott. Now. Please...." she moaned, shifting insistently against him, her body yearning for more than he was giving her.

Elliott grinned, fully hard, aroused at how desperate her need for him had grown. He needed no further bidding and tugged her clothes, baring her breasts wantonly to the world and his hungry gaze. "You have beautiful breasts," he murmured taking first one nipple then the other into his mouth, laving, and sucking, nipping until she squealed and pressed his mouth against her breasts desperately. He quickly freed his member from his trousers and pulled her toward him until she straddled him.

Exposed and vulnerable, yet hidden and secluded, her skirts spread out, her breasts bared to him, and her wet warmth pressing against his dick, he felt his heart in his throat. She was the most beautiful, entrancing creature he could imagine. "Ride me, Verity," he commanded as he entered her. "Keep your eyes open so that I can see them darken as you come. I want to watch your beautiful breasts as you ride me."

He could not help but groan as she began to move her moist centre pulling him into her core, her arse on his thighs, her body demanding him. "God, Elliott," she cried out in a strangled voice as she adjusted to his position.

"Take me deeper," he said, "I want to fill you."

Instinctively, Verity began to move. Elliott kept his hands on her hips helping her to move against him, her nub rubbing his body, his hands pulling her closer, ever closer, so that they both gained the maximum pleasure before he roared his satisfaction and she collapsed against his chest, her whole body shaking as wave after wave of sensation pulsed through her.

"Every time," she said breathlessly, "every time is better than the last."

He brushed a stray lock of hair from her face and kissed her sensitised breasts, making her shudder, before tucking them back into her gown. "I know, love, for me too. I know I shall never be able to get enough of you."

He took both of her hands in his. Every time he had tried to explain, something had gone wrong. This time he would ensure she understood him, with no reason to doubt him ever again.

"I would walk through fire for you, Verity. For without you, my life has no meaning. I love you, my duchess with all my heart and with all my soul. You are and always will be my one true love. I loved you when I first saw you. I loved you in our youth. I loved you in our years apart. I love you now, and I will love you with all my heart throughout our lives."

For a heart-stopping moment, he thought she was going to reject him, and claim he was reneging on their marriage agreement. But she smiled. "I love you, Elliott, I do not think I ever stopped. That is why our parting was so painful, and I could not get you out of my heart and mind. When my father told me you were nothing but a fortune hunter, and had found another woman with a better dowry, it broke my heart. I watched you ride from Swallowfield without a backward glance and my heart shattered."

He bent so that his forehead touched hers, "What a pair of star-crossed lovers we were, and seven years of happiness wasted."

She brushed that lock of hair back, "But we found each other again, so we must look to the future and never waste this second chance we have been given."

"Amen to that," he replied, dropping a light kiss on her lips. "Nothing shall come between us again."

They helped each other to straighten their clothing before walking back towards the house, arm in arm, just in time to escape the first few drops of rain falling from the gathering storm clouds, washing the proof of their joining into their land.

CHAPTER 36

True to his word, Elliott left to visit Sir William Hastings, though his grumbling made it seem that he had not realised that the magistrate lived nearly half the county away. Verity laughed, pleased that she had caught him. He made sure that she saw him instruct Jones to watch over her, and she nodded regally, humouring him and his 'brigands' from whom she needed protection.

She watched him ride away, blushing at how attentive he had been in the garden and in their chambers. Perhaps what he said in passion was true, and he truly did love her, desire her, and value her for herself. She turned back into the house, catching Jones' eye, and went about her work.

It was not until late afternoon, when Verity went to see Ella at the stables that anyone realised that she was missing. Beautiful was quietly munching hay in her stall and the groom said he had not seen Lady Ella all day. He was surprised because she always spent time in the stables or the outdoor school, playing with the kittens or watching the animals. Verity was puzzled, as she was certain that was where Ella had said she was heading immediately after breakfast. She checked with Ella's new maid and began to panic when told that she had not seen

Ella since she had dressed and gone down to breakfast, though she thought Lady Ella had said something about going to the village.

Verity was still thinking about Ella's uncharacteristic behaviour and considering taking a walk to the village herself when she heard a carriage draw up. Minutes later, she was dismayed as Audra Kingsley was announced.

"Well, Your Grace," the older woman looked around her before bobbing the briefest of curtseys, "it would seem that Elliott has spared no expense in improving the old place. The last time I saw it, there was damp everywhere and, quite frankly, it looked in danger of falling down. I advised Elliott to raze it to the ground and start again, but clearly, he knows your sentimental attachment to it."

"Mrs. Kinglsey," Verity replied, "this is something of an unexpected surprise."

"Surprises are always unexpected, my dear. That is why they are surprises," Mrs. Kingsley replied with a smile that, as Verity had previously noted, never reached her eyes.

"What I meant," Verity began, "is what brings you here?"

"What indeed?" Mrs. Kingsley replied cryptically.

"Although you seem to believe that our lives are somehow linked, I had not imagined that we should actually meet after my marriage to the duke," Verity said. "I certainly have not invited you to call, and Elliott has been kept quite busy."

Despite her calm, assured manner, she was frantic, angry, and hurting. His declaration of love had seemed sincere, and she had finally believed him whole-heartedly, but a small part of her could not help but doubt him. She hated herself for doubting, wanting to cling to what she was so sure they had built together, but was unable to stop herself. Mrs Kingsley had succeeded in planting and nurturing the seeds of doubt every time she saw her. Had everything Elliott had said and done since their marriage been a lie just to gain access to her bed? Had he intended to flaunt his mistress all along?

"I think at this point, it is customary for the hostess to offer tea," Mrs. Kingsley said, sitting down.

"I do not feel the need for tea," Verity replied evenly. The woman was beginning to make her flesh crawl.

"But I do," the interloper replied, standing and reaching for the bell pull.

The two women sat in complete silence as Fry brought in the tea tray and set it on the table between them. "Ah, the Sevres set. I always liked that pattern, though of course some might consider it a little dated now. Shall I pour?" Mrs. Kingsley asked, reaching for the teapot.

Verity could not believe the audacity of the woman who had waltzed into her home and was beginning to behave as though she was the chatelaine. "I think not," Verity replied, picking up the teapot herself.

"Sugar?" she enquired.

"Two lumps and milk, if you please," Mrs. Kingsley smiled, giving Verity the impression of a cat toying with a mouse.

"So," Verity said, taking a sip of tea and composing her features, "why are you here?"

"I happened to be in the area and thought I might call."

"I very much doubt that." Nothing this woman did was without careful planning.

"As it happens, I do have business in the area." Mrs. Kingsley smiled once more, and added, "I was most disappointed to have missed Elliott. He has gone to see Sir William Hastings, I believe. The Hastings and my family go a long way back."

Verity paused, her teacup partway to her mouth, "You are from this area?"

"You seem surprised, but yes, I know this area well."

"I am just surprised that our paths never crossed, and I am acquainted with many of the families in the area."

"My mother was not one for society and I was sent away to live when she died," Mrs. Kingsley explained with a brittle smile. "But let us talk of other things. You must be very happy now that your home is habitable. All it needs now of course is the production of the heir for which Elliott married," she went on, with a sly smile.

Verity could not help the blush rising on her cheek. Mrs Kingsley laughed harshly. "Ah, I see that Elliott is doing his duty in that regard, though make no mistake, men will enjoy a tup with any woman, for it means nothing more to them than scratching an itch. Oh," she continued mockingly, "did you believe that Elliott felt more for you? I had forgotten what an innocent you are. The world is a cruel place, my dear, and little is crueller than a woman finding she is in love with a man who does not return her love, and you do love Elliott, do you not?"

"I am really not prepared to discuss the nature of my relationship with my husband," Verity replied, firmly.

"You do not need to, my dear, for it is written all over your face." Mrs. Kingsley looked around the room. "I had rather hoped to see your sister. Is she not in residence?"

Verity paused for a moment, an instinct told her not to reveal Ella's absence to this woman. "Ella is out at the moment," she said.

"A pity. She will not remember it, of course, but I remember seeing her when she was a babe."

"You visited this house?" Verity could not keep the surprise out of her voice.

"Several times, in fact, with my mother, but that was a long time ago, and as I said, Lady Ella was but a babe and I was but a child myself." Mrs. Kingsley set down her cup and rose. "I must be on my way. As it happens, I shall be in the area for a few days, I have some business that must be attended to, so no doubt we shall meet again. Please give my regards to your sister and Elliott, of course."

"Elliott denies knowing you," Verity blurted out, ashamed that she had allowed the cruel woman to rile her so.

The other woman smiled. "Of course, he does," she said smoothly, not even glancing at her as she drew on her gloves. "Few men admit a mistress to their wives, now do they?"

With that, she swept out, leaving Verity standing aghast. The woman had seemed to haunt Verity in London, but how did she know they had removed to Swallowfield? Their removal from Orlando Court had been done swiftly, and there had only been enough time to get a message to Swallowfield to let the staff know of their arrival. It was as though someone, a servant, perhaps, was sending her information, but why? To torment their impoverished mistress? To allow Elliott to taste both wares and compare them? As for the revelation that she had visited the house with her mother when Ella was a babe, that was more than a surprise, yet the woman had seemed more than familiar with her surroundings; she had even seemed to recognise the old Sevres tea set which had been a wedding gift to Ella's mother.

As she looked out of the window, Verity was delighted to see Ella tramping over the lawn towards the house and kept watching her until she had entered the drawing room, kicked off her boots, and settled herself by the fire.

"The sun may be out, but it is definitely colder than it looks and the lane to the village is covered in mud," Ella began. "Have you had tea? I am dying for a cup."

Verity rang the bell. They sat in silence until the tea arrived.

"Ah, lemon biscuits, my favourite." Ella's eyes lit up. "Who was visiting? I saw a coach drawing away as I came across the lawn," Ella asked, reaching for a yellow biscuit.

"Surprisingly, it was Mrs. Audra Kingsley," Verity replied.

The hand reaching for the tray froze. "The one who claims to be Elliott's lover?"

Verity nodded. "And that is not all. She claims to have lived in the area as a child and even visited you as a babe."

Ella wrinkled her brow in thought. "I have no recollection of that," she said, taking a bite.

"She said you would not, but should we not have heard of her family at least?" Verity replied.

"Possibly not, if they left when she was still small."

"She said she was sent away when her mother died," Verity responded.

"Then we have no family name to ask after. She is Mrs. Kinglsey, it would be impossible to find her maiden name," Ella said thoughtfully.

"Possibly, but mayhap someone in the village might remember, the vicar perhaps, since he has been here almost since Adam and Eve were thrown out of the garden," Verity replied.

Ella laughed. "He's certainly old enough. Perhaps even Mr. or Mrs.

Clayton might know something, as they have served here since before Father's time. They know everyone in the village and probably knew their grandparents as well."

"That is a good idea, I had not thought of them, though Mrs. Clayton disapproves of gossip," Verity replied.

"I am sure for you she will tell you what she knows. You were always a favourite of hers. Well," Ella remarked, claiming her biscuit and leaning back into the sofa, "Mrs. Kingsley is certainly a mystery and not the only one I have encountered today," she announced.

"A mystery?" Verity leaned forward. "Do tell."

"Well, two in fact," Ella began, pausing to take another bite of biscuit, "but for the first, I received this note yesterday," she fished in her pocket, drew out a piece of paper and handed it to Verity.

There is a neglected house at the end of the village, set back from the road and hidden by birches. Be there at eight of the clock in the morning if you want to learn where the Grainger treasure is. Come alone and tell no-one.

Verity handed the note back with a grin. "Oh Ella, people have been talking about the Grainger treasure for centuries! Father had most of the estate dug up looking for it, and I for one am glad he never found it for he would have only squandered it. I very much doubt it even exists and if it did, I imagine someone found it years ago."

"I agree, but I confess I found it intriguing," Ella replied. "Anyway, I could not resist so I investigated the area this morning. I walked because had I taken a horse someone would have been sure to notice and insist I must take a groom with me. It is true, there is an abandoned cottage beyond the village, past the green, about a mile from the lane to the mill, on the road towards Midham. The garden is overgrown, and the trees obscure it almost completely. I knocked on the door, but no-one answered."

"And?" Verity prompted.

"It was unlocked, so I went inside."

"Ella, have you lost your senses?" Verity was horrified. "Anyone could have been inside. Thieves, kidnappers, highwaymen, footpads using it as a hideout. Elliott has gone to see the magistrate about precisely that!"

"Thieves? Highwaymen? Kidnappers and footpads? In this little backwater?" Ella scoffed. "I fear you have been reading too many Gothic novels, Verity. This was a little cottage, no vampires, haunted castle, maiden in distress, omens, or prophecies."

"Yet you were directed there by a mysterious note," Verity pointed out.

"Yes, well, on the whole I think someone was playing a jest. The cottage was almost bare apart from a few sticks of furniture, a couple of wooden chairs and a table, a dresser with a few pieces of pewter and a bed. I would say though, that someone must have been using the cottage recently as the table was scrubbed clean and the floor had been swept and there were the remains of some kind of meal. Perhaps some vagrant slept there for a couple of nights before moving on."

"Even so, you should at least have told someone where you were going," Verity admonished her sister.

"Well, the note said not to tell anyone, and in any case that would have spoiled the mystery somewhat." Ella grinned.

Verity shook her head. "There is no reasoning with you at times. However, I would just point out that should anyone know you had been out without a chaperone, let alone visiting strange houses, well, you would be ruined." Verity was mildly worried about Ella's flippant attitude, but truth to tell, this was the first time she had seen Ella so carefree and mischievous since before their father had died. This was the old, fun-loving Ella she had sorely missed.

"Oh pooh! For one thing, no-one will know and secondly, no-one will care, as I do not intend to wed so no gentleman will be remotely interested in what I get up to," Ella said airily.

Verity shot Ella a look, rehashing the old argument once more. She was never pleased with Ella's acceptance that her life would never have happiness or companionship. "One, you do not know if you will wed. You still may meet the right man and two, believe me, gossip has a way of catching out the best of us. Remember Lady Elise Blair who ended up married to Lord Wistowe because she was returning from the retiring room at some ball when he reached out, drew her into a shadowy corner and kissed her, thinking he was kissing his mistress. They happened to be wearing the same colour gown, and Lord Wistowe, as everyone knows, could not hit a target at the end of his nose. The whole thing was seen by the dowager Duchess of Wakefield who lost no time in making the thing public, the result being that the poor girl had to marry someone twenty years older than her that she had barely met, so never underestimate the power of gossip."

"I stand corrected," Ella replied, with little enthusiasm. "Though I do not..."

"You said there were two mysteries," Verity said, changing the subject.

"Ah, yes. As I was coming across the lawn, I met two of the gardeners who said that at the far end, near the path to the lane, where the grass is allowed to grow longer, they had found a mantrap—hideous thing. They were about to remove it."

"A mantrap? How on earth did that get there? Elliott cannot abide them, and even Father drew the line at them," Verity murmured. "Was it an old one perchance?"

"The gardeners were very clear that it had only been placed last night, as they had clipped around that area only yesterday afternoon."

"But who would set it and why there? Mantraps are meant to catch poachers and thieves, and at the edge of a lawn is hardly the place to catch anything other than perhaps the odd, unfortunate mouse," Verity mused.

"The younger gardener did say something puzzling," Ella said thoughtfully, "He said it was the second thing in a week."

"The second mantrap?" Verity exclaimed.

"Just the second 'thing,' that is all he said. Now, I must go and change for the grass was extremely wet and I'm damp through to my stockings," Ella rose, and at the doorway she turned and said, "I suppose if we want to know what the first thing was, we must go and ask the gardener."

"Hmmm," Verity replied, thinking that she would do just that.

It took twenty minutes for Verity to find the gardener who was sitting on an old wooden bench outside the potting shed at the far end of the walled garden, enjoying a pipe of tobacco when she found him.

Milton had been gardener for her father and had kept the grounds in as good a state as he could when all the other men had been dismissed, Elliott had retained him, and he once again held the position of Head Gardener.

"What can I do fer Yer Grace?" he asked, tapping the tobacco out of his pipe and pocketing it.

"Please, do not get up, Mr. Milton. I was simply wondering about the mantrap you found this morning," she began.

"Disgustin' things, shouldn't ort to be allowed." He pointed to the ground in front of him. "'Ad to set it off afore we could dig un out," he added.

Verity followed his finger; there was no doubt that if anyone had trodden on that vicious trap, they would have at the very least broken their leg, and at worst, it would have bitten straight through. The iron jaws had sharp teeth and the whole thing was solid and heavy.

"'Twas buried where yer and Lady Ella often did take a shortcut to the lane when yer were girls," Milton went on. "If it weren't for Lass, I should prob'ly 'ave been caught in it meself."

"Lass?"

Milton whistled and a black and white collie came out of the potting shed and nuzzled his hand. "Lass was runnin' a'ead when she came to a halt sudden like and started to bark as though the hounds of 'ell was comin'. She could smell summat were wrong yer see. Didn't like the smell of iron. Then the young lad saw the plate, that's the thing yer stands on and the trap springs."

"Goodness Mr. Milton, it sounds as though you had a lucky escape," Verity replied.

"I reckon I did. I were two inches away, that's all. Anyroad, the lad and I came back for tools while Lass guarded it. We 'ad to put a stick in to make it snap and look what 'appened to it."

Verity looked once more and saw that a sizeable piece of wood had been almost torn apart and crushed between the jaws.

"Someone meant someone 'ere 'arm, that's what I say," Milton continued.

"You do not think that it had been there for a long time, Mr. Milton? Perhaps something that has been overlooked for years?" Verity asked, knowing the answer.

Milton shook his head. "No, Yer Grace. It's an old one I grant yer. I 'aven't seen one like that since me grandper showed me one when I were a lad. But that was put there last night. We cut that grass regular an' we'd 'ave seen it. Yer father would've 'ad our guts for garters if the grass wasn't cut right, when we 'ad the staff. Before, things got yer know..."

"And this was never used to catch poachers on the estate?" Verity did not want to ask the question, but in his later years, she would not have put anything past her father.

Milton shook his head. "Never, Yer Grace, for all 'is faults, beggin' yer pardon, as much as he 'ated poachers, 'e 'ated these things more. Them as went before 'im might 'ave, but the last three earls, never."

"Then where did this evil contraption come from?"

"That I don't know, Yer Grace, but I'll be askin' a few questions down at The Dog and Fox. Somebody must know summat."

"There was one other thing, Mr. Milton," Verity began, "Lady Ella said something about this being the second thing. What, in that case, was the first thing?"

Milton's eyes narrowed, "What did 'er ladyship say exactly?"

"That she heard one of your men say that this was not the first thing."

"She should't 'ave 'eard that," he replied.

"That is as may be, but the fact is, she did. Now, Mr. Milton, please tell me what you know," Verity replied firmly.

"It's more'n me job's worth to tell yer."

"It will be more than your job is worth if you do not," Verity declared, using every ounce of composure and nobility she could muster. Verity's voice was calm, but her pulse was racing. Why would someone lay a vicious mantrap and something apparently equally wicked, and why was it being kept a secret from her?

CHAPTER 37

"*S*it yer down, Yer Grace," Milton said, indicating the bench. Verity sat and smoothed her skirts, knowing that Milton was not a man to be rushed. He took a moment to pack his pipe and tamp down the tobacco before striking a flint and lighting it. He pulled on it a few times before speaking. "Yesterday morn, after you and Lady Ella 'ad gone to t'village but afore yer came back, someone strung some fishing line between two trees, them two plane trees along the bridle path, near t' stile into t' meadow."

Verity frowned. "I do not understand."

"'Tweren't no ordinary line, silk 'ad been plaited together an' waxed to make it strong enough to take a person off their 'orse, but light enough so they wouldn't see it afore they rode into it," Milton replied.

"To take a person off their horse," Verity murmured.

"Aye, Yer Grace, or..." the old man drew on his pipe before continuing, "or take a person's 'ead off."

"You think someone intended to kill a rider?" Verity gasped.

Milton nodded solemnly. "I can't think of no other reason a person would do it," he responded.

"But why would anyone want to do such a thing?"

"That I don't know, Yer Grace."

"It does not make any sense, hardly anyone even knows about the bridle path, let alone uses it. Do you think the duke is the intended victim?" Verity asked. "He was a soldier after all. Do you think it could be someone who bears a grudge from his days in the army, or perhaps a business rival?"

"No, Yer Grace, I don't think it was intended for 'Is Grace. The fact is, 'Is Grace didn't know about the bridle path until we found that silk and 'e don't even know about yon mantrap." Milton took a deep breath before adding, "I don't think it were the duke as was intended 'arm, Yer Grace, 'e's a tall man, if it 'ad been meant for 'im it would 'ave been tied 'igher. No, Yer Grace, I think it were meant fer you or Lady Ella."

Verity was shocked. "I do not understand. Lady Ella or myself? Why on earth would anyone want to harm us? We have barely been out in society to make enemies, certainly none that would want to kill us."

"I'm sorry Yer Grace, I shouldn't 'ave said anythin'."

"But something clearly made you come to this conclusion Mr. Milton, and I should very much like to know what it is."

Milton tapped the tobacco out of his pipe with the side of his boot. "I'm not saying as it's you as made enemies, but yer father wasn't a popular man around 'ere, not in 'is later days. Yer won't remember, 'cos yer were too young to notice, but accounts with local traders went unpaid, cottages were left to rack and ruin an' rents was put up, an' folk who couldn't afford it were evicted. There was a lot of ill feelin'."

"But why would someone want to injure Ella or myself?" Verity was bewildered. "People in the village have always been nothing but kind towards us."

Milton paused. "I daresay they were, back then. Mebbe it's someone who's come back for revenge an' as the old earl's dead, they plan to take it out on yer."

"It makes no sense."

"Not everything folks do makes sense, and no good ever came from someone takin' revenge, but there's always them that does it for 'emselfs," he replied sagely.

Verity thought for a moment. "Since the duke bought Swallowfield, he has restored the cottages as well as the house, surely no-one can still bear a grudge."

"As I said, mebbe it's someone come back."

Verity paused again, unwilling to expose Ella. "I have found thar there is one cottage that has not been restored, slightly out of the village, almost hidden from the road. Would you know why that one is still untouched?"

"I'm familiar with the place. That one don't belong to t'estate no more," Milton replied, placing his pipe in his pocket.

"Then to whom does it belong?" Verity persisted.

"I don't rightly know. The family as used to live in it left afore yer was born. There was a fever in t'village, and one of the kiddies died as I recall, an' they just upped sticks an' went. Now, if yer'll excuse me, Yer Grace, I have work to attend to. Them roses won't prune themselves." The old man stood with a groan, indicating that the conversation was closed, but Verity had the distinct impression that he knew more than he was prepared to say.

"One more thing, Mr. Milton," Verity said as she rose too, "do you know of a woman named Audra Kingsley? Well, she is Mrs. Kingsley so her maiden name would obviously been something else, but she said she came to Swallowfield as a child, visiting with her mother and Audra is not a common name."

Milton pursed his lips. "Can't say as I do, Yer Grace, but then we gardeners don't usually get much further than t'kitchen."

"Thank you, Mr. Milton, I shall let you get back to your work."

Verity's thoughts were in a whirl as she returned to the house. Something was clearly very strange and very wrong. Swallowfield had always been a quiet and peaceful backwater, and there had never, as far as she knew, been anything much in the way of crime beyond the usual bit of poaching to which even her father had more or less turned a blind eye. Now Elliott was talking of footpads and highwaymen, which in truth she found less worrying than the discovery of mantraps and garottes on their own land. Milton had given her much to think about, but she knew there was one person who might be able to tell her more.

Mrs. Clayton smiled as Verity opened the door to her sitting room.

"Your Grace, it's a pleasure to see you, I was just going over the household accounts whilst having a cup of tea, I should be honoured if you would join me."

Verity smiled back. "I should be most grateful for tea, Mrs. Clayton," she replied, sitting down. As Verity had known it would be, the sitting room was both neat and cosy with a fire burning in the hearth and the table covered with an embroidered cloth. The walls were a pale green with dark green drapes at south facing windows which let in the sunlight. Not a speck or mote of dust was to be seen. Mrs. Clayton, garbed in a grey gown with snowy white cap and apron was a welcome sight. Two carved chairs were at the table and within moments, the ledgers had been replaced with a tray containing tea and biscuits.

"Now, my dear," Mrs. Clayton began, "I can see that something troubles you."

The older woman quietly sipped her tea, while Verity repeated the conversation she had had with Milton, concluding, "The thing is, I believe Elliott knew about the garotte in the woods, but he did not breathe a word of it to me," she finished.

"I imagine he didn't want to worry you, my dear," Mrs. Clayton replied.

"But it is barbaric, why would someone, anyone do such a thing?"

"That I do not know, but it would seem that someone somewhere for whatever reason bears a grudge against the Grainger family, and sad to say, your father made many enemies."

"Again, I do not understand, he had nothing at the end of his life. Everything had gone, Swallowfield, the lands, the money, it had all gone. What more revenge could anyone want?"

Mrs. Clayton thought for a moment. "There are those who are so deranged and withered that only complete destruction will satisfy their lust for vengeance."

Verity's heart lodged in her throat, her chest filling with fear. "Are you saying that this person will not stop until everything that is associated with Father is destroyed?"

Mrs. Clayton took a deep breath. "I..."

"You think it is a possibility," Verity interrupted, instantly thinking of Caro, of Ella. Of herself, she was sure that Elliott would protect her until she had had a child, even he cared little for her—and, she forced herself to remember, he loved her in truth!—but her sisters were so vulnerable.

"If a person is deranged, there is no knowing of what they are capable." Mrs. Clayton leaned forward and took Verity's hand. "I'm sure that the duke will do everything in his power to protect you. He loves you, of that I'm certain."

Verity choked, her bitterness tainting her words. "But how? It seems he cannot even protect me from his mistress who keeps popping up wherever I go."

Mrs. Clayton's eyes narrowed. "Who is this mistress?"

"Mrs. Audra Kingsley, she even came this morning. She said she used to visit here with her mother as a girl when Ella was a babe."

Mrs. Clayton shook her head. "The first countess was ill for much of the time Lady Ella was a babe, and as far as I remember, few visitors were admitted. Audra is an uncommon name. I feel sure I would remember it."

"There seem to be far too many mysteries at Swallowfield at the moment," Verity said darkly, taking a sip of tea before she went on to explain about Ella and her visit to the derelict cottage.

Mrs. Clayton drew in a sharp breath. "Do not go near that cursed place, Your Grace," she warned.

"Why on earth not? Come, Mrs. Clayton. It is not like you to be superstitious." Verity smiled.

"And I am not, but no good has ever happened to anyone who has lived there." Mrs. Clayton set down her cup with a clink, her hands shaking. "Your great-grandfather kept a mistress there. She had not been there long before she was drowned one morning. Your grandfather also kept a mistress there, but she died of a fever within six months of living there."

"And my father?" Verity prompted.

Mrs. Clayton shook her head despairingly. "I've no wish to speak ill of the dead."

"Come, Mrs. Clayton, you already have and surely you know by now that there is little you can tell me of my father that can shock me," Verity pressed.

"Your father did not have a mistress that he kept, my dear, but he had his way with the maids." Mrs. Clayton's eyes filled with tears in remembered pain. "I tried to protect them as best I could, but your father believed he could have what he wanted, and no innocent young girl or common woman such as myself could tell him otherwise."

"So he did not keep a mistress in the cottage?"

"Not to my knowledge, but many girls came and went through his door," was Mrs. Clayton's reply.

CHAPTER 38

*V*erity did not notice it at first, the small package had become hidden among the letters and invitations on the escritoire which had been delivered whilst she had been talking first to Milton and then to Mrs. Clayton, but upon opening it, she could not help but cry out. She did not need the note to tell her to whom the pendant and lock of hair belonged.

Ella, who had just come into the room, and was instantly by her side. "What? What is it, Verity?"

With shaking hands, she held out the note that had been wrapped around the items.

If you wish to see your sister alive, come to the abandoned cottage tonight at midnight. Come alone and tell no-one.

"Caro?" Ella's eyes widened. "It cannot be. But she is at school."

"Apparently not," Verity replied.

"She has been kidnapped?"

"It would seem so."

"What are you going to do?" Ella asked.

"What am I going to do?" Verity replied, her heart beating wildly, her fears realized. "I am going to do exactly what the note demands, what else can I do?"

"Then I am coming with you," Ella said firmly.

Verity looked at her older sister. For as long as she could remember, Ella had looked after them all. "No, Ella, you cannot, the note is very specific and whoever is behind it may harm Caro if we do not do as they say."

"They may harm you both," Ella pointed out. "Look, the note says nothing about a ransom demand, and if they wanted money, surely they would have kidnapped you rather than Caro, you being the duchess and the wife of a supremely wealthy man."

"We do not know what they intend or want, but I cannot risk Caro being harmed because I made the wrong choice."

"What about Elliott?" Ella persisted. "He will need to be informed."

"Elliott is not here and does not intend to be back until tomorrow. We cannot wait," Verity pointed out. "I promise I shall take care. I will steal out through the kitchen when everyone is asleep, the moon is full so I shall be able to see down the lane, and if we are lucky Caro and I will be back safe and sound before anyone knows we are gone."

"I cannot share your optimism," Ella replied. "Were it not for the fact that Caro is in danger, I would stop you from going, and demand that you wait for Elliott, however, I know neither you nor I could forgive ourselves if anything happened to one of the others. But you must have a care, the garden of the house is overgrown and should give you enough cover so that you might see something through a window of what awaits in the house before you enter."

"I shall certainly try, and I promise to be cautious," Verity said solemnly.

"I shall not rest until you are safely back." Ella hugged her sister tightly.

"Ella," Verity murmured, avoiding looking in her sister's eyes, "please tell Elliott what has happened if I do not return. He will come for me." Of that, Verity was certain. Even if Elliott loved another woman, even other women, she was still convinced that he loved her as well.

The two of them secreted away what they could think might be useful. A small knife, in case Caro was tied up. A small piece of bread in case they had not been feeding her. Dark, simple clothes that would allow her to be undetected.

Later that evening, it seemed that every floorboard creaked as Verity made her way through the dark house and down the back stairs to the kitchen. Fortunately, the key was in the kitchen door, and she quietly let herself out of the house and through the kitchen garden to the door in the wall that led out into the park. As she had expected, the night was clear, and the full moon illuminated her walk down the lane to the village. All was quiet, even the tavern was empty as she made her way down the road towards the cottage. She could see the dim light of a single candle in the window. Fortunately, the gate was hanging off its hinges, so she made no sound as she crept down the path and peered through the glass. Someone was sitting in a chair in front of the dying embers of a fire, their back to the window, but she could not tell whether it was Caro.

She was reaching for the door when it was suddenly flung open, and a pistol was pointed at her.

"Ah, Duchess, we meet again."

"Mrs. Kingsley?" Verity was shocked. Gone were the rich silks and satins, instead, the woman who stood before her wore a cream shirt, leather jerkin, men's trousers and boots, and with her hair was tied back in a simple stock.

"Come in," she said, opening the door wider, keeping the pistol trained on Verity's chest.

Verity stepped inside, glancing around her new surroundings. The room was as Ella had described it, the embers offered little heat, she held her breath as the figure by the hearth stood up. She could have wept with disappointment, for it was not Caro.

"Where is my sister?" she demanded, turning to face Mrs. Kingsley.

"At school, where she has always been," the other woman smirked, "though sadly without her pendant, of course. They really should pay their maids better."

"What do you mean?" Verity asked.

"Like all people with money, you never consider the lives of those without. It was easy enough to bribe the maid to cut a lock of your sister's hair and take the pendant," Mrs. Kinglsey replied, before turning to the silent figure by the fire. "Oh, I almost forgot, may I present my brother, Jude."

Jude stepped forward. "Jude, meet your half-sister. Shake her hand, Jude," Mrs. Kingsley spat.

"Pleased to meet you duchess," he said as he made an extravagant bow and held out his hand.

"Jude is perhaps not the brightest candle burning, but he always does as I tell him."

Verity looked from one to the other. "What are you talking about? Brother? Sister?" She was aware that her voice had risen.

"You think our father was satisfied with the milksop wives he bedded in order to get a son? That he gave up when met with failure after failure?" Mrs. Kingsley's voice was harsh.

"Our father?" Verity's heart froze.

"Yes, my dear, *our* father. We have different mothers but one father, and though you and your sisters were fortunate enough to be legitimate, we were not," Mrs. Kingsley said, her mouth twisting into a sneer. "Bastards we were born and bastards we remain because *our father*," she repeated brutally with disgust, "broke his promise to marry our mother and instead married yours."

Verity glanced at Jude. He was tall and broad shouldered, his voice deep and hinting at time spent in London. Past him was the door, which Mrs. Kingsley had locked.

"You won't get that far," Jude warned, following her gaze.

"I think you had better sit down, duchess," Mrs. Kingsley said, adding, "Jude, bind her hands. We wouldn't like our guest to escape."

"I most certainly will not," Verity began, yelping as a large pair of hands caught her by the shoulders and pressed her into the chair.

"Do as you're told, duchess," Jude grunted as he bound her hands with a stout rope.

"I do not understand," Verity said. "Any of this."

"Of course, you don't," Mrs. Kingsley began, "why would you, living your life of luxury first as an earl's daughter and now as a duchess? So I will tell you. You remember our sister Ella was injured in a fire when she was a babe?"

Verity nodded. "Of course, we were always told that a careless nursery maid left a candle burning which set the curtains alight."

A crack resounded around the room as Mrs. Kinsley slapped Verity across the face. "You will not speak ill of my mother. She was not careless. She had been dragged by the earl out of the nursery so that he could fuck her. She had already had one child with him. When Ella was disfigured in the fire, he dismissed her without a second thought, sending us both away.

"When Ella's mother died, our mother went to him, already big with his child, but he told her that if she bore him a son 'this time,' he would marry her. She should have known better, of course, but she was a simple, ignorant, uneducated girl and believed his lies. He sent her to a 'place of safety' in London while he sought for another wife in peace." Mrs. Kingsley's eyes burned. "Do you know what it was? Where he sent her?"

By now, Mrs. Kinglsey's face was inches from her own, the fury clearly in her eyes as she spat out the words, "It was a brothel, one he knew well and had used freely, and it was no place of safety! Even though her child but two months from birth, they put her to work; some men find bedding a pregnant woman arousing, apparently. Of course, when the babe was born, there was no place for her, brothels are no places for children, and she was worried about the looks that were given to her young daughter. She could not write to our father or pay for a scribe to do so for her, so she waited for him. When the madame offered to sell her daughter's virginity—*my* virginity—when came the time, she knew she had to leave."

"What happened?" Verity croaked.

"She made her way back here. Travelling impoverished, slowly, with two children in tow, proudly ready to present her son. but by that time, your father had married your mother for her dowry, but I suppose you knew that. The evil bastard was incapable of loving anyone other than himself. He gave my mother this hovel to live in provided that she kept me and Jude there out of sight, but within the year, she was dead. She lies in a pauper's grave in the churchyard. They said she died of a fever, but she died of a broken spirit, broken by your father."

"I am sorry, my father was a cruel man, I do not deny it," Verity replied. "I know it too well."

Mrs. Kingsley laughed. "How would you know the meaning of his cruelty? What did he do, deny you new ribbons for your bonnet? You know nothing of the depths to which he was prepared to go."

"You might be surprised," Verity replied, evenly.

"We used to watch you, Jude and I, from the ditches and bushes as you rode past in your carriage, clean, well fed, dressed in silks and satins, so don't tell me you know anything about cruelty. You had your sisters and your father, while we stayed in this hovel. No-one from the village came near because they thought it was haunted and no-one knew we were here because Mother had hidden us well, but we had nothing other than what we could steal, and we were good at it. We had no-one to look after us, if they'd have found us, they would have tried to split us up and send us to the workhouse, but we stayed together until your father realised that we were still living here." Audra's vehemence was evident as she spat the words like barbs as she paced.

CHAPTER 39

From the corner of her eye, Verity thought she glimpsed some movement through the window, a slight shadow that passed and disappeared as quickly as it had come, but she thought there was someone outside, though she heard nothing. Her heart began to beat faster with hope. Perhaps Ella had alerted someone or perhaps there were others, like Mrs. Kingsley and Jude who clearly wanted to do her harm. All she could think of, for the moment, was to keep the older woman talking.

"What do you mean, until our father found out?"

"He assumed that when our mother died, we had been taken to the workhouse, but his estate manager came snooping around the cottage and discovered us. I'd been taking care of Jude since he was born, we survived. Nobody missed the odd potatoes or carrots we dug up from their gardens and shopkeepers aren't bothered about what they throw out at the end of the day. When the earl knew of our existence, he paid to have us caught and taken away to a workhouse. I won't bore you with the details but let me tell you it was a far cry from the lap of luxury you were living in.

"I was taken as a housemaid as Audrey Bolton, and that's when my life got better. It was hard work, don't get me wrong, but it was easier than anything else in my life. There was plenty of food and I began to fill out my form. I knew I could trade on my looks by the way male visitors looked at me when they visited Mr. Kingsley. I knew this was my chance, there would be no other, so I worked, I worked hard, until I became head housemaid to Mr. Kingsley. He was an old man whose wife had died, and there were no children to challenge me, and he was lonely. It didn't take long before he was persuaded to marry me.

"Of course, what family he had were up in arms, but I knew I would win. What old man doesn't want a young woman on his arm, flashing tit, flattering him that he's as young and virile as he imagines himself to be. So plain old Audrey Bolton became Audra Kingsley. It wasn't pleasant having him try to get me with child, which I had no intention of doing, but thankfully the old boy expired eventually, not soon enough for me truth be told. And had he not had the good manners to die when he did, believe me I should have had no qualms about helping him on his way, but leaving his fortune to his grieving widow was something of the compensation I believe I was entitled to for having put up with the boring old fool for as long as I did. I then had the wherewithal to rescue Jude from the gang of thieves he was running with and begin to plot my revenge."

"Revenge?" Verity asked, "on whom?"

"Our father would have been my first choice, by denying my mother the wedding ring he'd promised and making Jude a bastard when he should have been the legitimate heir. Had he lived up to his promise, we would have had very different lives. But no, the old sod was dead and so was your mother, the one he married, when he should have married my mother."

"But that has nothing to do with me," Verity said, desperately trying to keep her voice even.

"You stole my life. You stole the life we should have had," Audra Kingsley spat. "Had you slipped into poverty as seemed likely, I should have permitted you to live. Indeed, it would have been amusing to see the daughters of the earl manage without their luxuries, but then you married a duke no less. I have tried several times to be rid of you. Unfortunately, Jude is not as skilled at driving horses as he had me believe, nor did he make an ideal footman and the snare and the garotte were rather based on the luck of you finding them, but now that I have taken matters into my own hands, I do not expect to fail."

"You have been trying to kill me?" Verity could not believe her ears.

"Of course, my dear, but you seem to be like the cat with nine lives. You dodged the cart in the village, didn't drink the poison at the ball, nor did you take the path through the woods or come across the mantrap." Mrs. Kingsley sighed heavily. "I find myself wondering why this husband of yours did not warn you to take more care."

"I have taken nothing from you," Verity began, hoping to find reason with her newly-discovered half-sister. "You said yourself that it is you that Elliott loves."

Audra Kingsley laughed condescendingly. "Elliott Thorne does not know me at all. We have never met. But how easy it was to manipulate your thoughts to the contrary. I thought I could be satisfied with that, driving a wedge between you and your husband, playing on your mind until I drove you mad, but I found I could not stand by and watch your privileged life become even more gilded, not when you had taken so much from us."

By now, Verity could see that not only fury lay in Audra Kingsley's eyes, there was madness there as well. The woman was not going to let her leave this house alive, of that, she was sure.

"Bring the candle here, Jude," Mrs. Kingsley ordered. He loped over to the window and picked up the candlestick.

"As it was a fire that caused the problem in the first place, I think a fire is a suitable ending to this tale, don't you? In some religions, fire is a symbol of purification. Your sacrifice will atone for the deeds of your father," she said, bringing the candle so close to her cheek that Verity could feel its heat.

Audra Kingsley ran a finger down her cheek. "Such soft skin, so unused to the ravages of work and weather, soon it will be even more ravaged than your sister's."

"If you kill me, you will be caught," Verity said as calmly as she could. "My sister knows where I am, and if I do not return soon, she will raise a hue and cry."

The older woman laughed once again. "Even if, as you say, Lady Ella knows where you are, she has no idea who you are with and by the time anyone arrives, it will be too late for you and Jude, and I will be long gone. The fire will have destroyed any hint that we were even here. Now Jude," she turned to her brother, "bring the rags to the table."

Verity watched with mounting horror as the woman carefully soaked the rags in some kind of spirit, brandy by the smell of it, and laid them on the table until she wound the last one around the rapidly melting candle.

"There," the other woman stood back to admire her handiwork. "I should say it will take a little over five minutes for the rags to catch light, so you will have ample time for reflection."

"Do not do this Mrs. Kingsley, Audra," Verity pleaded. "If it is money you want, I am sure Elliott will pay."

"You really do not understand at all," Mrs. Kingsley remarked as she picked up a cloak from a hook by the door. "I have no need of your money. The late, unlamented Mr. Kingsley left me well provided for. This," she gestured around the room, "this has been about avenging the cruel wrong done to my mother by your father."

"No," Verity shot back, "this has been about revenge, the two things are quite different. I am sorry for the way our father treated your mother and you, but surely you must see that it had nothing to do with me."

"The sins of the fathers are visited upon the children," the older woman quoted. "Come, Jude. When we leave here, we will go to the continent for a while. Would you like that? Mr. Kingsley was shrewd enough to buy a chateau where we shall reside until we decide where to visit next. Italy, I think. I have always wanted to travel and by the time we return, this little incident and you, duchess, will be long forgotten."

As Mrs. Kingsley and her brother sauntered toward the door, it burst open, cracking, left to hang drunkenly on its hinges. They both stepped back, Jude falling against the table, tipping the candle and instantly setting the rags alight. Within seconds, the table was ablaze and black smoke began to fill the room. There were shouts and through the smoke and flames. Verity could see a scuffle, and, to her horror, she heard gunshots. Smoke was in her eyes and throat, the flames getting ever nearer, she could feel the heat beginning to lick at her face.

"Verity!" she heard Elliott's voice.

"Over here," she croaked, hoping that her voice carried over the crackling and roaring of the fire which had taken hold on the curtains and was spreading across the floor. Before her was a wall of flame and the smoke was even thicker, she could barely see in front of her face.

Elliott's figure suddenly loomed in front of her, his face covered with a neckcloth. "Come. There is not much time, this place is likely to go up like a tinder box, the wood is so dry," he said as he began to cut through her bonds with a knife from his boot. He bundled her up and bolted from the burning building.

She allowed herself to be cradled against his chest, her throat burning, her heart sore. He only set her down when they were well away from the cottage, only then removing the neckcloth.

"Verity, my love, are you all right? Are you injured in any way?"

"No Elliott," she replied, her voice husky. "I am well. But what of you? I heard shots," she said, fearfully raking her gaze over his body, seeking any tears or injury.

"That woman and boy could not hit a barn door at ten paces. They did, however, manage to wing the old oak tree and a wheelbarrow which must have survived since the beginning of time, probably used by Adam in the Garden of Eden," he joked.

"And what of Mrs. Kingsley and her brother? Did they escape?" she asked, anxiously looking around.

Elliott shook his head. "They are in the safe hands of the watch and will be kept in the local Bridewell until they are questioned by the magistrate and eventually brought to court, the case against them is undeniable."

"What will happen to them?" she asked.

"I imagine they will hang. They tried to kill you, my sweet. When I think what would have happened had I not arrived in time," he said as he pulled her against him once again. She could feel the shuddering of his body and hear the thundering beat of his heart as he held her close.

"I think that perhaps Mrs. Kingsley is mad rather than bad, Elliott, and her brother is both ruled by her and...I think, there is some impairment with his mind, perhaps since birth. Would it not be kinder to put them in a place where they might be treated for their afflictions?"

"Their afflictions did not stop them from trying to do away with you," he replied harshly, adding more gently, "it will be for the magistrate to decide whether they knew that what they were doing was wrong."

"They are also my half-brother and -sister," she replied.

Elliott's surprise was cut short by the sound of the roof of the cottage crashing down in flames.

CHAPTER 40

*E*lliott could scarcely bear to let Verity out of his sight, even knowing that she was safe in bed, attended to by a physician. He had once again come so close to losing her, truly losing her, and he felt sick at the thought. She was in his heart and soul, and he loved her in ways he had not ever dreamed possible. He loved her wit and warmth, the way she could make everyone feel at ease, no matter their wealth, power or station in life. He loved her intelligence and compassion; there would never be another woman for him.

Even if she didn't have a body that responded so intensely to his when he made love with her, he would eternally love her anyway, needing no other woman. He knew that now, perhaps he had always known it, he had just never accepted it when he had been hurt and angry at her falsified rejection of him all those years ago. He was still angered that he had ever believed it. He should have known better than to believe that she would reject him without reason or explanation, but it had been easier to blame her than to think rationally. He had been a stupid, hot-headed fool.

And to compound matters further, he had forced her into this marriage, claiming it was solely of convenience, claiming that all he wanted from her was an heir, when in truth he wanted her, heirs or no.

What would he possibly be able to say or do to persuade her that he had changed? He stood up as the doctor entered the library.

"Your wife is young and strong, Your Grace. There is a little damage to her throat due to the smoke, but she should be as right as rain with a few days' rest," the doctor said.

"Thank God," Elliott replied, running a hand through his hair.

"I recommend a light diet for a day or so, something that slips easily down the throat. Beyond that, she will need to eat well, considering that she will need to keep up her strength, but ensure that she takes brisk walks while the weather is good. Physical strength is important before her confinement come winter," the doctor said as reached for his hat.

Elliott's hand stilled. "Confinement?" he asked.

"Oh, dear, I seem to have spoken prematurely." The doctor looked alarmed but smiled genteelly. "I advise you speak with your wife, Your Grace."

"Are you telling me that my wife is with child?" Elliott's eyes bored into the smaller man's.

"I think, all things considered, I had better leave you to a much-needed conversation with your lady wife," the doctor said and hurried from the room.

Elliott took the distance at a run, pausing to compose himself before entering her chamber.

Verity was sitting up in bed, a book in her hand, and smiled at him as he approached her. He suddenly felt awkward, though his heart was swelling. "Are you quite well?" he asked, the question sounding inane to his own ears. "The doctor said you should be fine after a few days of rest."

She smiled at him. "I am fine," she replied, setting the book aside. "I really do not see why I should stay in bed at all."

"You have had a terrible shock," he responded, sitting on the edge of the bed, taking her hand and raising it to his lips. "My God, when I think of what might, what would have happened had I not made it in time."

"But you did," she soothed. "How did you know? I had not expected you to return until the following day."

"I concluded my business with Sir William early, so I decided to ride back rather than spend the night. It was after midnight when I arrived back only to find Ella was pacing the room, half out of her mind with worry. She showed me the note and told me where you had gone. I gathered a few men and we set off straight away. We did not know who or how many we would face, but had there been an army, nothing would have stopped me from getting to you."

"Fortunately, there was only Audra and Jude," she responded with a gentle smile.

"But neither in their right minds, frankly, and both unpredictable." Elliott spared a sharp thought, wishing only pain and misery on the both of them.

"Poor Audra, life has not been kind to her," Verity murmured.

"You will forgive me if I cannot summon up a shred of sympathy for the woman. She plotted to ruin our marriage and kill you," Elliot replied coldly.

She smiled up at him. "But you saved me."

"Of course, I did, Verity. You are my very soul, my love. How could I allow anything but God Himself to keep you from me?"

He lowered his body onto the bed so that he lay alongside her and gathered her into his arms. "Your father had a lot to answer for, my love. He bears a great responsibility for the unhappiness and pain he caused. There is no doubt that his behaviour led to that woman's madness as well as our parting." He took a breath, if their marriage was to thrive, he knew that this last betrayal of her father must be spoken. "Your father showed me a note from you saying that you wanted nothing more to do with me, that I had been a dalliance, a flirtation until someone more wealthy came along."

She dropped her head against his chest, nestling into it perfectly. "How you must have hated me. But I wrote no such note, please believe me. Father was prepared to have me locked in my room until the wedding he had arranged took place."

He looked up at the drapes. It was so odd to converse so calmly and lovingly about so painful a time. He was glad of it. "I have to confess," he admitted gently, "I did hate you for a time. It was easier to blame you for all the shortcomings in my life than look at the things I needed to do to make something of myself."

She reached up and smoothed the errant lock from his brow. "Well, now I think we need to look forward together, and forgive each other for the hurt we unwittingly caused. There is nothing to be gained by letting the past dominate our future."

He smiled as he kissed her palm. "When did you become so wise? No, forget that. I think you have always been wise. Have we anything else to confess as we leave the past behind us?"

"I was also jealous when I believed you had a mistress," she admitted. "At times, I wanted to strangle Mrs. Kingsley with her own bonnet ribbons."

Elliott's face darkened. "When I think of the trouble that woman caused..." he growled, instinctively pulling her close against him.

"But now we know better," Verity interrupted, "and I should have known better than to believe her."

He cupped her face with his hand. "You know I have not led an unblemished past, so it would be foolish of me to deny it, but I make this promise to you now, I shall never take a mistress, and I shall never want to take a mistress. There is only ever going to be one woman for me, and she is the woman I am looking at now. My lover, my soulmate, my wife, and one day the mother of my children."

He bent his head and kissed her. It was a kiss not just of desire, but something deeper. It was a kiss of love and hope, almost a spiritual binding of two souls coming together, finally.

"We must endeavour to talk to each other properly, and listen to each other," Verity said, drawing back a little. "I cannot help but feel that a lot of the unhappiness we have caused each other could have been avoided had we just spoken the words."

"I agree," Elliott replied, twirling one of her locks around his finger. "So, in the spirit of talking, is there anything you would like to admit to me?" he asked.

Verity looked at him curiously. "Why do I feel that you already know what I am about to say?"

"Please, Verity, just tell me," he pleaded. "I need to hear your thoughts from your lips."

She took a deep breath. Then she smiled. "Very well. When Dr. Johnson had finished looking down my throat, I spoke to him about other things that I have felt recently, and in short, he believes I am with child."

Once more, Elliott gathered her into his arms and kissed the top of her head. "You cannot imagine how happy this news makes me," he exclaimed jubilantly. "I only wish I could alert the world immediately."

Verity bit her lip.

"What?" he asked, "what is troubling you?"

"I only hope it is the heir you so want," she answered, her eyes downcast. She could not bear it if, now that they had finally come to a peace in love and hope, she saw disappointment in his eyes were she to bear him a daughter.

He placed a finger under her chin. "Please look at me, Verity," he said softly. "It is of no consequence whether our first child is a son or a daughter so long as it is healthy. It is of no consequence if we have no other children, as long as we are together. We are about to become a family, a true family. I know from what you have said that your life with your father was less than pleasant, but I will do all that I can to ensure that our life in no way reflects him. I want us to be a real family. More than anything, I want us to grow old together, loving each other as much as, if not more than, we do now."

"Elliott," she said, planting a kiss on his palm in turn, "I truly cannot imagine loving you more than I do now."

"But we have so much time to make up, my love," he said and smiled down at her. "In fact, I should like to do just that," he added, his hand drifting down to rest on her still flat belly. "Were it not for the babe. I do not want to injure it, or you."

Verity could not help herself, and she threw back her head and laughed until there were tears streaming down her cheeks and all the tension she had felt over the last few weeks melted away.

Elliott crooked an eyebrow. "I was not aware that I had said anything so amusing. I will protect you, even from my own attentions when you are in this condition."

"Well," she gasped, catching her breath, "your reticence is both surprising and ill informed. I am already pregnant. I do not think I can get more pregnant if we make love now. The babe is safely away from even the most arduous activities you can think of."

"Witch," he growled, his eyes glowing as he quickly dispensed with her nightrail and his own clothing before kissing her deeply, wanting her to know that all the love in his heart was hers and always would be. He pressed his nude body along the length of hers, melding them together as one. His tongue sought entrance to her delicate mouth as his fingers gently teased her nipples with his fingers, then he trailed his hands languorously down her navel towards her core. He slid down and kissed her breasts, trailing kisses where his hands had been, until he reached her core. Verity gasped as he slid his tongue inside her, sucking and laving until she could bear it no more.

Quickly, so quickly, did his wife whisper, "Please, Elliott, I need you inside me. Now." His beautiful, responsive, delectable, perfect wife who completed him in every way needed him to complete her as well. To be at one with him, to accept his body and his heart into her own.

"With the greatest of pleasure, my love," he said, quietly, raising himself so that his cock was poised at her entrance. "Look at me Verity," he said softly. As he moved within her, she looked into his eyes and her breath caught. There it was, all the love in the world, shining in his eyes. It had been there each time he had made love to her, but this time, she understood.

They moved together in perfect rhythm until they both cried out their release. When their breathing returned to normal, Elliott rolled onto his back and tucked a pillow on his arm so that Verity could rest her head on his chest. He rarely spared a thought for Verity's father, but for all his faults, and there were many. This one thing he had at least got right when he had set out to ensure, at the end of his life and which went a little way to atone for his sins was that the daughter, he had wronged might have the chance to marry a duke.

EPILOGUE

Six Years Later

*V*erity paused at the door of the dining room. Everything was in place for the dinner they were to give later in the evening. The mahogany table was polished to perfection and laid with their finest crystal and silverware, the Christmas roses and evergreens not only lent an air of festivity to the room as well as the scent of cinnamon, cloves, nutmeg and ginger from the oranges decorating the sideboard. The silver candelabras shone, and the long, elegant beeswax candles stood ready to be lit when the guests arrived. In the kitchen, Cook would be putting the last-minute touches to the dinner of turkey, goose, and ham as well as the pies and special puddings.

That morning, both she and Elliott had been out with their children, Francesca, Lily, and Teddy to collect the evergreens with which they had spent the afternoon decorating the mantels and tables. Little Teddy had gone back with his father and men from the estate to bring home the yule log, which was sitting in the fireplace ready to be lit. Verity and her daughters had spent the rest of the afternoon, cutting silk and gold paper to decorate any surface they could find. Their skills with scissors, at ages five and four, meant that the decorations had a lop-sided charm. What they had lacked in skill, they had more than made up for in enthusiasm.

As she stood there, an arm snaked around her waist. "Are they all sleeping?" Verity asked her husband, who insisted on taking their children to bed and reading stories to them whenever possible, something Verity knew was missing from her own childhood and that she suspected was done by very few dukes of the land.

"Teddy is already dreaming of the carved animals he hopes to receive. Francesca is no doubt dreaming of sugar plums, and Lily is hoping for a doll, but yes, they are all sleeping. I clearly have a knack for getting the children to sleep, it is either my wonderful reading of a story or my voice which induces sleep, and I can never quite discover the ending of the tale." He laughed at the expression on his wife's face.

His eyes darkened as he took in Verity's appearance. Even after pregnancies, she grew thrilled when she saw lust overcome his eyes. The emerald green silk fitted her to perfection, emphasising her narrow waist which had not thickened with the bearing of their three children and her full breasts, which had increased with each pregnancy. He sucked in a breath. "Am I imagining this or are you with child again, Your Grace?" he asked.

"And what makes you say that Your Grace?" she asked demurely, struggling to contain her laughter.

He leaned forward. "For one thing, as you know, I shall never be able to keep my hands off you, and for another, one of the first signs that you are *enceinte* is the fact that your already magnificent breasts," he said, grazing his hands over them possessively, "become even more magnificent," he whispered in her ear, sending a shiver of excitement through her body.

"I would say then, that come the summer, we should be making space in the nursery for one more," she said slowly as she smiled back at him.

"That is the most wonderful news," he cried as he spun her round and kissed her soundly, adding, "Would that we could cancel tonight's dinner and spend it alone."

"I would not hear of it. Your brother will be here directly, and my sisters have talked of nothing for days, quite apart from the fact that Mr. Govan will already be on his way," she replied, cuffing his shoulder.

"Ah, Mr. Govan, I have often wondered quite what a role he played in the writing of your father's contract. I sometimes get the impression that there was more to it than met the eye," Elliott conjectured.

"Do you regret it?" Verity asked.

"Good Lord, no, never for a moment and I never shall. To be honest, Mr. Govan could have made a pact with the devil for all I care, so long as it brought me to you."

"I think," Verity replied, smiling, "that you just reached the ending of our tale."

Don't miss out on your next favorite book!

Join the Satin Romance mailing list
www.satinromance.com/mail.html

THANK YOU FOR READING

Did you enjoy this book?

We invite you to leave a review at your favorite book site, such as Goodreads, Amazon, Barnes & Noble, etc.

DID YOU KNOW THAT LEAVING A REVIEW...

- Helps other readers find books they may enjoy.
- Gives you a chance to let your voice be heard.
- Gives authors recognition for their hard work.
- Doesn't have to be long. A sentence or two about why you liked the book will do.

ABOUT THE AUTHOR

Anna lives in a lovely village in Hampshire England with her own romantic hero, otherwise known as her long-suffering husband and has two grown up children. An ex-teacher, she has taught many subjects from religion to drama but has always had a passion for history and would love a time machine to experience life in Georgian England, though suspects she would have been one of the maids washing the cups rather than delicately sipping tea from them.

When she's not thinking about life in the nineteenth century, she enjoys travelling and learning about different customs and cultures, especially the food. Anna also loves to walk in the beautiful Yorkshire Dales which provides much inspiration for her writing. She also plays the piano and it's her ambition to be able to play well enough so that the cat doesn't leave the room.

ALSO BY ANNA AYSGARTH

www.ingramcontent.com/pod-product-compliance
Lightning Source LLC
Chambersburg PA
CBHW021642260626
47154CB00016BA/987